VIRGIN

Also by Robin Maxwell

The Secret Diary of Anne Boleyn
The Queen's Bastard

VIRGIN
Prelude to the Throne

A Novel

ROBIN MAXWELL

ARCADE PUBLISHING • NEW YORK

FIRST EDITION

This is a work of fiction. Names, places, characters, and incidents are either products of the author's imagination or are used fictitiously.

Library of Congress Cataloging-in-Publication Data

Maxwell, Robin, 1948–
    Virgin : a novel / Robin Maxwell. — 1st ed.
        p. cm.
    ISBN 1-55970-563-9
    1. Elizabeth I, Queen of England, 1533–1603—Fiction. 2. Catherine Parr, Queen, consort of Henry VIII, King of England, 1512–1548—Fiction. 3. Great Britain—History—Edward VI, 1547–1553—Fiction. 4. Seymour, Thomas Seymour, Baron, 1508?–1549—Fiction. I. Title.

    PS3563.A9254 V57 2001
    813'.54—dc21   2001022051

Published in the United States by Arcade Publishing, Inc., New York
Distributed by Time Warner Trade Publishing

Visit our Web site at www.arcadepub.com

10 9 8 7 6 5 4 3 2 1

Designed by API

PRINTED IN THE UNITED STATES OF AMERICA

For Anne Boleyn, her daughter Elizabeth, and Catherine Parr, whose courageous and extraordinary lives have endlessly informed, enriched, and inspired me

ACKNOWLEDGMENTS

I gratefully acknowledge my hardworking agents Kim Witherspoon and Maria Massie, who restored my faith in their profession, and my publishers Jeannette and Dick Seaver, who with loving acceptance made possible the flowering of my career. My cheerful and indefatigable publicist Phillipa Tawn, agent associates David Forrer and Alexis Hurley, and editorial assistant Casey Ebro made the day-to-day business of this author's life a pleasure. I thank my always erudite copy editor Ann Marlowe and Amara Dupuis, who typed this manuscript and supplied so much encouragement.

Fellow author/historian Vicki León urged me to write this fascinating but rarely told episode of Elizabeth's life, and my husband Max Thomas — as always — provided me with love and the perfect environment in which to execute it.

VIRGIN

Chapter One

"The King is dead. Long live the King."

It was not by mistake that Edward Seymour, Duke of Somerset, had, for this somber pronouncement of Henry the Eighth's passing, brought together perhaps the only two individuals in Britain who would have cause to fall into the sincere and copious weeping that young Elizabeth and Edward Tudor now commenced. It was hard to say if the boy's tears and sobbing at his uncle's words should be attributed to the loss of his beloved father or to the sheer terror of ascending the throne of England at the age of nine.

Despite a turmoil far greater than Edward's — for her place in the scheme of things was, and had always been, convoluted in the extreme — the thirteen-year-old Elizabeth emerged as comforter to her half brother's hysterical grieving.

"Edward, Edward," she crooned, brushing away her own tears with the palm of her hand. She accepted a handkerchief from the appropriately condolent Somerset but, rather than using the cloth herself, wiped the boy's nose with it. The king of England allowed the intimacy as natural, the two having shared a deep and abiding affection one for the other ever since he had been a small boy.

"May Edward and I be alone, my lord?" Elizabeth inquired of Somerset with polite dignity. She could see his lips tighten at the request, but the royal uncle backed away deferentially and pulled the nursery door closed behind him. Edward had fallen onto his bed in a new fit of weeping.

Elizabeth was steadily regaining her composure, as much owing to her genuine concern for the miserable little boy who lay, perhaps for the last time, on his nursery cot as to the knowledge that seeing her father never again would be only slightly less often than when he was living. Elizabeth had loved her father, loved him far more than he had ever loved her. There were times, she had to admit, when he had been unendurably cruel to his younger daughter. Elizabeth finally sat herself at Edward's side and watched his slender body heave.

"I am an orphan, Elizabeth," he said between choked sobs.

"As I am . . . and your sister Mary." All of Henry's children had long been motherless. Their half sister, Mary, had lost Queen Katherine of Aragon more than ten years before, after an enforced banishment from each other's comfort and company at the king's pleasure. Elizabeth had been barely three when her own mother, Anne Boleyn, was executed for adultery and treason. But poor Edward had lost his to a fever just weeks after his birth. Cruel prophesies at the time had promised that when he came to the throne King Edward the Sixth would be a murderer, as he had started his life by murdering his mother in childbed. So he had never known the demure Jane Seymour, Henry's third and most beloved wife — the woman who had given him the son he had changed the world to have. The woman next to whom he had demanded to be buried.

"You're an orphan, Edward, but you have me, and you have Mary. You know we both love you very much."

"Who will tell Mary?" he asked, sniffing back his tears.

"I'm sure your uncle Somerset will see to it." Elizabeth's own relations with Mary were bittersweet at best, as the tragic history their two mothers shared was an ever-present barrier between the half sisters. "And our father has made very sure that you will be well handled in your minority, Edward," Elizabeth continued. "Sixteen members of the Privy Council, including your two Seymour uncles, were carefully chosen to oversee the regency. You shall have *sixteen* fathers."

"No one like His Majesty," Edward wailed.

"I know that." Elizabeth's lips twitched involuntarily and tears sprang unbidden from her eyes with the truth of her brother's sentiment.

Henry *had* been a truly magnificent man, even in his wretched old age. Until recently, with the excruciating pain in his ulcerous leg prostrating him for months at a time, he would confound his Councillors by suddenly insisting he be taken from his sickbed to hunt. There at the blind, his corpulence barely supported by his famous wide stance, the elegant archer would shoot all of an afternoon, his arrow rarely missing its mark. Then he would collapse in pain, raging violently at everyone around him, all the time cringing with inward revulsion at what the "handsomest prince in Christendom" had finally become.

"And how can you forget the Queen?" said Elizabeth, composing herself. "She has been mother to us all for years now." Henry's sixth and final wife, Catherine Parr, had done more for the royal children than courtesy demanded. Far more. Kind and generous in the extreme, she had not only lavished the little prince with affection but had miraculously rescued Henry's two bastardized daughters from poverty and obscurity, bringing them back from exile into the Tudor family fold. More important, Catherine had remonstrated with Henry until he had reinstated Elizabeth in the succession — an extraordinary act that she could never repay. Further, the Queen had personally seen to the young princess's education and insisted that, when this day came, Elizabeth should come and reside under the roof of the Queen Dowager.

"I do love Catherine," Edward whimpered.

"Of course you do. Now come, sit up. We have been expecting this for a good long while."

The little boy, dressed in the richest finery, sat up, face red and swollen, his legs dangling over the side of the bed. His feet did not yet touch the floor.

"No one can take the place of our father, but think, Edward. You are the *king of England* now. You've been preparing for this day since you took your first step, spoke your first words. You are brilliant, at least Master Cheke says so," she added teasingly. "You already have the manners of a great nobleman. You are a fine athlete, just as your father was. You understand how battles are fought. You've memorized every port on the coasts of England and the Continent. And you know four languages."

"My French is still poor."

"But your Greek is marvelous. And that's the one that matters most. All else will follow. I tell you, Edward, you will be so utterly consumed with the business of state that you will forget you even *have* sisters."

"I shall never forget you, Elizabeth. Or Mary either. It's just . . ." Edward's lips began to quiver again.

"I cannot tell you not to grieve for our father. Heaven knows I shall miss him" — Elizabeth's voice cracked with emotion — "but you were his greatest joy. His greatest hope." Tears began gathering in Elizabeth's eyes. "Much . . . was sacrificed so that you could be born." A fleeting image of her mother kneeling at the block, and knowledge that the day following her execution Henry had betrothed himself to Edward's mother, caused Elizabeth to shudder. "You were *everything* to him, brother. Everything. You must make him very, very proud."

With that Elizabeth burst into tears. Edward, suddenly the comforter, placed an awkward arm around his sister. Then, laying his head upon her shoulder, Edward, King of England, began weeping anew.

Chapter Two

Hooves thundering on the damp spring earth, the geldings galloped side by side, their riders urging their racing mounts as they had since Elizabeth and Robin Dudley had been children. Elizabeth pulled ahead, grinning triumphantly at her competitor, her horse flinging clods of soggy grass up behind it.

"Ha! Ha!" she heard Robin crying, spurring his horse faster. He would catch her soon enough and pull ahead laughing as the wind whipped his long hair. And so it went, one overtaking the other, through the meadows and the wood, bounding across narrow streams till the animals were spent and the pair, reining in their horses, reluctantly dismounted.

They fell to the moss-covered ground breathless, reclining, hands under heads in the oak's dappled shade. There was no one, thought Elizabeth — save Kat — with whom she was more at home than this childhood friend. She turned her head and found Robin, eyes closed, sucking in great gulps of the fragrant air, and smiled. He was a handsome boy, almost exactly a year older than herself, and she suddenly realized that sometime in the past months he had finally overtaken her in height, his voice becoming deep and manly. His betrothed, Amy Robsart, was a very lucky lady indeed, Elizabeth mused. For not only was she promised a handsome young husband instead of a toothless if wealthy old widower for her marriage bed, but Robin lusted for the girl, and she him. They could hardly wait the two years for their wedding. Such a match was very rare, and some even whispered that it was doomed, for carnal desire in a marriage was not in the natural order of things.

In the next moment, eyes still closed, young Dudley spoke. "My father met with Amy's father yesterday."

"Robin!"

"What?"

"You've done it again."

"What did I do?" He turned on his side to face Elizabeth, bent his elbow, and propped his head on his hand. He wore a slightly amused expression and was, as always, extremely attentive.

"Just then I was thinking of the future Amy Dudley and in the next moment you mentioned her father."

"So I've read your mind again," he said, picking an oak leaf off the shoulder of her black riding gown. Only four months since her father's death she was still officially in mourning.

"Well, I don't like it," said Elizabeth with mock petulance, for she *did* like his uncanny ability very much. Certainly her beloved nurse, Kat Ashley, loved her, and the Queen Dowager had been exceedingly kind and affectionate, but no one in the world cared enough about what Elizabeth was thinking to read her mind.

"Then I shall not do it again," he said with an ingenuous grin. He, of course, knew how flattered she felt to be so well known and cared for by him.

"What did they talk about, your father and Lord Robsart — besides their children's lusting after one another?"

Robin's face colored with embarrassment, but the great reserve for which his father, John Dudley, was well known had recently begun to flavor Robin's character as well. He ignored Elizabeth's lascivious reference when he answered.

"Their concern is growing every day at the way our government is being run. And the Privy Council is furious at Edward Seymour —"

"The Duke of Somerset," Elizabeth corrected with a touch of sarcasm.

"Indeed the *duke,* and self-proclaimed at that." Robin sat up, the intimacy between them giving way to the fourteen-year-old's political diatribe. "They're saying that he and Lord Paget were busy changing your father's will even as he lay dying."

Elizabeth winced but did not interrupt. Now that she was living out in the country at Chelsea House with the Queen Dowager, Robin — through John Dudley — was her most valuable source of information about the goings-on at court. As she'd suspected it would, her brother's correspondence since his accession, whilst remaining cordial, had become less and less frequent.

"The pair of them, Somerset and Paget, simply usurped control from the Councillors King Henry had chosen to guide Edward, and Somerset took it for himself. Now he's sole Protector and no one else has a say in the King's business — unless of course you count the *Duchess* of Somerset. And she's a horrible, conniving old cow."

"Robin!"

"Well, she is."

"I think this is your father speaking, and he's still angry at Somerset for taking away his admiralty and giving the post to his brother."

"You're quite wrong, Elizabeth. My father's not angry at all, despite the fact he's a better man for the job than Thomas Seymour will ever be. What the 'demotion' means is that my father is able to stay close to court now, which is desirable, and that Seymour will be forced by his duties to ship off to sea for the better part of the year. We're all a good deal better off without him. My father says he's the most grasping, unscrupulous man ever born on English soil."

"Is that what he says?" said Elizabeth, mildly amused.

"Seymour was unsatisfied with all his new titles and properties," Robin went on, "and was wildly jealous that his brother snatched away the regency for himself. He's still steaming about the lowly place he was given in the King's coronation procession. I tell you, the man gives ambition a bad name." Robin smiled then, his demeanor lightening with the irony of his last statement. It was well known that his own grandfather Edmund Dudley had been executed for his ambitiousness, and John Dudley, though more reserved in his own political pursuits, was no stranger to powermongering.

"You may be right about the Duchess of Somerset," said Elizabeth, "but I think my brother is better off for having one firm hand guiding him than sixteen. Nobody can ever agree on *anything* in Council, you know that, Robin. And by the time they'd got through arguing, Edward would be completely confused and never know which side to take. He's just a little boy, and his uncle, from what I have heard, is a pious and high-minded gentleman of many accomplishments. He's a scholar, and a famous soldier —"

"And so harsh and snappish he makes grown men cry," Robin finished for her.

"Really?" Elizabeth's interest was piqued. "Whom did he make cry?"

"Lord Rutland for one, in the Council Chamber. And he's obsessed with subduing Scotland. He's already gathering forces to invade."

"I believe he's *right* to care about Scotland," argued Elizabeth. "They're allied with England's oldest enemy. If ever France wanted to invade us they could come marauding across the Scottish border."

Robin stood and moved to his mount. As he lifted the front foreleg and examined the foot, he continued speaking. His natural ease around horses had already earned him a reputation as one of England's finest young horsemen.

"You make a good point. It's just his arrogance that riles people. His unshakable belief that the protectorate is his God-given right. And worst of all . . ." Robin hesitated for a very long moment.

"What is worst of all?" demanded Elizabeth.

"Worst of all is the way he treats the King. He ignores Edward entirely. Your brother might as well not be alive. He's never consulted on *anything.* And only four months into his regency Somerset's adopted the royal 'we.'"

"I think you're being rather too hard on the duke. And his brother."

"Maybe on the duke, but not on the Lord High Admiral. I tell you Thomas Seymour is scheming wicked schemes. There are rumors about, you know."

"The ones that have him asking for my sister Mary's hand in marriage? I've heard them. I don't believe them."

"And his courting Anne of Cleves?"

"I don't believe that either."

"He asked the Council for *your* hand, Elizabeth," said Robin pointedly.

Now Elizabeth stood, flushing with indignation as she straightened her riding habit.

"That is simply a lie," she said crisply. "You really should keep to political commentary, Robin Dudley. Gossipmongering doesn't become you." She stood at her horse's side and silently waited for a foot up. Robin complied instantly and she took the saddle. She felt, as always, the grace and natural ease with which he deferred to her. Although Elizabeth had only recently regained her title as princess — and at thirteen, with a robust Tudor brother at the beginning of a long and glorious reign, was accorded virtually no chance of ever sitting on the English throne — Robin Dudley treated with her as he would a queen. And it was for this reason, thought Elizabeth as she rode back to Chelsea House with her best friend at her side, that she loved him the most.

Chelsea House was a lovely country castle fit for the queen that inhabited it. Situated on a gentle curve of the Thames, its red Tudor brick walls and turrets were topped with dozens of chimneys. Broad mullioned windows flooded every chamber with light, allowing a cheerful atmosphere even on the darkest winter day. On the north side was a glorious park and woodland, well stocked with red and fallow deer, and it was from this direction that Elizabeth now approached on horseback.

Chelsea House was a large establishment, Catherine's own servants numbering more than two hundred, besides the Princess's personal household staff. But they were a happy, congenial lot, and more so in recent weeks with the exciting and mysterious comings and goings of the Queen Dowager's lover.

Riding through the outer courtyard gate, Elizabeth was first met by the armed yeomen's appropriately reserved smiles and nods, then by cheerful hellos from the battalion of gardeners who stopped their hedge trimming to tip their caps to her. When she reached the stables the liverymen and stable hand who helped her down from her mount and came to lead the horse away were decidedly warm and solicitous, inquiring if Elizabeth would be riding later that day and, if so, which animal would be her preference. By the time she walked through the great carved doors of Chelsea House the greetings of the Queen Dowager's ladies standing in a gossipy clutch near the entryway, and of the maids scurrying up the great staircase, were profuse and respectful in the extreme.

"Good afternoon, Princess Elizabeth," said Lady Tyrwhitt with a smile and curtsy.

"I do hope you had a lovely ride," Lady Milton said shyly. She was the youngest of Catherine's waiting women.

"Very lovely, thank you," replied Elizabeth, and started up the stairs.

"I believe the Queen has been asking for you, Princess," Lady Tyrwhitt called after her.

As she climbed the broad stone steps of the sweeping stairway and gazed down at the grand entry and the gaily dressed waiting ladies, Elizabeth's heart swelled and tears suddenly threatened. She was loved and respected in this royal household, once again "Princess Elizabeth." Certainly she had been born to that title, and as an heir to the Tudor throne, fawned over and protected as a valuable asset to her father's kingdom. But all that had changed with Anne Boleyn's humiliating downfall and death. Not yet three, Elizabeth had been bastardized, her title revoked by Henry's decree, and exiled into wretched poverty. Her household allowance had been so pitiful that she had, year after year, been forced to squeeze into gowns she'd long outgrown. Her few loyal servants were paid but sporadically. The story was widely told — though Elizabeth herself did not remember — that at the end of the day on which the disastrous change in her circumstances had occurred, she had questioned her keeper, saying, "How is it that this morning I was Princess Elizabeth and this evening merely Lady Elizabeth?"

As she moved down the main corridor and made for her apartments in Chelsea's south wing, she recalled how her condition and reputation had suffered further at the execution of her young cousin Catherine Howard, Henry's fifth wife. Accused and convicted of adultery before and after her marriage to the King, Queen Catherine was widely compared to her kinswoman, "the goggle-eyed whore" Anne Boleyn. Afterwards all women of the Howard line, including the eight-year-old Elizabeth, were said to have wanton blood running through their veins. The reputation had persisted to make Elizabeth's life an endless humiliation — until Henry's marriage to Catherine Parr. This kind and intelligent noblewoman, who'd borne no children of her own, knew more about mothering than most women who had. She'd lavished her affection on all of Henry's brood, but of the three children, Elizabeth had benefited most specifically.

Edward, Henry's long hoped-for boy, had always been doted upon and was given the brilliant education expected for the heir to the English throne. Mary had suffered a miserable life after Katherine of Aragon's downfall and, like Elizabeth, had been bastardized by Henry's decree. But by the time of Catherine Parr's coronation, Mary was already an adult, with Catholic retainers and foreign allies to support her place in the royal landscape.

It was Elizabeth, of all the children, that lived in the most wretched of purgatories. Catherine Parr had swept the gangly redheaded nine-year-old from oblivion and infamy, restoring to her not simply her honor but the promise of a rich and dignified future.

"Princess Elizabeth," she whispered to herself with a smile as she was admitted into her lavish apartments. There, standing beside the Princess's canopied bed, now spread from corner to corner with fine new gowns, was Elizabeth's beloved Kat, nurse and waiting woman since her fourth year. Katherine Ashley had been a rock of salvation in the terrifying storm of Elizabeth's life. She had been doting, fiercely protective, and audaciously outspoken in her disapproval — even to King Henry himself — of the cruel treatment to which her young charge was subjected. The woman had fallen in love with the sad-eyed, precocious little creature and, whilst treating her always with the respect due a princess, title or no, she never spoiled the child. Herself an educated woman, Kat never allowed Elizabeth with her quicksilver mind to run roughshod over her. Bad behavior was punished sternly, but good was rewarded with lush praise and many embraces. Too, there had always been an understanding between them, a directness and a sometimes painful honesty made necessary by the harshness and constant peril of Elizabeth's circumstances. She could at any time, by the King's whim and pleasure, be cast off, accused of treachery — even "disposed of" as, in the past, other inconvenient youngsters of royal blood had been.

Even as a small child Elizabeth was taught by Mistress Ashley the politic behavior that might save her limb and life. She became adept at the abundant obeisances that must needs be shown her great father on the few occasions she'd been called into his presence. She would kneel three times before addressing him, proffer handmade gifts that spoke of her undying devotion to the greatest king in the world, and acquit herself admirably with her Greek and Latin and scripture if, at a moment's notice, she was called upon to perform. Despite this, and to Kat Ashley's undying chagrin, Elizabeth retained an untainted love for her father that no vile treatment or ignoring could sunder. She was ever proud to be Henry's daughter, and delighted to be the only child of the three that bore a striking physical resemblance to him.

"What are these?" Elizabeth demanded gaily, moving up behind Kat, wrapping her arms around the woman's waist and peering over her shoulder at the dresses. At thirteen the Princess was nearly as tall as her nurse.

"The Queen has made you a present," replied Kat. "Or should I say a whole new wardrobe."

Elizabeth, gawking now, moved to the bed to examine the silks and brocades more carefully. Though they were all in the blacks and grays of mourning, they were nevertheless exquisite gowns in cut and design. "Surely she cannot mean for me to have them all? I'll choose the one I like best."

"She means for you to have them *all*." Kat now wore an indulgent smile. "Come, give me a kiss, young lady. You've been gone the whole morning and half the afternoon. Your tutor is becoming annoyed."

Elizabeth moved into Kat's arms for a brief but warm embrace. Just then Thomas Parry, the Princess's longtime servant and now her household accountant, strode into the room.

"Good afternoon, Princess," he greeted her cheerfully. "How was your ride? And how is young Dudley?"

"Both were excellent," she replied.

"My good wife Blanche will have a word with you when you have a moment, Mistress Ashley. What's this?" he cried when he saw the fine cloth bounty laid out on the bed.

12

"The Queen Dowager's generosity, it would appear," answered Kat.

"Or perhaps a case of high and happy spirits overflowing to the members of her household," he suggested with an obvious smirk.

"What have you heard?" demanded Kat, her nose fairly twitching with desire for a tidbit of juicy gossip.

Elizabeth pretended to examine the charcoal beaded gown but listened with the greatest of interest.

"So the newlywed has a hankering for more dirty linen than in her own bedchamber?" Thomas teased. Indeed, Kat had recently married John Ashley, though there had been some rumor that she'd had a previous lover torn from her in order to satisfy her parents' wishes.

"Just *tell* me, Thomas Parry. What are they saying in the kitchen?"

"Yesterday the Lord High Admiral came to Queen Catherine again just before dawn. They remained secreted in her private apartments all through the day, and he left after dark."

"Ooooh, the wicked widow," crowed Kat devilishly.

"Come now, Mistress Ashley, be kind." Parry continued in a jesting vein, though it was suffused through and through with simple truths. "The woman deserves a love match, married as she was three times for duty's sake." Thomas flushed suddenly in Elizabeth's presence, remembering that one of Catherine's "duties" was the Princess's own father.

"You needn't blush, Thomas," Elizabeth said, giving up her pretense of studying the gowns. "If the Queen loves Thomas Seymour and he loves her the same, then I am happy for them both. I daresay my brother the King will feel the same. He adores Catherine and wishes her well. And he loves his uncle, too."

"'Tis the *other* uncle worries me, he that rules the King."

Kat shot Parry a threatening look, one not lost on Elizabeth.

"It's all right, Kat. I know the Duke of Somerset holds sway over Edward," said Elizabeth with all the worldly wisdom she could muster. She was mightily grateful for Robin Dudley's timely intelligence. "He changed Father's will and wrested control from the sixteen Councillors he'd chosen for the regency."

Kat's and Parry's eyes went wide as saucers to hear the girl talking.

For want of a decent interval between the old king's death and a lesson in the current politics of treachery, Kat had not yet apprised Elizabeth of the duke's handling of young Edward.

"Despite the fact that Somerset takes no heed of the King's wishes," Elizabeth went on, "I still believe my brother will prevail in this matter. He'll let Catherine and Seymour marry if they ask. The one I would watch carefully is that conniving old cow married to the duke."

"Elizabeth!" cried Kat in dismay.

Parry was trying unsuccessfully to stifle his laughter.

"It's that young Dudley puts these foul oaths in the child's mouth," insisted Kat.

"At least he keeps this 'child' *informed*, Katherine Ashley," replied Elizabeth tartly.

"Aren't you the rude little snippet!" Kat was outraged.

"I'll be going now, ladies," said Parry, edging out of the fray. "Don't forget to have a word with Blanche, Mistress Ashley." He closed the door behind him, leaving the Princess and her nurse squared off and steaming, neither of them prepared to give an inch and both prepared for warfare. A moment later the door opened again, only wide enough for Thomas Parry's head to poke through it.

"Saved from the wrath of God, Lady Princess." He winked. "The Queen Dowager wishes a word with you. *Pronto.*"

Elizabeth smiled sweetly, gave Kat's flushed cheek a quick peck, and escaped before her nurse could fathom that she had once again been beaten at her favorite game.

"Your Majesty." Elizabeth curtsied gracefully before the Queen Dowager and allowed herself to be embraced. Catherine Parr, thought Elizabeth, looked more radiant than she ever had. A mature woman at thirty-three, this day she had the air of a maid — eyes bright, unrouged cheeks a natural glowing pink, lips relaxed into a graceful smile.

"Good afternoon, Princess Elizabeth," said William Grindal, who stepped forward now. Her tutor and the Queen, it appeared, had been chatting on two stools set before a brazier in Catherine's study.

"I hope you've not be waiting for me in the schoolroom, Master Grindal," said Elizabeth, mildly alarmed.

"No, no. I received your message that we'd not begin our work until three."

"Grindal has been visiting with me, Elizabeth. We've been discussing your studies."

"Thank you, Your Majesty," said Elizabeth, pleased with this news. It was a wonder, she thought, that the Queen, preoccupied as she was with her love affair and her household, should still have time to worry about Elizabeth's education.

"Come, sit," instructed the Queen as Grindal pulled up another stool. They all sat, the women taking a longer moment to rearrange their skirts. Even without the rigid stays beneath her bodice, Elizabeth's tall slender body would have remained, after the long years of posture and deportment training, perfectly erect in the backless seat. Lately, though, she had had to overcome shyness in the presence of men, even her beloved Grindal, for her small breasts had begun to bud.

"We were arguing the merits of enlarging your study of mathematics," began the Queen. "Your Greek and Latin, logic, and other languages are of course superb, but the former, so says your tutor, is somewhat lacking."

"I admit I do not much love numbers," offered Elizabeth earnestly. "Shall I increase the mathematics, then?"

"Not necessarily," Grindal replied. "A debate now rages in Cambridge about the merits of teaching that science within the boundaries of a humanist education. One Roger Ascham, a don there and a brilliant fellow, claims that studied too rigorously, mathematics thwarts the soul."

"*Tempora mutantur, nos et mutamur in illis,*" said the Princess.

Grindal and Catherine laughed delightedly. They were both mightily proud of Elizabeth's shining intellect.

"True, very true, Princess," Grindal agreed. "And so do you believe that 'in these changing times' mathematics will prove an important course of study?"

"Much as I hate to admit it, I do think so," she replied.

"Interesting," said Catherine. "With this argument against mathematics, things have come full circle."

"How so, Your Majesty?" asked Grindal.

"I was thinking of my grandmother Fitzhugh, and your father's grandmother Margaret Beaufort," she said, looking at Elizabeth. "The two were friends around the turning of the century. And the New Learning had not yet taken hold. Highborn girls were promised no education save elementary law and arithmetic, enough to manage their husbands' estates whilst they were off fighting foreign wars for months, even years at a time. But their mothers sensed a change coming and a need for their daughters to know more. Happily for us, all the tutors whom they imported for the girls were teaching humanism."

"Many of those mothers quietly sat in on their daughters' lessons," interjected Grindal.

"Indeed," agreed Catherine. "This was the first generation of educated women. King Henry's grandmother Beaufort was both well positioned *and* a passionate champion of education for girls as well as boys. The school she and my grandmother, and later my mother, fought to establish at court fostered not only your father and your friend Robin Dudley's father, but your aunts, your sister Mary, and myself. Your mother too, for your grandmother Elizabeth Boleyn was part of that inner circle of women who loved learning."

The unexpected mention of her mother made Elizabeth flush with sudden shame, but Catherine went on.

"They struggled, learning to fight men with the greatest weapon on earth — their intellect — and they finally won the right for gentlewomen to receive the same classical education as boys. Greek, Latin, the sciences. *Mathematics.* And here we sit today debating the merits of teaching it at all."

"Full circle indeed," said Grindal, smiling with enjoyment at the Queen's remembrances.

"Will you come and continue our conversation in a fortnight, Master Grindal?" inquired Catherine pleasantly.

"My pleasure and my honor, Your Majesty," he said, standing to take his leave. He bowed to both ladies and made for the door.

"Elizabeth will be up presently," called the Queen after him. "I'll just have a few more words with her."

The door shut behind him. Queen Dowager and Princess found themselves alone and comfortable in the quiet of each other's presence. Elizabeth warmed her hands at the brazier as the late afternoon chill crept into the room. Watching Catherine's face — one some considered attractive, others prim — it occurred to Elizabeth that her stepmother was not merely enjoying her company in the quiet. She was actively collecting her thoughts. Elizabeth began to grow impatient, wishing to know those thoughts, though of course it would have been impertinent to do anything but wait. Finally Catherine spoke.

"There is more to your education," she began, "than what Master Grindal and your chaplain and your music and dance instructors can teach you. Of course you know this." She looked to Elizabeth for affirmation, but saw instead a face filled with confusion. Catherine continued. "One of my greatest teachers, Elizabeth, was your mother." She paused, knowing the upwelling of emotion this would produce in the girl. In fact, Elizabeth was well and truly speechless, her lips tightening into a thin, straight line.

"Anne Boleyn possessed one of the most brilliant minds of her day. Many dismiss her intellect and her contribution because of her . . . infamous end. I never knew her personally, but my sister Anne Parr waited on her when she was queen, and her friend and chaplain Archbishop Cranmer served and befriended me when I was married to your father. They both had nothing but the highest regard for Queen Anne. As a girl, just your age, I watched her closely but from afar. You see, I'd lived my whole life with my mother and sisters in Henry's court and inner circle. Your half sister, Princess Mary, was my dear friend. I observed Anne's unparalleled rise to power and her equally rapid fall from grace. I learned many of the rules of queenship from Anne Boleyn, some by good example, many more by her mistakes."

Elizabeth found she could hardly sit still, so discomfiting were Catherine's words. She wished the Queen Dowager would stop this talk about her mother — her rightly reviled mother, to whom Elizabeth owed not simply her bastardy but also her father's shabby treatment for most of her childhood.

"Like your mother," Catherine went on, ignoring Elizabeth's

discomfort, "I was ambitious, but the ways in which Anne achieved her objectives were sometimes harsh. When an enemy was brought down — in the case of Cardinal Wolsey, for example — she gloated openly. Though he was widely hated, her manner earned her enemies of her own."

Catherine could see Elizabeth fairly cringing at her words, but plunged ahead. "Once her hard-won queenship was established, she made what I consider to be one of her deadliest blunders. She refused to share any of her power with other women of the court. She guarded it so fiercely and so singularly that her ladies — many of them more highborn than herself — came to resent her deeply. When the balance of power began to shift, many of these women spoke out against her, happily bore witness to her alleged adultery, which led to her death." Catherine paused thoughtfully, her expression reflecting seemingly fresh emotion rather than an old memory. "Perhaps your mother's greatest folly was due not to arrogance or ambition but to a dearth of experience. Perhaps she did not understand your father nearly as well as she supposed she did. He was a complicated man with complicated motives —"

"Why are you telling me this, Your Majesty!" Elizabeth finally blurted. She sprang from her seat and began pacing, hands flailing helplessly at her sides. "I do not want to hear about my mother. I do not!"

"Elizabeth, Elizabeth," crooned Catherine. "Please, I promise I'm not telling you this to torture you. Let me finish. I've told you of the mistakes Anne made, and how I learned from her poorly chosen methods, but more important were her *contributions*. In ways, she and I were sisters under the skin."

Elizabeth turned and stared at the Queen Dowager, who was smiling with that sweet mildness the Princess so loved in her. "Your mother was a champion of the New Learning, and that in itself was of great importance, for she carried on the traditions of learned women going back to Margaret Beaufort. But more important, she was the very ringleader of Protestant reform. Few people know this, Elizabeth, but your father placed her at the head of a coterie of powerful men in his government, and together this group devised the master plan for

Henry's divorce from Katherine of Aragon and broke the power of the Catholic Church in England."

"I still do not understand, Your Majesty," said Elizabeth, exhausted with upset and confusion, "why I need to hear this."

"Because it is *queenly* intelligence, my dear," replied Catherine in a suddenly steely voice, "and you must begin to understand such things."

"But I shall never *be* queen. My brother sits on the throne and, despite what the Catholics would have the people believe about his sickliness, he is a healthy young boy. When he comes of age he will marry and beget heirs. And even if he should not for some reason have children, Princess Mary takes precedence over myself. What need have I, then, for 'queenly intelligence'?"

Catherine was silent again as she studied the normally calm, pale-skinned girl who now, flushed bright pink, stood before her, nervously wringing her long-fingered hands.

"Kings and queens rule, Elizabeth, not so much by blood as by the Fates, and the Fates have no master. You may never rule England, but just as easily, *you may.* Indeed, you may become a queen through marriage. So as long as you are under my protective wing I will see to it that you are prepared for any eventuality. Therefore" — Catherine took a long, slow breath, and the fierceness of her demeanor was suddenly transformed to ironic amusement — "whilst I am gone for the next fortnight, you shall oversee Chelsea House."

"I?" Elizabeth's jaws fell open and she gaped wide-eyed at the pleasantly smiling Queen Dowager.

"You'll see to the planning of the meals — and take especial care in the buttery. There's been something of a rebellion amongst the milk-maids." Catherine suppressed a smile. "Of course the laundresses need constant overseeing or they'll overstarch the linen. The candlemakers need the least watching, but the gardeners can be difficult in planting season. I've already told Master Beem, my cofferer, that you will be inspecting the books regularly —"

"Your Majesty, I —"

"— and your signature will suffice for any bills that come due in my absence."

"I thank you for your confidence in me but . . ."

"I was hardly older than you when I took over my first household," said Catherine firmly. "These are things a great lady, even a princess, must learn to do. You have excellent servants around you for guidance — Mistress Ashley, Master and Mistress Parry. I have every confidence in you, Elizabeth."

"But my studies?"

"I expect you to continue your studies, of course, though Master Grindal has been informed of your additional duties. I'm sure he'll give you some latitude."

"Where are you going?" asked Elizabeth, finally coming to her senses.

"'Tis a secret," replied Catherine with a decidedly wicked smile. "Now go along and see your tutor. He'll be wondering why I've kept you so long."

"Yes, Your Majesty." Elizabeth curtsied and moved to the door. She turned back and regarded Catherine Parr with bemused affection. "Thank you . . . I think," she said.

Catherine laughed. "You are going to be fine, Elizabeth. You are going to make me very proud."

The overseeing of Chelsea House had in fact been daunting. Despite the good counsel of her servants, Elizabeth was faced every day with a hundred new tasks and decisions to be made. It was discovered that the whole stock of apples in the root cellar was rotten and must somehow be replaced, for the fruit was the Queen Dowager's favorite. A shipment of wool cloth from Flanders arrived moth-ridden and had to be sent back. Catherine's barge sprang a leak and a boatbuilder had to be found to repair it. Elizabeth fell into bed every night exhausted, though her mind continued racing, so that sleep evaded her for hours. And whilst Grindal made some allowances in her rigorous schedule of studies, he had no doubt been instructed by the Queen Dowager — who had clearly meant to test the Princess's limits of endurance — to continue what for an average pupil would have been a full course of education.

It happened that on the day of Catherine's return home Elizabeth was preoccupied with several rounds of cheese that had gone bad, so when Lady Tyrwhitt poked her head into the buttery to say that the Queen's carriage had just come through the gates, the Princess was taken entirely by surprise. She hurried to a looking glass and tucked her flyaway red curls into the combs of the simple coif she'd lately been wearing, and noticed with dismay that her bodice and kirtle were spotted with oil. But there was no time for perfection. She must be at the door to greet the Queen when she arrived.

The great front doors, lined on either side with Catherine's servants, were swung open just as Elizabeth reached them. Catherine Parr entered her house — but, thought Elizabeth in that instant, it was not Catherine Parr at all. A strange thought, but strongly felt nonetheless. It was not just the extreme radiance of the Dowager Queen's face nor the spring in her normally dignified gait. *The very soul of her had somehow changed.*

Seeing Elizabeth, Catherine embraced her with an almost crushing fervency, then pushed the girl back to arm's length to look at her. When she noted the condition of Elizabeth's gown and hair, she began to laugh.

"Look at you, Elizabeth," she said. "A proper lady of the house with half the larder on your bodice."

"I'm sorry, Your Majesty. I was quite taken by surprise at your return and I —"

"No apologies! My house is still standing" — she looked around at her smiling servants — "and my staff has not mutinied. Whilst I'm sure you'll have some stories of hair-raising domestic mayhem to tell, it appears you've survived the fortnight reasonably intact." With great affection Catherine pushed one of Elizabeth's errant curls behind her ear.

In the next moment a commotion at the still open doors caused all eyes to turn and witness the explosion into Chelsea House of what was more a force of nature than a man. Lord High Admiral Thomas Seymour — tall and elegant, broad-shouldered, slim-hipped, with a great red beard framing a boldly handsome face — wore a smile that easily outshone the sun. As he came, a whirlwind through the hall, he greeted each and every manservant and waiting lady with a hearty backslap or a brotherly kiss.

21

Elizabeth, as if glued to the spot, watched as the women were reduced to tittering girls. The men, unsure what had just occurred, themselves began to smile and shift from foot to foot, bantering with each other in relaxed laughter.

Kat, the Parrys, and the rest of Elizabeth's household had just descended the staircase from her upstairs apartments when Catherine, beaming from ear to ear, announced, "I should like to present my husband, Lord Thomas Seymour, High Admiral of the King's Navy and Baron of Sudeley."

The response was a burst of sincere applause, but when Thomas strode to Catherine and, pulling her into a bear's embrace, kissed her full and passionately on the mouth, any decorum left in the house dissolved into hearty shouts of laughter and congratulations. When he finally released her, his eyes fell on Elizabeth standing nearby, stock-still and staring incredulously at the unexpected and outrageous display.

"By God's precious soul!" he fairly shouted. "She's even more beautiful than you told me, Catherine." Then with a bow more low and gracious than any man had ever honored her with, Seymour took up Elizabeth's delicate white fingers and kissed them. "Princess Elizabeth," he intoned solemnly, "I am *ever* at your service."

"My lord Admiral" was all she could utter before her servants, Kat at the fore, pressed forward to be presented to him. Elizabeth was so stunned by the man's presence that although she was vaguely aware he spoke individually to each of her retainers, charming and disarming them every one, she was at the same time somehow absent, and, whilst conscious, paralyzed altogether. She prayed that she would not be called upon to speak again, for she was quite sure she would be unable. By God's grace it was Catherine who next spoke.

"I thank you all heartily for so warm a welcome home. And I thank my daughter Elizabeth" — Catherine turned and caressed the Princess with her eyes — "for making sure my new husband and I had a home to return to."

More laughter and applause as Catherine and Thomas made their exit to the palace's east wing. Elizabeth's servants gathering around her, themselves all atwitter, never realized that the fabric of the Princess's existence had begun an unravelment that would, though at present imperceptible, come to threaten the lives of them all.

Why, Elizabeth asked herself, do I not remember him as he is now? The question kept repeating as she walked through Chelsea's corridors on her way to Lord and Lady Seymour's private apartments. Surely she had seen the Admiral as recently as Edward's coronation celebrations. The little king had even commented to Elizabeth on how gallantly his uncle had performed in the lists. Of course, Thomas would have been unrecognizable in heavy armor. But at the feasts afterwards, and in years past, she would have seen him at all the court events. In those days had he not been so grand, so boisterous, so marvelously handsome? Or had she simply been a child with no eye for such qualities in a man?

Stop! she commanded herself. She must waste no more time in such thoughts. He was in a way her stepfather now as well as Edward's uncle, and as much her family as the Queen Dowager. Thomas Seymour was part of Elizabeth's future life, and she would find a way to control the unwelcome and entirely untoward emotions that his mere presence inspired.

Kat had been no help. She herself seemed smitten with the man. It was the-High-Admiral-this and the-High-Admiral-that a hundred times a day. Though Elizabeth remained mum, Thomas was, in the first weeks of his presence at Chelsea, the center of every conversation. Elizabeth was witness to discussions of Thomas Seymour's character and exploits by nearly every member of the household — from Thomas Parry on how Thomas had distinguished himself as a soldier and diplomat in Henry's French wars, from the cook on his culinary habits and appetites and demands, even from the laundress on how large his shirts were, for his shoulders were so broad and manly.

Everything and everybody reminded Elizabeth of him.

She paused outside Catherine's door to collect herself. The Queen Dowager — she still retained the title — had summoned her, and she must do her best to appear calm and normal. The guards uncrossed their halberds to give her admittance, and she entered the grand bed-chamber. Catherine was nowhere to be seen, but to Elizabeth's horror, Thomas Seymour lay stretched, fully clothed but in an attitude of complete nonchalance, across the bed, head resting in his hands.

"Good day, Princess," he said in a deep and alluring voice, never bothering to rise, never taking his eyes from her. In fact, unless it were her imagination, it appeared to Elizabeth that he was examining her closely from foot to head, perhaps lingering on her torso and breasts, and the exposed whiteness of her upper chest and neck. She began to blush furiously and could think of nothing to say. Was she always to be tongue-tied around this man? she wondered with annoyance. And why was he still lying on the bed so indolently? She forced herself to inhale slowly, to calm herself — a small but worthy trick that Kat had taught her — and in a few moments her head cleared.

"Good day, my lord," said Elizabeth, astonished at how relaxed she actually sounded. There was even a slight air of mocking in her voice she had hoped to achieve. "I do hope 'tis not illness which keeps you from rising to greet me."

He smiled that smile which illuminated the world around him.

"'Tis your loveliness, not my laziness, that jellies my knees and makes me incapable of standing, Princess," he answered. "If I tried, I fear I would fall helpless at your feet. And then you would laugh at me."

Elizabeth had already in perfect seriousness uttered, "I would never laugh at you, sir," when she realized she had fallen into the trap of his charming arrogance. In the space of a simple exchange it was she, in fact, who lay helpless at *his* feet. She was, however, spared further humiliation when Catherine entered from the adjoining dressing room. As she passed the canopied bed, the Queen Dowager had only time to extend her hand to her stepdaughter and say "Elizabeth —" before Seymour sprang like a snake from his supine posture, grabbed his wife's waist, and pulled her down on the bed next to him.

"Thomas!" she cried, but she was laughing happily as she struggled in so undignified a manner in the presence of the Princess. He was covering Catherine's face and neck with kisses. Finally he released her, and she sat up trying to catch her breath and regain a semblance of dignity.

"Come here, Elizabeth," she said, suppressing the remainder of her smile. "Come, sit with me. And you," she added with a mock glare at Seymour, "sit up." He obeyed as a chastised child would a mother, propping his back against the headboard, his feet stretched out before him. The two women sat with their feet hanging off the edge of the bed.

"Your stepfather is a prankster, Elizabeth. He is incorrigible."

Elizabeth smiled uneasily, even more at a loss for words than before.

"Here is our problem," Catherine continued. "We have married, as you know, but we've done the deed without the King's permission."

"Without my brother the *Protector*'s permission," Seymour added with what Elizabeth believed was an edge of bitterness.

"Despite the King's affection for me, and mine for him, Henry chose that I should not be part of Edward's upbringing. So I've not had much leave to see him these last months," Catherine said, smoothing the hair that had been ruffled in her wrestling match with Seymour. "We know how close you and your brother have remained," she continued, "and were wondering if you felt we were still sufficiently in his good graces to approach him . . . *directly* about our marriage. 'Tis after the fact, and we fear the duke's feathers will be ruffled —"

"The duchess's feathers, more likely," interjected Thomas, his eyes rolling heavenward.

"If the Protector is angry, but we have the clear support of the King, we believe we can weather the storm a bit more handily."

Lord and Lady Seymour were now staring at Elizabeth expectantly.

"You wish *my* opinion?"

"We do, Elizabeth," said Catherine. "You know your brother's heart better than anyone."

Elizabeth grew quiet and serious, proud to be consulted on so weighty a matter. She thought for a very long moment. She silently recounted everything she had been told about Edward, about the Protector and his wife, and about Thomas Seymour. Finally she spoke, her tone and expression grave.

"I think you'll find the support you desire from my brother. He does love you very deeply, Your Majesty. As it is with myself, you are the only mother he has ever known." Elizabeth paused thoughtfully. When she next spoke, she looked down at her hands rather than risk embarrassing herself with an untoward display of emotion. "As for you, Admiral, Edward much admires yourself. He was aware of our father's affection and the favors he granted you before he died. And whilst the time has been short since King Henry's death . . ." It was getting harder and harder for Elizabeth to go on. "I think Edward would wish your happiness and blessings even above protocol. Of course it has already been done" — now she looked up and saw the pair of them listening intently to her words — "and cannot be undone. I would suggest you write to him. If you fear interception" — she looked down at her hands again — "from the Protector, I mean, you might place the letter within one I send, for I do not think the duke . . . fears me . . . enough to censor my correspondence with Edward."

With that, Elizabeth sighed deeply. She had never before spoken so long or commandingly on a subject of political importance. But when she finally looked up at the faces of her stepparents she was relieved to find them smiling, pleased, and holding hands. Her own heart soared to think she shared such intimacy and possessed the power to make those she loved happy.

"I think that when we write, we should broach the subject of the jewels," said Seymour to Catherine.

"I do not know, Thomas. Perhaps leave it till later."

Elizabeth was staring at them quizzically.

"My brother-in-law —" Catherine began, but Seymour interrupted.

"Your *sister*-in-law," he said. "The pair of them are conspiring to keep from Catherine certain pieces of jewelry your father gave her whilst they were married."

"Why?" asked Elizabeth, heart swelling to be so well trusted as this.

"Because the duchess now holds herself above the Queen Dowager. Because she's a —"

"Thomas." Catherine placed a gentle hand on his arm. "We'll have the jewels in good time. For now I think we should thank our stepdaughter for her counsel and her offered help." She turned to Elizabeth. "If you would write your own letter to Edward, we'll have ours ready by tomorrow. Thank you, Elizabeth." She embraced the girl enthusiastically.

Seymour leaned forward and grasped the Princess's delicate hand, clasping it warmly between his two strong, manly ones and smiling gratefully.

Elizabeth smiled back, hoping desperately that the expression on her face did not reveal the chaos she suddenly felt at Thomas Seymour's touch. The sweet sense of familial affection had, in the space of a moment, evaporated like the dew on a summer rose. She stood and, perhaps too abruptly, begged her leave. As she exited the bedchamber she heard through the door Catherine's sudden squeal of laughter. The thought that Thomas had grabbed the Queen Dowager caused Elizabeth to blush furiously — and to burn with terrible jealousy.

I must gain control of myself, she thought with conviction. He is my stepfather and she my beloved mother.

But as Elizabeth hurried back to the safety of her apartments, she was anything but convinced.

Chapter Three

The sun had not been up an hour and already the Princess and Master Grindal were embroiled in a debate so heated that the temperature in the chilly Chelsea House schoolroom was rising quickly.

"Clearly," insisted Elizabeth with conviction, "Plato meant for his descriptions of Atlantis in the *Timaeus* and *Critias* to be taken as allegory or metaphor for his notion of the ideal state."

"It seems anything but clear to me, Princess," her tutor replied tartly. "Why would Plato have had to invent Atlantis to expound on his ideas of a utopian society when he had previously, and more than once, expounded upon them in his other works, without any geographical references?"

"Then you are saying you believe the great civilization to have been a *reality?*" Elizabeth demanded with more than a touch of skepticism.

"I am merely pointing out that on no less than three separate occasions in those works," said Grindal, "Plato took great pains to assure the reader that his account of the lost continent was not myth, but the true history of the world, handed down from Egyptian priests to his own ancestor Solon. He wrote many other works which *were* allegorical, and in those he allowed the reader to know them as such."

"Still —" Elizabeth insisted.

The heavy schoolroom door swung open. Elizabeth and Grindal turned in unison to see Thomas Seymour ushering into the room a girl the Princess knew to be nine years old, but whose tiny, doll-like figure looked to be no more than six. Though Elizabeth had seen her only once or twice before, there was no mistaking Lady Jane Grey. No one of the court children was more deadly earnest, bookish, or somber than poor little Jane.

"Good morning, Princess, Master Grindal," said Thomas. "Elizabeth, you know your cousin Jane."

The miniature person attired in an unadorned, high-necked gown of brown wool curtsied without smiling, first to Elizabeth and then to the tutor, looking neither of them in the eye.

"I'm happy to say young Jane has become my ward," announced Seymour, his normally loud voice somewhat subdued. He began a circuit of the schoolroom, casually fingering books without looking at them, spinning the world globe as he went by it. It was the first time he had made such an appearance, and to Elizabeth he appeared strangely stiff in his movements, as though the atmosphere of erudition and the smell of ink and vellum made him uncomfortable. "She's taken up quarters in the north wing with her servants," Thomas said, then addressed Jane. "I think you'll be happy there, will you not, my dear?"

"Oh yes, my lord." She looked up at the admiral with what Elizabeth supposed to be her happiest and most adoring smile, but the girl's sadness was so palpable that the expression appeared pathetic.

"Would you like to join us now, Lady Jane?" asked Grindal gently. "We're just debating some of the finer points of Plato."

"I'm very eager to begin, Master Grindal," she said, trying to meet his eye, "but I'm awfully tired from my journey —" she looked away embarrassed — "and my head is aching badly."

Elizabeth spoke up suddenly. "Why not let me take you to Master Roberts? He's our apothecary. He'll have something for your head."

"No, thank you kindly," said Jane. "I think I shall lie down. I'll join you with great enthusiasm tomorrow morning."

Seymour, uncharacteristically reserved, nodded to Elizabeth and Grindal and, placing a hand on Jane's shoulder, led her out. When they had gone Grindal sighed and stared thoughtfully out the classroom's leaded window.

"She is very sad, is she not," said Elizabeth.

"I think she is the saddest child I have ever known. Her tutor is a friend of mine. He says she possesses a most brilliant mind, and it is set entirely upon her studies, which have become her entire life. They alone give her joy, for what constitutes the rest of her existence is so appalling."

"How can that be?" asked Elizabeth, puzzled.

"Lord and Lady Dorset are the most heartless of parents. We are not a society that dotes on our children, you know that, Princess, but the Dorsets go far beyond normal insensitivity, all the way to cruelty. Never is a kind word spoken to the girl. She is whipped and beaten for behavior for which other children would be praised." He paused briefly, then continued. "I am not in favor of the practice of purchasing wardships. It has always seemed to me a form of slavery — buying and selling small children for profit in the guise of giving them a superior education in another man's household. But I must say, in this case I believe the Lord Admiral's wardship of Lady Jane is a godsend for her." He looked gently into Elizabeth's eyes. "I know you will show your cousin the greatest kindness."

"Of course I will. We'll try to give her a little joy." Elizabeth smiled wryly. "Here at Chelsea House there's more than enough happiness to go round."

Chapter Four

God is good, thought Elizabeth, watching the sun break out, all in an instant, from behind a swiftly retreating storm cloud. The Thames was set to glittering, its riverbanks coming alive in the light. From the deck of the Queen Dowager's barge Elizabeth could see the commoners who'd flocked to the shore to watch the vessel float majestically downriver, taking the tide to London. She wondered if, when they'd woken this morning, the people's first thoughts, like hers, had been of Edward. It was the King's birthday, and whilst all of England celebrated, Elizabeth had opened her eyes with an especially thankful prayer that her dear brother had been born. Certainly she adored him, but had he not survived his birth, she mused, her father would have died a deeply unhappy man. Now England had its third Tudor king, the dynasty was intact, and Elizabeth was a beloved princess of the royal house. It was good to be alive.

The rest of her party had come on deck with the advent of the sun, and she regarded them with quiet affection. The Queen Dowager and John and Kat Ashley were immersed in lively conversation. Catherine, Elizabeth observed, looked especially pretty when she spoke, her rather plain features becoming animated by the energy of her fine intelligence and interesting ideas. And now that the period of mourning for Henry was over, all the ladies had donned their merriest colors.

So too, she noted, had Thomas Seymour. He might be a peacock with his luminescent greens and blues, the French lace collar, the silk stocking revealing the curves of a muscled calf. Finding herself staring, she turned her attention to Lady Jane, with whom he conversed. Elizabeth had observed that whenever Thomas spoke to Jane Grey his tone became subdued, his manner somber. The conversations were, however, punctuated by his attempts to coax a rare giggle from the almost morbidly serious girl.

There! She was laughing now. Thomas, Elizabeth thought, had the rare gift of making people happy.

"Princess Elizabeth."

She turned to find that in her reveries she had missed Thomas Parry's approach.

"Parry! You sneaked up on me."

"A bear climbing out of the water onto the deck of this barge could have surprised you as easily," he said, looking in the direction of Elizabeth's line of sight. Thomas Seymour's bulky arm had just gone round Lady Jane's birdlike shoulder.

Elizabeth flushed furiously and averted her gaze over the rail at the river.

"Thank Christ the weather's changed," said Parry, gracefully changing the subject. "'Twould have been a shame had the festivities been ruined by rain."

"True. October can be so dreary," Elizabeth agreed, grateful for his tact.

"I'll be having a word with the Protector about your accounts," said Parry. "He's been late for several months now with your household allowance."

"Shall I speak to Edward directly?"

"I think the duke may be similarly late — or perhaps simply stingy — with the King's allowance. Edward may not be the one to approach for redress on this."

"I cannot believe Somerset would withhold Edward's money."

"It's some time since you've been at court, Princess. Things have changed."

"How so?"

"You'll see for yourself in the next few days. Then we'll discuss it. All right?"

"Fair enough," said Elizabeth. She enjoyed her servant's easy way with her. Thomas Parry was devoted and loyal, and he had happily begun treating her with the respect due an adult in the past months. He suddenly leaned down and whispered in her ear.

"You look very lovely today, Princess."

"Thank you, Parry."

"Roses in your cheeks," he went on. "And you've grown tall as a woman."

Talk of the physical made Elizabeth suddenly squeamish. It reminded her of her gangly body's recent surprises — the budding breasts, the red-gold hair sprouting under her arms and between her legs. She'd recently begun her monthly courses, and the female rituals that accompanied them had been presided over by the clucking ladies Ashley and Parry.

"Isn't she a sight!" exclaimed Parry suddenly. The barge had turned a bend in the river and the palace at Hampton Court had come into full view. It was perhaps the grandest of Henry's castles, with its many buttressed walls and high peaked towers, bright-colored banners flying from the gilded vanes glittering in the sun.

Trumpets sounded as the barge docked at the palace's long wooden quay. Vessels were arriving one after the other, bearing noble passengers and their trunks stuffed with all manner of finery for the three-day birthday celebration. Elizabeth disembarked and, followed by her servants, entered the River Gate. More trumpets echoed in the palace's enormous central courtyard, and now a yeoman holding a bullhorn to his mouth called out the arrivals.

"The princess Elizabeth! Lord High Admiral and Lady Seymour! . . ."

Thomas's head swiveled instantly to glare at the yeoman's announcement. His face went quite red, and when he turned back to Catherine, who walked regally at his side, her arm in his, he was fairly spluttering with rage.

"Did you hear that! They've left off your title as Queen Dowager!"

Elizabeth could see that Catherine too was shaken, but her extreme poise ruled the moment. She pulled Seymour along and into the palace, mounting a wide stone staircase to the residences.

"It's all right, Thomas. We will see to it," she said.

"I'll see to my brother's neck!"

"Shhh — don't give them the satisfaction of seeing you angry."

"Let them see!"

"My darling," she soothed him with her voice. "We will have our day."

"*And* the jewels."

"And the jewels," she repeated indulgently. "We have just to find the proper moment —"

"To wring the good duchess's neck."

"Husband!"

Seymour sucked in a breath to calm himself. "You're right, sweetheart. They'll not succeed in their nefarious plots."

"And we have Edward," she reminded him.

"Yes," he said, brightening noticeably. "We have Edward."

They had arrived at the apartments assigned them — Catherine and Thomas a large suite, and the Princess and her retinue an adjoining one beyond it. In the two suites, two sets of servants had begun unpacking the gowns and doublets to uncrush them.

Elizabeth found her rooms very grand, but through the still-open communicating door she could hear Seymour grumbling again as he stared out the mullioned windows across to the north wing. Elizabeth moved closer, pretending to fetch a basket of slippers, and dumping them out so she could pause and eavesdrop on her stepparents.

"You see which apartments my brother and sister-in-law have appropriated?" Seymour said to no one in particular. And as no one responded, he answered himself, "The *queen's* apartments. Your old rooms, Catherine. They see themselves as king and queen. 'Protector' quite clearly did not suffice."

"Will you stop now?" Catherine said, her voice scolding, but as she came up behind Thomas her arms twined about his slender waist. She leaned against his back and laid her head to the side. "I can feel your heart beating," she said in the voice of a woman contented.

Seymour turned and took her in his arms. "*Now* what can you feel?" he asked with gruff sensuality.

Flummoxed, Elizabeth dropped the leather slipper she'd been

holding and Thomas's eyes fell on her kneeling outside his door, she having had no time to look away. A moment later he turned his gaze from the Princess and covered Catherine's mouth in a deep and devouring kiss.

Elizabeth, cringing with humiliation, darted back into her bedchamber. By the time Seymour looked up from the kiss, all that was left in the doorway was a toppled basket and a half dozen scattered slippers.

Waiting for a moment to approach Edward at the start of the small family dinner in his private chambers, Elizabeth observed her brother closely. In the eight months since his accession he had grown considerably. Now ten, he was a tall boy but slender, and so pale of skin that many thought him unwell. But he was actually quite sturdy, and exuded a proud, pulsing energy that reminded her of their father. Princess Mary, all in black despite the cessation of mourning, had just received a warm kiss from Edward. He seemed mightily pleased with her gift, which Elizabeth could not make out, Mary's back being to her.

It had alarmed Elizabeth to see Mary drop to her knees as she approached the King, not three times as they had their father, but *five* times. She wondered if the protocol must extend therefore to herself, though it seemed to her not only excessive but slightly ridiculous, and she then resolved for three. Mary moved away and Edward stood alone, suddenly looking quite small next to the immense, heavily carved Bed of State. Feeling suddenly and inexplicably weak-kneed, Elizabeth stepped forward, gift in hand. When she finally stood before Edward, towering over the miniature king, she dropped to her knees once, twice, three times as had always been customary. But when she rose from the third, Edward's expression silently commanded that she continue her obeisance. Twice more she made the elaborate curtsy, knowing that all eyes were on her to discern whether it was the King's pleasure or displeasure that was bestowed upon his youngest sister. Her faced burned with sudden humiliation at having to grovel to the little boy whom she had coddled as a babe and comforted in his weeping just months before. When she rose from her final curtsy, however, Edward's face was glowing with such sincere happiness to see her that the moment of embarrassment was forgotten. He stood on his tiptoes to kiss her cheeks.

"Your Majesty," she said. "They told me you were growing like a weed, but I'd say more a sapling."

"And you're looking more like our father than ever."

"What! Hairy and rotund?" exclaimed Elizabeth, feigning outrage.

"No, silly," he giggled. "I mean as he did in the portraits of him as a handsome young man."

Relieved that Edward and she retained the sweet familiarity they'd always shared, Elizabeth held out her gift, wrapped in blue velvet and tied with silver cord.

"Happy birthday, Edward," she said smiling.

He took the package in his hands and felt the weight of it. "'Tis light," he said, squeezing the present with his fingers through the wrapping. "Hawking gloves? Embroidered stockings?"

Elizabeth answered only with an unreadable expression.

"Mary gifted me a purse full of gold coins," he bragged.

"Then you will be disappointed in my gift."

"I shall not."

"I promise you will be," said Elizabeth, wondering if the five curtsies had been an idea of Mary's which, along with a purse of gold, was meant to curry favor with the impressionable young king.

"I cannot guess," Edward announced finally, and tore open the wrappings to find a cambric shirt, almost every inch exquisitely embroidered in silk threads of purple, silver, and gold.

"It's beautiful!" he cried, holding the shirt up before him to examine it. "Did you really do it all yourself?"

"Every stitch. Till my fingers *bled*," she exaggerated dramatically.

"I love it," he said, his face glowing with sincere gratitude.

"As much as the purse of gold?" Elizabeth teased.

Edward thought about his answer carefully. Elizabeth could see that the boy, already schooled for some years in statecraft, had never during their bantering conversation forgotten he was king, that the pert young woman before him was a princess, a potential ally or usurper, as well as a pawn to be used in future political maneuverings.

36

"In some ways I like it less, and in some better," he said.

"Pray tell," said Elizabeth, amused.

"Who would *not* like a purse of gold the best of all?" he replied with a mischievous glint in his eye. "Uncle Edward is so stingy, I have no spending money to gift my friends and servants. Now I do." Then his eyes softened and, looking at the embroidered shirt, he said shyly, "But you honor me with the hours you worked to make me this shirt. For this, I like *your* present best."

"Your diplomatic skills are impeccable, Your Majesty," said Elizabeth with much gravity.

"And I like it better," he continued, surprising her with his earnestness, "for it comes from a good Protestant and not a Papist." His mouth twisted into a frown. "I do worry about our sister's faith."

"It will do you no good to worry on it, brother," said Elizabeth thoughtfully, "for she will never change it."

"I, for one, will continue trying to help her see the light," said Edward. "And the Protector for another."

"Luck to you both," said Elizabeth evenly, "but Mary's faith is as deeply ingrained as her mother's was. And she's every bit as stubborn."

"Your Majesty." It was the cool and level voice of Somerset. "Shall we be seated and dine?" His perfunctory smile at Elizabeth was so brief as to be dismissive. It was the first time the duke had acted so rudely to her, but she knew better than to object. When he had seated Edward at the center of the U-shaped trestles near the fire, he returned to Elizabeth.

"May I show you to your seat?" he inquired unctuously.

"Thank you, my lord," she replied.

Somerset led Elizabeth to a bench at the far end of the table. Across from her, at the other end, sat a disgruntled Catherine and Thomas. As she took her place far from the royal canopy under which Edward now sat and under which she had always held a place since her return to the royal family, Elizabeth considered the influences to which her brother would be subject for the next eight years until he reached his majority. Those influences would indeed affect her own fate, and she hoped fervently that the High Admiral was wrong about his brother and sister-in-law's motive. Ambition was to be expected from a family as old and noble as the Seymours, but taken to its extreme the trait was dangerous to everyone within its reach — dangerous unto death.

So far the weather had cooperated. Spotty clouds vied to prevail over crisp blue sky, but there had been no rain to spoil the day of outdoor festivities. The early morning hunt to hounds had got Elizabeth's blood pounding and the color rushing to her cheeks. Nothing made her feel more alive than to ride, the faster the better — to feel the wind on her face, the muscular beast pounding beneath her.

The celebrants had returned to the palace for the first of several changes of dress for the day. Now the noblemen and ladies wandered amidst the many entertainments in the central courtyard — wrestling, tennis, bowls, archery, running at the rings, casting the bar. And of course gambling. Above all, this was the nobles' favorite pastime.

Elizabeth had heard it whispered that Edward was very cross this day. The bear chosen for the royal bearbaiting — the young king's favorite event — had died en route to London, and despite a frantic barrage of orders and dispatches, another animal had not been found in time. Though she told no one, Elizabeth was relieved. She had always liked the sport well enough, but in the last several years the savagery in the ring and the even more violent bloodlust of the audiences had given her nightmares. Perhaps, as Kat frequently reminded her, she was at a tender age and her bodily humors in constant flux were rattling her mind.

As she stood for a while watching the graceful acrobats leaping and tumbling, forming pyramids, and walking across the grass on their hands, she began to feel a strange sense of having been here before, done this very thing before, though not in her recent memory. It was something vague and very long ago, and she struggled to recall. When, in an almost dreamlike daze, she turned to the sound of jingling bells and her eyes fell on the troupe of Morris dancers dancing, a vision exploded before her eyes, clearing her mind.

She was a tiny girl held in her father's arms at a celebration much like this one, watching the Morris dancers, their high kicks jingling the bells sewn to their costumes. She was dressed in a yellow satin gown matching

38

Henry's magnificent yellow satin doublet. Very proudly, he displayed the little red-haired princess to his celebrating courtiers. Elizabeth giggled and tugged the King's red-gold beard. He laughed so hard, she bounced on his heaving stomach, and everyone laughed to see the King so cheerful.

"Elizabeth."

The sound of her name spoken snatched the princess from her reverie. Elizabeth's eyes regained their focus and she was rewarded by the sight of Robin Dudley, his handsome face at fourteen taking on the contours of manliness, a soft reddish sprouting of beard and mustache on his upper lip and jaw.

"Why have you arrived so late?" Elizabeth demanded. "You missed the hunt."

"We missed the tide. All my sister Mary's fault," he said pointedly as Mary Dudley came up behind her brother and poked him playfully in the ribs for his accusation. Then she curtsied prettily to Elizabeth.

"Good morning, Princess. Don't you listen to my brother. It was *his* fault we were late."

Smiling, Elizabeth gave Mary Dudley a peck on either cheek. She liked her friend's sister very much, for besides being darkly beautiful, she was sweet and intelligent and, like her brother, had always been perfectly kind to Elizabeth. Too, the girls shared deep affection for Robin, who enjoyed teasing them equally well.

"My fault!" he exclaimed. "Whose fifteen gowns to impress young Henry Sidney had not been packed in time?"

"Are you to be betrothed to Henry Sidney, Mary?" inquired Elizabeth with interest. "What a fine match that would be."

"Our fathers are talking," she said, suddenly shy. "But I admit I do like the match."

There was a small friendly commotion behind them as the rest of the Dudley family made their way through the crowd. The parents, John Dudley, lately created Earl of Warwick, and his wife Joan, were followed by their three other boys, John, Ambrose, and Guildford, each more handsome and winsome than the last.

John Dudley was smiling broadly and his wife, hanging on his arm, gazed up at him with unadulterated adoration. Despite the family's reputation for ambition, engendered in good part by the execution of Robin's grandfather Edmund, Elizabeth was intrigued that there had never been a hint of scandal with regard to the Dudleys' marriage. It was apparently sound and happy, inwardly as well as outwardly, and Joan had been as good a mother to her brood as she had been a wife to her husband. Elizabeth had pondered if this shining example of womanhood had contributed to the habitual kindness and loyalty Robin had always shown herself, even before she had regained her status as princess. How, Elizabeth had often wondered, would her own life have been different, if *she* had had such a mother?

The Dudleys joined Robin and Mary in paying their respects to the Princess but did not linger. Mary departed with them, leaving Robin and Elizabeth to themselves. The pair began to stroll through the playground, looking for what would best entertain them.

"Your father seemed cheerful enough," observed Elizabeth.

"My father is a fine actor."

"What do you mean?"

"He's fit to be tied, Elizabeth. It was bad enough that Edward Seymour usurped the regency for himself, but now his brother is planning an even more outrageous coup."

"The Admiral?" Elizabeth was forced to quickly turn her face away from Robin as she spoke of Seymour, for just the thought of him made her blush furiously.

"The 'Admiral' indeed," said Robin. "Are you aware he's not attended to his obligations under that title since it was granted him? He hasn't been anywhere near the shipyards or the naval offices for months. But that's not what's making my father so hot." Robin took Elizabeth's arm and steered her through the crush to the courtyard's North Gate and surreptitiously pointed out two gentlemen standing together tête-à-tête. Anyone observing the men could see by the intensity of their expressions and the sharp punctuating hand gestures that Thomas Seymour and Jane Grey's father, Lord Dorset, were plotting together.

"What are they planning?" asked Elizabeth, curiosity suddenly overwhelming her.

"Nothing less than Lady Jane's marriage — to the King."

Elizabeth giggled with the surprise of such an idea. "My brother and Lady Jane?" she said incredulously.

"Think about it, Elizabeth," Robin insisted.

"Well . . . they are cousins. She's English, and these days the people like their queens English. Jane is very bright, and Edward would require an intelligent wife . . . and they do like each other."

"You're missing the point, Elizabeth," whispered Robin impatiently. "Thomas Seymour bought Jane's wardship from Lord Dorset for this purpose alone. Don't you see? They mean to make her queen and, through their relationship to her, gain close access to the throne."

Elizabeth was silent for a long moment as Robin's arguments echoed in her head. She felt confused, unsure where her loyalties lay, assaulted more and more frequently by wild thoughts and untoward emotions.

"Well, Edward has to marry *somebody*," she finally blurted. "Why not Lady Jane?"

"Elizabeth —"

"Robin, I've come to celebrate my brother's birthday. I don't wish to spend the entire day worrying about politics! Now, is it bowls or archery?"

"Dice," he answered with a devilish grin.

"Dice it is," said Elizabeth, smiling happily. "Allow me to show you the way."

It was that time of day peculiar to the noble class when, after a morning and afternoon of strenuous physical games, the body demanded to be refreshed by rest in preparation for the long evening of feasting, drinking, and dancing that lay ahead. All those of sufficient stature or favor with the King had retired to their apartments, and those not fortunate enough to be quartered in such luxury napped on cots squeezed into friends' chambers or upstairs corridors made temporarily into dormitories.

John Dudley had been the Councillor closest to Henry, save Edward Seymour at the last, and his apartments in the palace were well established and suitably grand. The Duke of Somerset had not possessed the audacity, though his wife had suggested it, to displace the Dudleys from their rooms. Now the family had assembled for their rest. As the other sons collapsed with feigned exhaustion — for at their ages energy was a boundless commodity — Robin Dudley stood with his back to his seated father, pulling off the man's boots.

"I'll just give you a little help, son," said John, giving Robin a foot in the rump that pushed him forward, pulling the boot off as he went.

Robin turned grinning. "Thank you, Father," he said, and they laughed.

John Dudley loved his family dearly. He was particularly proud of his handsome sons. Each had been blessed with his own great strengths, and none had had the misfortune of any desperate shortcomings. Certainly he was most fond of John, his eldest, as all fathers could not help but be. By virtue of being firstborn, young John was heir to the entire family fortune. But the elder Dudley bore Robin a large measure of affection. Though he'd never spoken such thoughts, he believed there was greatness in the boy. He was sure of it. Only fourteen, Robin had a mature and temperate nature and an elegant style. He seemed to understand instinctively the importance of loyalty, which showed itself most clearly in his devotion to Elizabeth, whom Robin had befriended when the girl had still been a pariah to King Henry's house. Despite high spirits and a flair for grandiosity, the boy had a certain sense of reserve as well. He knew when a quiet conversation was called for and, touchingly, proffered sensible advice to his friends and family when he knew they were troubled. Conversely, he could tell when *not* to interfere or control, but simply to listen to the problems of others.

John Dudley took a place in the center of the wide canopied bed.

"Is there anything I can get you, Father?" asked Robin, standing by his side.

"Nothing, thank you."

Robin moved to the window seat to remove his own boots and, gazing out the glass, caught sight of Thomas Seymour hurrying across the palace yard.

"I see the Admiral is not taking his rest," he said.

"Does that surprise you?" asked his father.

"No, but . . ." Robin did not finish, but a question hung in the air.

"What is it, son?"

"Why are *you* not up and about, scheming your own schemes?"

John Dudley smiled at the audacity as well as the perceptiveness of his son's question and took a moment to consider his answer before he spoke.

"I think of my well-laid plans as I do fruit trees."

Robin looked perplexed.

"The seeds are planted. I nourish them, watch as they take root, grow, take shape. Time, sometimes many seasons, must pass before they're ready to bear fruit. A man cannot pluck the fruit until its proper time. If he does take it before perfect ripeness, he will be bitterly disappointed. And all the work, the planning, the waiting, will have been in vain."

"Have you many fruit trees planted, then?" asked Robin, enjoying so edifying a conversation with the father he adored.

"Several, though none whose fruit are near ripeness. 'Tis vital, Robin, that for now I practice patience, eschew overtly ambitious schemes, appear a mild and unthreatening figure to everyone at court and in Council. Edward Seymour, with his harsh and arrogant behavior, makes more enemies every day. And his brother Thomas — that man is a reckless fool. He hardly has need of my scheming to dig himself a grave. So, for the time being I can take off my boots, put up my feet . . . and watch my fruit trees come slowly into blossom."

Thomas Seymour was, indeed, scheming. As the boy king rested in his great Bed of State and his gentlemen of the wardrobe bustled about preparing the elaborate garments he would wear for the evening's entertainments, the Lord High Admiral sat on a bench in the King's antechamber with Thomas Fowler, a young man of twenty-three whose sparkling blue eyes and crooked grin gave him a somewhat sly but altogether handsome appearance. He was just the sort of gentleman with whom the King enjoyed surrounding himself. Edward had never discovered that Fowler had been placed in his service — *planted* to be more exact — by Thomas Seymour.

"How *much* money?" asked the Admiral.

"Considering that your brother gives the poor boy no spending money at all, I would say *anything* would please him," answered Fowler knowingly.

"And you're certain this is the way to his heart? He's always cherished my wife's affection —"

"Money, my lord. Gold pieces. I'm absolutely sure of it."

"All right, I'll see to a handsome purse within the week. And, Fowler . . ."

"Yes, my lord?"

"Does he confide in you?"

"Oh yes, my lord," said Fowler, the right side of his mouth curling higher than the left in a crooked smile. "When you and the Queen Dowager sent your letter begging for his support of your marriage, he showed the thing to me before he pled your case to the Protector."

"Very good," said Seymour, absently fingering the wiry hairs of his beard, silently skipping weeks, even months ahead into the future of his artful calculations. "Tell me when you think he will be ready to hear us on the subject of the Queen Dowager's jewelry."

"First send him several purses," instructed Fowler.

"Three? Four?"

"Say four. And another good one just before Christmastide. He will be very grateful to have money for gifting his closest retainers on New Year's Day."

"Like yourself," said Seymour pointedly.

"Indeed." Fowler was equally pointed, and unabashedly so.

"Then how soon after Christmas shall we broach the subject of the jewels?" demanded Seymour impatiently.

"Two weeks. No more. Children forget gratitude very quickly. Then have the Queen Dowager write a letter herself."

"Not from me as well?"

Fowler trod lightly, as if moving across a crust of thin ice. "His feeling for your wife runs very deep, my lord. She is the only mother the King has ever known — though of course he is very fond of you as well," he added quickly. "Many times he's spoken to me of your spectacular performance at his coronation lists." Fowler was warming to this fine opportunity to disseminate praise to his patron from Edward. "I think the King wishes to grow up to be like you — in the manly sense."

"And in no other sense?" Seymour demanded irritably. He was finding himself ever more cross with Fowler as the audience went on, never knowing if the young man was sincere or slyly impertinent. "Not as an example of a statesman or a diplomat?" he insisted.

Fowler took on the expression of one who, in the midst of a losing battle, has discovered an impregnable stone barricade behind which to hide. "But, my lord," he intoned, smooth as a snake, "King Edward had his father Great Harry as his example of those attributes."

Thomas Seymour found himself humiliated by his own hubris. There was nothing to be done but finish his business with this arrogant fellow. He stood, and so did Fowler. The Lord High Admiral was pleased that he towered over the young man. In fact, he wished right now to tweak his ear very sharply. Or worse. Instead he was gracious. Fowler was his closest link to the King and he could not afford to anger him. Still, thought Thomas Seymour, when the struggling courtier had outlived his usefulness, he would pay for his impertinence. It would not be long now.

"Oh! Begging your pardon, Your Majesty!" exclaimed Sally Wilton. The girl had come flying round the corner, her arms crowded with cosmetics jars and hairpieces, and collided with Catherine Parr astroll in the corridor of Hampton Court's north wing. The girl, one of her minor waiting women when she'd been queen, was horrified at the cloud of wig powder now enveloping them both and began curtsying frantically, eyes lowered.

"Oh, Your Majesty, I'm so very sorry!"
"All right, Sally. No harm done," said Catherine in a kindly voice.
"Thank you, madame, thank you."
"You go on your way, now. Do not keep your mistress waiting."
Another curtsy and Sally was gone, only to be followed round the corner by a young courtier whose face she did not recognize. He

regarded Catherine with sanguine politeness and a mere nod in her direction. "Lady Seymour," he said and went on.

How different were the two greetings, Catherine remarked to herself — one from King Henry's court, one from King Edward's. Or should she say the court of the Somersets? To one she was the beloved Queen Dowager, so titled until King Edward's marriage. To the other she was merely the High Admiral's wife, requiring little more than disdain. The courtier, thought Catherine, was most probably one of the Protector's "new men." The privilege normally reserved to the King — the raising of subjects to eminence — had been unceremoniously usurped by her brother-in-law and his wife, along with many other sovereign prerogatives. All of these new men and ladies would of course follow their maker's lead and shower disrespect on any remnants of the old regime. And of course the Duke of Somerset's fiercest competitor was his brother Thomas. The Duchess of Somerset meanwhile had claimed that Catherine, by marrying a man so far beneath her station, had forfeited her rights as Queen Dowager. Clearly the yeoman's instructions to publicly announce Catherine only as "Lady Seymour" also announced the duchess's perceived precedence over Catherine.

No matter, thought Catherine; I have finally, after three tedious marriages for duty, made a marriage for love. She was ever warmed by this thought, this blessing shared by so few of her class. Nevertheless she had found herself this afternoon, as the ladies and gentlemen of the court were being coiffed and dressed for the evening's festivities, drawn back to the royal residences where she had lived for several years as queen of England.

It had been a rare time in her life, filled with equal measures of joy and dread. She had so loved the king's children, each differently but deeply: Princess Mary, dear friend since school days, who had weathered banishment and bastardization by her father; Princess Elizabeth, a tender girl of nine when Catherine had been crowned, and similarly exiled by Henry; Edward, a sensitive four-year-old who had never known maternal love until Catherine came into his life. She had assembled from the scattered shards of Henry's life a true family — one he at first grudgingly and later sincerely enjoyed, and from which Catherine derived the only true pleasure of her reign.

The marriage to Henry had been a triumph of self-will and intellectual gamesmanship. She knew him as well as any woman alive, for she had been part of the Tudor family circle since infancy and had watched each previous marriage unfold, blossom, and wither. But she had never loved the King. In the years before he commanded her into his bed she had begun to fear and loathe him. The great and beautiful prince he had been in his youth — virile and athletic, as pious and scholarly as he was fun-loving — had devolved into a murderous and decrepit mountain of flesh, his stinking, pustulent leg an advertisement of the power-corrupted soul that lay within. Even Henry's faith, once inviolable, by the end of his life was as constant as the flight of a tennis ball batted back and forth across a net. He would hang, draw, and quarter traitors for refusing to uphold Catholic tenets on the same day he would burn heretics for their Protestant ideals.

Once Henry had worshipped women for their intellect, preferring a sharp mind and quick wit to a pretty face. But by the time of her predecessor Catherine Howard's ascendance, he had chosen his wife for her docility. Even Catherine, brilliantly educated and well known for her agile mind, had had to stifle herself, pretend she was a mere student to Henry's all-knowing teacher, in order to save herself from scheming Councillors who would have liked to see her headless on the block.

Catherine stopped to examine a corridor wall where her family's coat of arms had once hung. It had been hastily taken down after Henry's death, replaced by the Seymour crest. She was thrust suddenly into thoughts of the past: her brief widowhood after Lord Latimer's death, before Henry had asked for her hand — remembered the heady days of Thomas Seymour's courting and the thrill of their trysts, recalled the rightness of her pleasure after twenty stifling years of young life married to old men, recollected her and Thomas's hours of strategizing over how they would approach the King for permission to marry. Then the dawning horror that Henry's intentions for his own remarriage had, in fact, settled on Catherine. There had been many tears on her part, much raging on Thomas's, but of course there was nothing to be done except acquiesce. Henry had, no doubt, learned of their affair, but had been undeterred — for he had concluded that Catherine, Lady Latimer, was the perfect wife for himself, committed neither to the Catholic Gardiner faction nor to the progressive Protestants that included the Seymours and the Dudleys. The King simply announced his intentions to Catherine and, with the stroke of a quill, caused Thomas Seymour to disappear — sent him abroad on a years-long series of diplomatic and military engagements.

Catherine had had to grit her teeth, plaster on a gracious smile, and comply, saying that God had placed this duty before her and she would not shrink from it. If part of her relished the opportunity to use the prodigious wit and political know-how she had acquired over years of life in the inner circle, that part was overshadowed by the profoundest grief at having lost her love and the physical pleasure she had found in Thomas Seymour's arms. But her survival, she knew, was dependent upon a believable portrayal as Henry's contented and happy queen. And so she'd become Henry's helpmate and nurse, spending hours, as he gave audience to Councillors and ambassadors, with his ulcerated leg propped upon her lap. She endured his caresses and his oppressive, sweating nakedness in the great Bed of State.

For happiness' sake, she began the rejoining of the Tudor family and, most important, returned the princesses to the succession. She accompanied Henry on the grandest summer progress of his reign, then stood as regent and protector of the infant Edward, Henry's heir, when the King departed for the French wars. She drew her ladies of intellect and devoted humanism round her in an ever more protective cocoon, and schemed very carefully to bring learning to the masses.

Always smiling, gracious, and kind, Queen Catherine had won Henry's trust and devotion. But always she feared him. Detested him. Watched as his once razor-honed mind fell into decay and his stony will eroded, so that the merest whisper from either faction could send him careening from one extreme of persecution to the other. She watched helplessly as the King allowed her dearest childhood friend, Anne Askew, to be viciously tortured on the rack and finally burnt at the stake for belief in her Protestant faith. Sometimes Catherine marveled that she herself had survived the attempt by the Gardiner faction to have her arrested and executed as a heretic. They had schemed against her so carefully, but she had groveled to Henry, pretending that her religious beliefs were the thoughts of a mere humble wife who needed her husband's guidance. This had appealed greatly to his pride, and at the last moment he had called off her attackers, as hunting dogs would be pulled back from the cornered deer before they could rip it limb from limb.

But her sacrifices were not all in vain. Having regained Henry's trust, she began quietly instigating the reforms she and her women had dreamt of — not so much reforms of the Protestant faith as their beloved humanistic ideals.

Then Catherine had watched Henry wither and begin to die. It was all she could do to control her elation, for in those months, as the factions inevitably began taking their positions and honing their future plans, Thomas Seymour was called home from abroad. At court in his presence she remained coolly reserved, the faithful queen, when all the time she was silently shouting Thomas's name, feeling his strong hands on her body, smelling the male musk of him, hearing him whisper her name as he moved inside her.

Catherine was astounded at her own patience waiting for Henry to die. She arranged for Elizabeth to come to live with her at the Chelsea Dower House. She feigned appropriate grief on Great Harry's passing, and felt nothing at her exclusion from the protectorship of the boy king Edward. Her duty was done. Finally she was free to live for herself. To live for love. True, there had been talk of Thomas's overweening ambition, the machinations surrounding marriage proposals to the princesses, and even to Anne of Cleves. But from the moment of his return he had been ever attentive to herself, and he'd dismissed the marriage proposals as ugly rumors. She had, of course, believed him. How could she not? He loved her, had thought of no one in the previous years but her, and she adored him. The moment she had installed herself and Princess Elizabeth and their households at Chelsea, she and Thomas had begun their clandestine trysts. A mere four months after Henry had been laid to rest, they'd been secretly married.

Sometimes she wondered if her happiness was blinding her. There had been moments of late when Thomas's behavior alarmed her. His desperation about retrieving the crown jewels bordered on the ridiculous. And she had seen how he sometimes looked at Elizabeth. . . . No! she chided herself. There was nothing to worry about. It was simply

Thomas's way. Everything about him was bold and outrageous. Even reckless. That was why she loved him. She had been a patient and understanding wife to a far more dangerous character in Henry, and the reward for a marriage to Thomas was so much greater. She could hardly wait for the next time they would share a bed. . . .

"Lady Seymour."

The woman's voice jolted Catherine out of her thoughts, the fantasy's torrid sensuality causing her to blush as she turned to face the Duchess of Somerset.

The high color in Catherine's cheeks and the surprised expression pleased the Duchess, and she smiled patronizingly. "Haunting your old residences, are you?"

It took a moment for Catherine to comprehend the disrespect with which the woman had addressed her. She silently engaged her opponent with a steely gaze. "I hope you and the duke are comfortably ensconced in the queen's apartments." The arrogance of appropriating the royal rooms had been angrily commented upon by many of the Privy Councillors who'd been unseated by Edward Seymour's unilateral Protectorship, but none of their opinions were sufficient cause to change the couple's high and mighty accommodations. "To be honest," Catherine continued, regaining her composure, "I miss these rooms not at all. I was, in fact, just thinking that I am far happier in my modest household with your brother-in-law than I was in these rooms married to the king of England." She smiled sweetly to punctuate her statement.

The duchess's face was hard. "You can afford such nonchalance. Your husband the High Admiral" — she said the title with a sneer — "is quite ambitious enough for the both of you."

Just then Thomas Seymour was approaching the women unseen from around the corner, returning from the King's apartments and his meeting with Fowler. Hearing his name and recognizing the voices, he quietly fell to one knee and, facing the wall, pretended to be tying a bootlace.

"Lord Somerset has treated Thomas very shabbily," said Catherine. "Truly, such behavior does not befit the dignity of someone in so high a position. Much as your husband aspires to royalty, Duchess, 'tis clearly not in his blood."

Seymour sensed the path along which this argument moved and began praying silently that these two snarling cats would not touch upon the subject of the royal jewels. Fowler and his plan — a sensible one — were already in place.

"My husband treats Thomas as he would any arrogant and self-serving subject," the duchess insisted.

"Subject!" cried Catherine, unable to control her outrage. "You two *do* place yourselves very high indeed."

Momentarily flustered, the duchess quickly regained her composure. "Thomas is the King's subject, and Edward's responsibility is to protect the King from such men," she said. "Such *greedy* men," she added.

"*You* dare speak of greed!" said Catherine, her voice rising shrilly.

"I do. What else should Thomas's interest in the jewels be called?" was the duchess's retort.

Behind the corner Seymour winced, but the Queen Dowager answered, unaware she was being led into a trap.

"Those were a present from Henry to myself." Catherine's voice wavered. "You and the duke are taking this stand only to humiliate me."

"Why, Lady Seymour," said the duchess with condescending sweetness. "You interpret this far too personally. My husband is simply doing his job. You see, legally, the jewels belong to England."

This was not an argument with which Catherine had thus far been confronted, and she became momentarily flustered.

"Have the jewels, then!" she shouted. "I do not care if I ever see them again!"

"Very good," said the Duchess of Somerset coolly. "I'll let my husband know you and Thomas will be pursuing the matter no further."

Furious, Thomas stood up and strode away, muttering evil curses at his brother, his sister-in-law — and his wife. How could Catherine have been so stupid! He had married her for her brains, not her beauty or feminine charms. He'd married her for her wealth, and for the ability and intelligence she had brought to bear while she'd been queen. As queen dowager he'd assumed she would continue to wield the most power of any woman in the kingdom.

And now he had witnessed her being bested by his conniving harridan of a sister-in-law. Perhaps he had been wrong about Catherine, he thought with a sudden sinking feeling in his belly. Perhaps he had set his sights on the wrong woman. Something, he decided, his jaw tightening, something would have to be done.

From without, the fresh-built wooden banqueting hall, long and large and tall as it was, gave no indication of the splendor within. There, ten thousand points of flickering torch- and candlelight set the gilded walls ablaze, brought to life the myriad figures in the hung tapestries, and in the high cupboards along the wall, set all the King's riches of silver and gold to sparkling.

Therein, to horn and string and drum, England's noblemen and ladies danced and masqued in honor of young Edward's birth. Beneath the royal canopy the King, poised on the edge of his throne, seemed altogether merry at the spectacle. He was still puffed with pride at his own magnificent entrance to the entertainments, astride a white horse caparisoned in forest green with silver trappings, himself bedecked in a doublet of purple and gold. All had loudly cheered his arrival, and the boy's normally stern expression exploded into smiles and childish laughter.

This evening, Edward had instructed his musicians to play more *voltas* and *galliards* than slow, measured dances, and so the air was thick and warm with the revelers' exertions. Cheeks were flushed, spirits high, and pulses racing.

On nights like these Elizabeth lived to dance. Energy boundless, she stopped only when the music did, dancing each and every number played. She was envied by the ladies for her grace and exuberance. Gentlemen fought for the honor of partnering her. Robin Dudley had already had the pleasure three times this evening, but as Lords Clinton and Arundel playfully bantered for the next dance, young Dudley slipped behind them, grabbed Elizabeth's hand, and guided her to the center of the hall where couples had already gathered, waiting for the music to begin. He gave her a wicked smile.

"What a knave you are, Robin Dudley," said Elizabeth with mock indignance.

"You like dancing with me the best. Admit it."

"I'll admit to no such thing," she replied, trying to suppress a smile.

"Look there," said Robin, his tone shifting suddenly to seriousness. "There's your knave. He's up to something."

Elizabeth followed Robin's gaze to the throne, where Thomas Seymour, arrayed in shimmering orange and gold, was bending over the King and whispering in his ear. Edward nodded in agreement with his uncle, then stood suddenly. As Elizabeth and Robin watched, he strode across the hall, certainly aware that all eyes were on him, and stopped before an astonished Lady Jane Grey. The little girl's mouth actually fell open as the King of England performed a deep, flourishing bow and, taking her hand, led Jane out onto the dance floor. The moment the miniature couple had struck their poses the music began. This was one of the few slow *allemandes,* and so conversation was possible throughout.

"What did I tell you?" said Robin smugly.

"Jane is Edward's cousin," Elizabeth replied evenly, "and they are friendly. Why should they not dance?"

"Oh, they *should* dance. They'll dance a king and queen if your stepfather has a say in it."

"Say what you like, Robin, but Thomas Seymour is no villain. He's very good to me and exceedingly good to Jane."

"Not as good as he is to himself," Robin replied, leading Elizabeth into a swiveling half-turn. Directly in her line of sight was Thomas Seymour again. He had moved to Lord Dorset's side and, head lowered to the ear of Jane Grey's father, conferred with the other man. Both wore what could only be construed as conspiratorial smiles, their eyes fastened on the dancing Edward and Jane. As Seymour and Dorset began to laugh, Robin brought Elizabeth round to face him, again neither of them missing a step of the *allemande's* rhythm.

"Smugness doesn't become you, Robin," she said.

"Perhaps. But I *am* right."

"If you insist." Elizabeth sighed, then smiled. She'd caught sight of the Queen Dowager on the sidelines, watching her dance with Robin. Catherine's face was aglow, as though deeply pleased by the sight of her stepdaughter.

*

Indeed, Catherine was happy. Through her own devices she had secured Elizabeth's place as an honored princess in the royal court of England. Despite the earlier unpleasantness with the Duchess of Somerset, Catherine felt nothing but enjoyment this evening. The King looked very well and made a pretty couple with little Jane. Thomas had nearly taken her breath away when he'd come to fetch her for the banquet. There was no handsomer or more dashing man in the pavilion, she thought. Her life, she decided, was perfect — full and rich with love. She reflected that she had not openly declared that love for him for much too long. As she watched the dancers on the floor an idea was born — she would tell him a moment before the last *galliard* of the evening. Husbands and wives who for the previous hours had partnered with divers men and ladies would, as unspoken tradition demanded, come together for this special dance. There were high leaps and ladies swung far in the air, their falling bodies pressed for a sweet and fleeting moment to their partners' bodies. It was a small public intimacy she relished. Yes, she would whisper her most ardent affection for him in the moments before the *galliard* began, lending yet more sensuality to the dance, for Thomas had always said that so reserved a woman as herself succumbing to passion excited him.

The *allemande* had ended and Catherine could see the gentlemen and ladies seeking out their partners for the last dance. Eyes modestly downcast and smiling to herself, she waited for the moment Thomas's hand would be extended to hers and the manly voice would ask for the pleasure of her company on the dance floor. All round her taffeta and velvet rustled, and murmured requests were proffered and accepted. The sidelines cleared and the floor filled. Still Thomas did not appear. Finally the Queen Dowager lifted her eyes and searched the hall for her husband. There he was! Just now skirting the dance floor coming in her direction.

Her heart thumped hard in her chest. Her lips bowed in a contented smile, but in the next moment the smile collapsed into dismay. Thomas was reaching out his hand to another lady, half hidden by Lord Winchester. When Winchester turned to his wife and took her onto the dance floor, the lady was revealed.

Elizabeth? Not possible! He would dance this dance with his wife, not some young virgin. Catherine's mind reeled. Perhaps she was mistaken. Perhaps this was not the last *galliard* after all. Perhaps —

But then the music began. It was in fact the *galliard.*

"May I have the pleasure, Your Majesty?" Catherine turned to see her brother, William Parr. He must have noticed her discomfiture, she realized, and with good grace and charity spared her from the disgrace of being left partnerless for the dance. But tears had begun to sting Catherine's eyes and a sudden wave of nausea overtook her.

"Thank you, William, but I'm feeling unwell. I told my husband he should ask another lady. In fact, I think I will retire."

"Shall I see you to your rooms, Majesty?" he asked with genuine concern.

"No, no . . ." The music was loud and pounding, and dancers' cries drowned out all attempted conversation.

"I'll find my own way!" Catherine shouted, then turned and fled the pavilion.

Elizabeth, for a moment suspended in midair, was transported with rapture. She fell gracefully into Thomas Seymour's waiting arms and he flung her round him in a full circle before setting her lightly on her feet again. As they danced her heart swelled, for he had never for a moment taken his eyes from hers, held them with such intensity she would have turned away but for his command that said, Stay with me, relinquish my gaze never. She obeyed him as her feet and arms obeyed the *galliard*'s prescribed steps and rhythms and flourishes.

Elizabeth watched as Thomas leapt staglike. Then he swept her into his arms and, hands gripping her waist, thrust her heavenward. A cry escaped her throat, and when she fell to earth it was into a full embrace, his body pressed tightly to hers. It was only for a moment, and unseen by the revelers all round them, but she felt his heat, felt his breath, felt — sweet Jesus — the hardness between his legs. He released her but did not twirl her round him as he should have. He simply stared into her eyes until the music caught them up, announcing the next set of steps, and they began again as though nothing at all had occurred.

But something *had* occurred, thought Elizabeth, wild with the dance and the sound and the furious confusion in her head.

He returns my feelings! she thought, terror mixed with her joy. He thinks of me as I do of him! Oh, Thomas, she cried silently, Thomas, my love, my love . . .

Spirits had run so high that evening that after what was to have been the last *galliard,* the King — to the revelers' delight — ordered that the musicians play on. Servers brought cups of watered wine and ale to the dancers, and another round of festivities began at the moment they were meant to be finishing.

The Duke of Somerset stood, one hand resting on the arm of Edward's empty throne, gazing about the banqueting hall. The King was happily engaged on the sidelines surrounded by a group of fawning courtiers. The Protector could see his wife, attired more exquisitely and expensively in French lace and cloth of gold than all the other ladies this night. She was just now having court paid her by Lord and Lady Wilton. This was a most agreeable sight, for before the couple had always been disrespectful in the extreme. Things were as they should be, thought Somerset, unable to keep from smiling. Indeed, all was right with the world.

"Why don't you just *sit* on it, Edward. The throne, I mean."

Somerset had no need to turn to the speaker to identify the sarcastic voice of his brother Thomas. He forced himself to retain the pleasant countenance he had assumed, for he did not wish anyone to see how angry and discomfited his younger brother could, in the space of a breath, make him feel.

"Good evening, Thomas," Somerset said mildly, ignoring the "throne" reference, clearly the opening gambit of one of Thomas Seymour's annoying verbal competitions. "Are you enjoying yourself?"

"Splendid occasion," said Thomas. "The duchess your wife is simply sparkling tonight — or is it perhaps Catherine's *necklace* that's sparkling? I cannot be sure."

"I understood from my wife that the jewels were no longer an issue," said Somerset, finally turning to look at his brother, who was similarly struggling to keep his composure.

"The 'issue,'" Thomas said pointedly, "is the disrespect that you and your *wife*" — he spoke the word as if it were a curse — "continue to heap upon the Queen Dowager."

"Disrespect?" said Somerset innocently. "We have never meant her any disrespect."

"Then why was she publicly announced merely as Lady Seymour when we arrived?"

"A simple oversight," said Somerset dismissively.

"And was it an 'oversight' that at the King's birthday supper she and I were seated at the very farthest end of the table?"

There was a silence whilst Somerset collected himself, deciding whether or not to engage with his brother in a duel of wits. Such an activity would no doubt leave him with a headache, but the man was more than an irritant. Thomas was, in his wilding ways, very dangerous to everyone around him and could wreak havoc with Somerset's own plans. The intentional slights to Thomas and Catherine had not, as he'd hoped, had the effect of announcing the Protector's superior position over the couple, but only served to enflame his brother. The equanimity that Somerset had valiantly attempted to maintain now faded as he realized that there *was* no solution to the problem of Thomas Seymour. He would, as long as the Protector was in power, be a bone in Somerset's throat. "I think," he said, his voice choked with growing fury, "that you should learn the meaning of gratitude."

"Gratitude?"

"Yes, Thomas, gratitude. You've been given the admiralty of the King's Navy, and the barony of Sudeley. You've married yourself a high-born lady."

"A queen!" Thomas fairly shouted. Several people turned to see the brothers arguing — exactly what Somerset had wished to avoid.

"And you've got plenty of money to go on with. I therefore wish to hear no more complaints about your situation, or I will see to it that you are stripped of those titles and leases that have been so generously granted you by the Crown!"

Somerset was gratified to see the color rise in Thomas's face, and when his brother turned and strode away without another word, the Protector felt a thrill of victory surge through his being. But as he watched Thomas skirting the edge of the dance floor, stopping to say a few congenial words to every high courtier he met, Somerset saw that his brother was altogether unperturbed by his tongue-lashing, *as if it had never occurred.*

The glow of victory faded, and in its place in Edward Seymour's mind began to grow a cold, unreasoning fear.

Chapter Five

She stood tall and naked in a spring meadow, pale green grasses tickling her ankles. A mild breeze from one side set her long loosened hair caressing her cheek and neck and small rounded breast, the rosy nipple rising and hardening to the curls' touch. A smile played about her lips, for the feeling was so delicate and lovely. Yes, such a sweet sensation, sweet, joined now by the touch of air moving the golden bush in the vee of her thighs, mmm, the faintest touch, sweet sensation, lazy as the spring day. Her eyes lowered and found to some surprise no breeze, but a gentle hand brushing the silky hairs of her virgin mound. The man on his knees seemed to worship at her feet, the hands now descending slowly the length of her slender ivory legs, his touch so soft it barely disturbed their pale down. She felt his warm lips kiss her bare feet, the tongue flicking the clefts of her toes. She swooned with the loveliness, not merely the sensation of flesh on flesh, but the thought of a man's utter worship of herself. It warmed her soul first, and as his lips and hands began to move, slowly higher and higher, again her body's heat rose. She reached out her long white fingers to follow and, as if blessing the man, touched the crown of his auburn mane. He raised his head and she saw it was Thomas. Beloved Thomas. He resumed his ascent, the heat once more suffusing her torso and limbs, now congealing into pure liquid pleasure in the central place, the secret place so lovely and sweet. Unbearably warm, his breath unbearably sweet. Hot red-gold curls brushing her nipples. Suddenly, oh, an explosion of sweetness, there, oh, oh . . . !

Elizabeth's eyes flew open as she gasped with surprise. It was not simply in-taken breath that flooded her being, but *shame*. She lay face up, naked under lawn sheet and coverlet, as she always did, her red-gold curls now falling round her shoulders brushing, as in her dream, the soft of her breasts. She exhaled and sighed deeply, as though she had escaped the sensual ordeal somehow intact, yet somehow irrevocably changed. What had just occurred? What world had she been inhabiting in her dreams? Had she been possessed by some unmentionable demon? Surely such pleasure was a serious and punishable offense. And with Lord Thomas Seymour! At the thought of him, Elizabeth blushed furiously, even as she told herself that such embarrassment was entirely private and therefore unnecessary. Kat Ashley lay asleep and snoring softly on the pallet next to the canopied bed in which Elizabeth lay.

Her mind resumed the logical analysis of what had happened. No one had ever mentioned such a miraculous sensation. Married women and girls of loose virtue gossiped endlessly, sometimes laughing behind their hands at some shared and lascivious secret. Was this it? But surely what they knew, their guilty pleasures, were to be found with men of flesh and blood, not the solitary act attended only by a dream creature who looked, who was none other than Thomas Seymour, a married man! Still a virgin, thought Elizabeth, and I have yet committed adultery!

An unexpected giggle escaped her throat, and she rolled over to bury her face in the pillow, muffling her laughter. It would not do to wake Kat this way. She would insist upon knowing the source of Elizabeth's merriment, and as the Princess had never, ever been able to lie convincingly to her nurse, her humiliating secret would soon be revealed.

She heard the squeak of the heavy bedchamber door as it slowly opened. Blanche Parry must be up and about already, bringing the warmed water for Elizabeth's morning ablutions. But she was not yet ready to face the day, still wished to wallow in memory of the delicious dream. She would pretend to be sleeping. Let the woman go about her business and —

A sudden weight came down on her body. Hands grappled with her bedclothes, and a boisterous shout of "By God's precious soul!" rang through the chamber.

Elizabeth's heart came nearly bursting out of her chest. Shrieking loudly, she wrestled for control of the sheets now threatening to be wrenched away, revealing her slim nakedness. As she turned, squirming, to face her attacker, she came face to face with the visage of

Thomas Seymour, his eyes bright to madness, his white teeth revealed beneath a leering smile.

"My lord!" Elizabeth squealed just as the sheet was snatched from her grasp to allow full view of her breasts.

His eyes feasted on the sight for only a moment before Elizabeth snatched the white lawn up to her neck again. Then Kat came aboard the storm-wracked ship and, thumping the Admiral aside with her shoulder, threw her ample body crossways over Elizabeth's slender one, leaving Thomas with a view of the good woman's nightgowned rump.

Her muffled voice was still loud and commanding enough to bring the staunchest criminal to his senses. "God's blood!" she roared. "Have you lost your senses, Admiral?"

At the sound of the reprimand Elizabeth fully expected apologies to begin flowing, but what she heard as she gently pushed her waiting lady aside was jolly laughter from the man. Laughter!

"By God's precious soul!" he bellowed again. "'Twas a *jest,* Mistress Ashley, a jest!" His laughter, rolling and echoing in the bedchamber, outrageous as it was, proved infectious, and suddenly Kat Ashley was giggling like a schoolgirl as Elizabeth sat rigidly holding the sheet to her neck, face hot with embarrassment.

"My lord, you took us both by surprise," said Kat. "Snatched us out of a dead sleep."

"My point exactly," he replied, making no move to leave the bed, but instead sitting up with his back to the headboard beside Elizabeth. She stared straight ahead, refusing to meet his gaze. "It's well past six," he insisted. "The Princess should be up and dressed for her morning ride."

"If you leave us, I will dress her," answered Kat, but the indignance was wholly gone from her voice.

"And what will she wear this morning?" Seymour demanded, and with casual familiarity reached out and squeezed Elizabeth's knee under the covers.

She was reminded of his hands but moments before, *in that place — just there —* in her dream, and again flushed crimson. Then he leapt off the bed and strode to the wardrobe, flinging open the doors.

"Shall I choose for you?"

"No!" cried Elizabeth, finally finding her voice. "You must leave my room at once, my lord."

He turned slowly to face the women, an amused grin defying Elizabeth's command. "Oh, I *must,* must I?"

"Yes," said Elizabeth, her confidence slipping away like milk through a sieve.

"You command me in my own house, then?" he asked as if sincerely interested in her answer.

"'Tis the Queen Dowager's house," was Elizabeth's feeble retort.

"And I am her husband. So, 'tis *my* house, you see."

Elizabeth elbowed her nurse for some assistance, but Kat Ashley seemed stupefied, altogether flummoxed at the circumstances. The best she could mutter was, "The visit at such an hour *is* unseemly, Admiral. My lady's reputation —"

"Your lady is my stepdaughter, and *I* say what is seemly in my own house. But I will leave you now." He fixed Elizabeth with a stare so raw and direct that she was forced to avert her eyes. "Let me see you in the olive green with gold braid this morning, Princess. It sets your milky skin aglow." Then he was gone, striding out the bedchamber door.

The great heat and force of his presence suddenly absent left Elizabeth and Kat strangely more bereft than relieved. The nurse, perhaps ashamed that she had acted so weakly, jumped up and like a large clothed hen began clucking busily about the room in preparation for Elizabeth's morning *toilette.* The girl sat stunned, watching but not seeing Kat's frenetic rounds of the bedchamber, immobile with utter confusion. One moment Thomas had appeared to her in a shockingly sweet dream, the next he was all flesh and booming voice and, far from worshipping at her feet, had taken liberties and commanded her as a husband commands a wife.

Which was real? Elizabeth wondered silently. What was happening to her? Who on earth could she tell? Certainly not Kat, who had behaved so oddly in the presence of this red-haired giant. And certainly not Queen Catherine.

The door cracked open again. Both lady and nurse, breath catching in their throats, turned and saw Blanche Parry, still in her morning robe, enter with a pitcher of water.

"'Tis only myself," she said matter-of-factly. "You look like a pair of owls. Who were you expecting to come through that door then, Satan?"

Kat clucked dismissively and Elizabeth pulled the covers that Thomas Seymour had wrested from her back over her body, then slid down till she was hidden completely. She was not ready to face the day, not with her mind a roiling cauldron of emotions.

"I'm staying abed," she announced to her servants through the sheet and coverlet.

"You're doing nothing of the sort," said Kat, who took the covers down off Elizabeth's face. "'Tis a beautiful morning for a ride. Go and have a wash while the water's warm."

As she reluctantly rose, Elizabeth could see that Kat had already laid a riding outfit across the foot of her bed. It was the olive green velvet with gold braid.

When Elizabeth saw what had been chosen for her to wear, her heart began to pound anew. She glanced at Kat and realized with alarm that the woman, altogether oblivious of the fact, had fallen under the spell of the Admiral's magic.

Nothing, thought Elizabeth, would ever be the same.

Chapter Six

Thomas Seymour pressed himself against the corridor wall and watched a still sleep-weary Kat Ashley scurry by to the fool's errand on which he'd sent her. His servant had whispered in her ear just before dawn that a messenger from Suffolk was at the front door with a letter for her. Thomas had heard a piece of gossip that Mistress Ashley's old sweetheart lived in Suffolk, and he judged that the woman would be curious enough about such a correspondence to abandon her post.

The ploy, happily for Seymour, had left Princess Elizabeth deliciously alone in her bedchamber, perhaps still asleep. The greater her surprise, he'd discovered in the last weeks of these early morning visits, the greater his own arousal. It had become something of a game, he conceiving ever more shocking strategies to take Elizabeth by storm in her bedchamber, she attempting to outwit him by her own devices. First she had taken to wearing nightclothes in order to never again be caught naked as she had the first time he'd come to her. Then she'd begun waking early to be fully dressed when he appeared. She'd sometimes gone into the schoolroom, sitting prim and straight over her Greek translation, even before the sun was up. He'd followed her there, too, having a merry time chasing her round the desk till she'd fled shrieking back to her nurse.

But all of her cries and protestations he knew to be halfhearted. She *enjoyed* his attentions, he was sure of it. And why shouldn't she? He was a great man at the height of his vitality and good looks. Even women of wit and sophistication — his wife Catherine was one — were slaves to his charms. How could so tender and nubile a girl as Elizabeth resist him, no matter how outrageous his advances?

This day he had slipped out of bed extra early, sending Ellen

Wilcox, still groggy with sleep, to fetch Kat from her bed. Seymour had worried that the nurse would suspect a ruse, but she had indeed been fooled. What Mistress Ashley would discover at the front door was a playful letter from himself inquiring after her "great buttocks," if they had grown or not, for he much admired them. She would feign embarrassment and give him a stern remonstrance, but he knew she would be mightily complimented by his attentions, unseemly as they were. Kat liked him very well. He knew this by the way her eyes fell on him when they stood together, the carriage of her shoulders, and the tilt of her head. With all her fine manners, Kat Ashley had the heart of a bawd.

He slipped into Elizabeth's chamber and found the girl quite alone and, blessed Jesus, in her bed *asleep.* The sight of her so helpless and milk sweet, her red hair spilling from beneath her nightcap onto the white pillow, stirred him violently. It was all he could do not to lock the door behind him and ravish her on the spot. But he steadied himself. It would not do for his purposes to lose all control. There was a method to his madness that only he understood. He would tease and cajole and flatter her to distraction, then ignore her, turning the want to need and need to a frenzy of desire. He could see her mind was a muddle of passion and guilt in equal measures. Indeed, his plan was working perfectly.

Elizabeth stirred, moaning in sleep. His arousal grew sharper. He must move quickly, for Kat Ashley would be returning momentarily. He threw off his robe so he stood in only a thin nightshirt and slippers. Then he climbed onto the bed and carefully straddled her body, pinioning Elizabeth between his widespread thighs. Thus positioned he struck, his fingers finding her waist and sides — and began tickling. She cried out in terror even before her eyes flew open. Recognizing her tormentor, she looked frantically around for Kat but found her gone. They were alone! Her squirming and struggling caused his tickling fingers to fall "accidentally" on breast, belly, or hip, and her shrieks finally, with the ceaseless onslaught, turned to helpless laughter. He was laughing too, laughing like a boy, delighted with his own prank.

"Stop! Stop!" cried Elizabeth, gasping for breath.

"Never!" shouted Thomas.

She, agile as a cat, suddenly rolled out from under him, sprang from the bed, and bolted for the door. He dove with outstretched arms and caught her nightdress, halting her flight. He wrenched her back as he leapt to his feet and suddenly she was in his arms, face to face. They were breathless, nothing separating their bodies but two thin night-gowns. She could not, he realized with animal pleasure, be unaware of his sex, fully erect and pressing into her belly.

"Come now, Elizabeth, give your stepfather a kiss."

Her eyes flashed wildly and, with more strength than he realized she possessed, she pushed Seymour's shoulders back with the flat of her hands and screamed, "No!" Her face was bright with anger, her breathing ragged.

"Be still. I only meant to show you some affection," he uttered. "Truly."

She sniffed and replied sharply, "I may be a green girl, but I'm no fool. These visits are creating a scandal in this house. You must stop coming alone into my apartments like this, my lord."

He did not reply, but stared deep into her eyes, attempting to re-lay the warm message he could not speak in words.

"You *must* promise me that," she persisted.

"I shall never come into your rooms alone again," he intoned solemnly.

"You swear?"

"On my honor."

"My God!" shrieked Kat, who stood like an angry bull in the doorway. "You tricked me, Thomas Seymour. And now look at you. In your nightshirt, and the Princess . . ."

He grinned sheepishly at Kat.

"Get back in bed, Elizabeth," she commanded. "And you leave at once, my lord."

"If you insist, Mistress Ashley," he said, grabbing his robe.

As Elizabeth turned her back on Seymour, he swatted her play-fully on the backside.

"Out!" cried Kat, and came at him as if to attack.

As he dodged the fuming nurse, he pinched her buttock and

whispered in her ear before scooting away, "They *have* grown to a wonderful size."

"Oh, oh! You're a terrible man!" she shouted, but was unable to hide the affection in her voice.

Heads poked out doors to see the figure of the lord of the manor disappearing down the corridor in his nightshirt and slippers. They exchanged disapproving glances and clucked at the scandalous commotion which had, almost daily in the past weeks, changed the once stately Chelsea House to a bawdy house. 'Twas a bad business, this. It would come to no good end.

As promised, Thomas Seymour never again came alone for his mad morning romps into Elizabeth's bedchamber. When next he arrived, in fact, his wife was with him.

As the pair fell on Elizabeth's cowering figure beneath the covers and commenced tickling her, she had but a moment to wonder if her eyes were playing tricks, or perhaps she was dreaming. The two of them were in their nightgowns. Catherine's thin, straight hair fell in wild disarray about her shoulders, and her eyes gleamed with so manic a brilliance that the Princess hardly recognized her much-loved stepmother. It was terrible to witness this paragon of virtue and erudition transformed into some mad creature pretending a gaiety that even Elizabeth could see cloaked appalling desperation.

This frightful visit came as a complete surprise. To Elizabeth's chagrin, Thomas had for a fortnight stopped coming altogether, after the visit during which she elicited his "promise" from him. She had been — though she could not say it aloud — more miserable than relieved. His absence left a gaping hole in her life. The first several days of his ignoring her had been tolerable, for she was buoyed by a fine-honed edge of anticipation. She dreamt incessantly of him and always pleasantly. There had thankfully been no recurrences of her carnal night fantasy. Instead, her dreams were suffused with the gentle glow of romance. *Thomas bringing her a knot of red and white posies. Thomas riding to rescue her from an evil water spirit at the edge of a misty lake.* He was always a gentle friend in the dreams, never the boisterous package of virility that he was in the daylight. He was somehow soft in his being, but strong, always strong.

It was this man in her dreams with whom Elizabeth fell madly and hopelessly in love.

Thomas's absence from her bedchamber lengthened into a week. Two. She became frantic. She'd catch sight of him riding out from the stables well after she'd come back from her morning ride. He was tall in his saddle, more graceful than a man his age and great size had a right to be. At meals, he was unerringly decorous to her, and maddeningly more attentive to Catherine than he had ever been before. The Queen Dowager warmed to this attention at first, but as the days progressed, Elizabeth saw the woman's mind being drawn tighter and tighter, as a lute string might be stretched. Catherine's temper grew short and she would screech abuse at Elizabeth or Lady Jane, then after an outburst she would smother the girls with apologies. One moment she was serious to tears, the next giggling so uncontrollably she'd have to excuse herself from the room.

This morning the lute string had finally snapped. Catherine was not herself. As they struggled, wrestling and tumbling amidst the bedclothes with Catherine muttering lewd obscenities, Elizabeth grew more and more frightened of the woman. She was a strange chimera — the Queen Dowager's body inhabited by the soul of a coarse wench.

Kat, paralyzed by the sight of Catherine in so unseemly a state, stood by wringing her hands, her jaw flapping with disbelief. Occasionally she would reach out as if to snatch Elizabeth out of the lion's pit, only to pull back for fear of being bitten. Catherine, strange as her behavior might be, was still the highest lady in the land. Who was Kat Ashley to restrain her?

"Stop, stop!" Elizabeth gasped just as Thomas Seymour lunged across her body to grab and tickle his wife. Catherine shrieked with surprised delight and in turn grasped a handful of his hair, pulling him to her for a kiss. Their moist faces, glowing with the heat of exertion, were inches from Elizabeth's own, and when their lips parted, the couple turned and smiled crazily down at the girl. Thomas sank his face into Elizabeth's neck, nuzzling her noisily. Taking her cue from him, Catherine followed suit and buried her face in Elizabeth's shoulder, now bare, for her shift had pulled down, exposing a breast as well. In the awful panic of the moment, Elizabeth saw that her nipple was hard and erect, and Thomas had stopped his nuzzling to gaze at it.

"Kat! Kat, help me!" Elizabeth screamed in mortification.

The sound of her charge's voice finally roused the nurse from her helpless stupor. With a loud cry she flung herself on the pile of writhing bodies. Unheedful of all consequence, she shoved aside the grappling attackers and laid her own body lengthways across Elizabeth's.

"Out, out, both of you! For shame, for shame!"

"Come, Catherine," Seymour cried laughingly. "Queen Kat has spoken."

With wide eyes Elizabeth peered over her nurse's shoulder and saw Thomas reaching for his wife. But the Queen Dowager was staring down at the bed, at Kat's prone figure protecting Elizabeth's slender frame with her own. A look of abject horror swept across her face as if she had only then realized what she had done. Then Seymour gathered Catherine by the waist and took her from the room.

"I don't know what's come over Her Majesty," said Kat as she pushed herself off Elizabeth and lay panting beside the girl on her bed. "She ought to be ashamed."

Elizabeth was bereft of all speech. She had prayed for Thomas's return. Despite her guilt, she had prayed to Jesus for one more moment of intimacy with him, no matter how outrageous and sinful the circumstances. Then he had come to her bed with Catherine. What was he thinking? Did he not love and desire herself? Wait, wait! What was she saying? He was a married man. Married to the only woman she had ever called mother.

Kat had finally caught her breath. She sat up and smoothed her nightgown around her.

"And what of her husband? Should *he* not be ashamed as well?" asked Elizabeth, searching desperately for some raft of sanity in this ocean of chaos.

"He is a man, Elizabeth, and cannot be held accountable for his lusts."

"Does he lust for *me,* then, Kat? Do you think — ?"

"I meant, I mean —"

"Does he lust for me!?" shouted Elizabeth, suddenly forgetting the ugliness of what had just occurred.

"Shh!" hissed Kat and, pulling away from Elizabeth, she climbed down from the bed. She began searching frantically for her slippers on the floor. "Of course he does. And why wouldn't he? His wife is middle-aged and plain. She's bedded with three old men for husbands. . . ." Kat was on her knees now, searching for the slippers under the bed, and seemed temporarily to have forgotten that one of those old men had been Elizabeth's father. "You, sweet girl, are as radiant and beautiful a virgin as any who's walked on this earth. Who would blame him for de-siring yourself. Hah!" Kat cried, and came up with the slippers in hand. "If you ask me," she continued, sitting on the bed and putting the slip-pers on one at a time, "you and the High Admiral make a sight more handsome couple than he and the Queen Dowager."

"Katherine Ashley!" cried Elizabeth, trying to sound horrified but barely stifling her delight.

"Well, 'tis true, but you forget I said that. Do you hear me?"

"Yes, Kat," said Elizabeth demurely.

"Now, I've got to get dressed and down to the kitchen. They'll all have heard of this by now and I'd best do what I can to quash the ru-mors before it's made out worse than it was. We'll have all our meals sent up today and pray that His Lordship and Her Majesty come to their senses. Might as well get yourself back in bed, then," Kat added. She shook her head as though trying to rearrange the mess of thoughts and emotions within it and bustled into the adjoining room to dress.

Elizabeth lay back, closed her eyes, and in seconds had conjured the face of her beloved. The back of her long pale fingers caressed her own cheek and slender neck and, hidden under the covers, found the pink rosette centered in the small mound of her breast. It was erect and still hard, and the gentlest touch made her womanly place quiver de-lightfully.

Suddenly, she cared very little for the scandal of it, allowed her worry for the Queen Dowager's state of mind and any consequences to recede to the most distant shores in her world of dreams. She loved

Thomas Seymour and he lusted after her. Nothing, she thought lazily, nothing under heaven could be sweeter.

"I'm afraid I've some unhappy news, Elizabeth."

The Princess looked down at the Queen Dowager sitting alone at a desk in the schoolroom. The Princess had come there as she always had, continuing her Greek translations during her tutor's absence. This day she had been surprised to find her stepmother.

"I've already informed Lady Jane . . ." intoned Catherine morosely.

"Grindal?" cried Elizabeth, staring round wildly as though searching the room for her teacher. She turned to face Catherine, whose eyes were red-rimmed and shimmering with tears of grief, though the dark circles beneath them and the deepening lines of worry at the corners of her mouth and forehead, Elizabeth knew, had been forming for many weeks before this.

"He died on Wednesday."

Elizabeth's hand flew to her mouth to cover the twisted shape of its grieving. "We knew he had taken ill, but not so sick as to die," she said.

"The plague took him," Catherine said simply.

"Plague!" cried Elizabeth. "So, he travels to Cambridge for a holiday and instead dies of the plague? What sense is there in that?" Tears had begun streaming down Elizabeth's cheeks. "He cannot be dead!"

"I'm sorry, my dear." Wearily Catherine stood. She could not bear to meet her stepdaughter's eye, and instead moved for the door. "He was a good friend, Master Grindal. He will be missed." Then with nary a comforting embrace, the Queen Dowager departed.

Elizabeth looked down at her volume of Xenophon and the unfinished translation beneath the inkwell. With an angry sweep of her arm, she knocked them all from her desk. Everything around her was crumbling, and everyone had become insane. She needed desperately to find some solace or she, too, would go mad.

Tears still blinding her, she turned on her heel and walked quickly down the long corridor from the schoolroom to the manor's front door. The chilly morning air stung her wet cheeks and she wiped her face unceremoniously with the back of her sleeve. She headed for the stables.

Elizabeth galloped wildly across the rolling meadows and through pastures, scattering herds of grazing sheep, ignoring the rutted roads and twisting lanes altogether, for this was the quickest route to Warwick Hall and the comforting presence of her best friend in all the world.

The Dudleys lived in modest splendor. Robin's father, John, had been, along with Edward Seymour, the most trusted advisor of Henry VIII. Aside from the Tudors who were royal, the Dudleys and Seymours were unquestionably England's most prominent and important families, figuring in the country's politics since Great Harry's father had stolen the throne from Richard III and killed the last Plantagenet king on Bosworth Field. For their loyal service to the Crown, the Tudor kings — Elizabeth's grandfather, father, and now her brother — had bestowed upon the two families the greatest wealth and authority possible. Elizabeth's and Robin's lives were, therefore, inordinately and inexorably bound, and it was well that there was a deep and sincere sympathy between them.

A frequent visitor to Warwick Hall, Elizabeth was shown in immediately by the house servants. Moments later Joan Dudley had greeted the Princess and enfolded her in a warm embrace.

"Margaret," said the older woman, "bring the Princess some cold ale," then, to Elizabeth, "You're very flushed, my dear." She examined Elizabeth's perspiring face. "I hope you're not ill."

"Sick at heart perhaps, but not unwell. Thank you for asking, Lady Dudley. Is Robin about?"

"You'll find him in the forest with Ambrose and their birds. At breakfast I mentioned a taste for plump quail and they said they'd find me some."

"Then will you excuse me?" said Elizabeth distractedly and turned to go.

"Your ale, dear . . ."

But Elizabeth was already gone.

It did not take her long to find the boys, for Elizabeth had hawked and hunted with them in these woods and meadows for years. From a distance it would, for anyone else, be difficult to tell apart the two Dudleys — now riding hell-bent across the field. Ambrose was older but Robin was tall for his age. To Elizabeth's eye, however, the distinction was obvious — Robin's assured posture in the saddle, his extra-broad shoulders on the slender frame promising a magnificent man as he matured into them. Once she had him in her sight, Elizabeth felt herself calm immediately and slowed her mount to a trot. There was something so reassuring about Robin Dudley's presence, some unfathomable kinship that soothed her. All pretenses fell away when they were together. She trusted him entirely.

Now Robin extended a rigid arm before him. A moment later a hawk swooped from the sky and, great claws first, landed on the boy's padded sleeve. A limp bird, no doubt one of Joan's quail, hung from its beak. Elizabeth watched Ambrose wheel round and gallop back toward his brother, who had already stored the kill in his saddle pouch and was now placing a plumed hood over the head of the proud hunter.

She rode to meet the boys as they came back across the meadow, smiles of genuine pleasure on their faces at the sight of her. But as soon as the initial greetings and pleasantries were done, Ambrose grabbed Robin's pouch, now crammed with fresh-killed quail, and excused himself, knowing very well whom the Princess had come to see. He spurred his mount and started back for Warwick House.

The friends had not been alone more than a moment before Robin demanded, "What's wrong, Elizabeth? Tell me."

"Grindal is dead," she replied, and burst suddenly into tears.

Robin jumped down off his horse and came quickly to Elizabeth's side. She allowed herself to be helped down and enfolded in Robin's awkward embrace. She had never cried in his presence before, even at the death of her father, and despite their comfortable friendship he found himself at something of a loss. He therefore remained silent, allowing her to cry. But instead of the tears gradually subsiding, the outpouring of emotion grew wilder until the girl was heaving with sobs.

"Elizabeth, Elizabeth," he muttered helplessly.

"Oh, Robin . . ." she wailed piteously. "Oh, God . . ."

"What is it? Tell me what's wrong. You must tell me. What has happened?"

She choked back her sobs and pulled out of his arms. "Now look what I've done," she said. "I've soaked your jacket." She began to blot his shoulder with her sleeve.

He gently grabbed her wrist to stop her and kissed the back of her hand before taking both hands in his own. The gesture was so dear that Elizabeth burst into fresh tears.

"Stop, Elizabeth," he crooned. "Take a breath and calm yourself." He waited until she did as she was told, then he wiped her tearstained face with a clean handkerchief he'd found in her saddle pack. "That's better. Now listen to me. You have my deepest condolences on Grindal's death, but this" — he gestured, indicating her recent outburst — "this has nothing to do with him, has it?"

"No," she admitted, but offered nothing further.

"No? Then what is it? Must I drag it out of you? Is the Queen Dowager ill?" He saw Elizabeth's hand fly up to cover her quivering mouth, but the Princess did not answer. Exasperated, he took Elizabeth by the shoulders and gave her a shake. "Tell me!" he shouted.

"She's not ill," Elizabeth finally blurted, "but she's gone mad."

"What? How can that be? Catherine Parr is the most sane and levelheaded woman in all of England. I do not understand. What has she done to deserve such a description from you, of all people?"

"She came into my room in the morning, in her nightgown . . . her hair unloosed . . ." Elizabeth was struggling to push the words out. "She fell on me, wrestling . . . and tickling me and . . ."

Robin was listening hard, but the words were nonsensical. "How does that make her mad, Elizabeth? Perhaps your stepmother has become more playful since her —"

"*He* was with her!" Elizabeth cried. "He has been coming into my room in the mornings, barelegged in his nightclothes and —"

"Seymour?"

"Yes."

"Thomas Seymour has been visiting you in your bedchamber in his nightshirt?"

She nodded.

"For how long?"

"I do not know. Weeks. Not every day . . ."

"And the Queen?"

"Just once. But she was not herself, Robin."

"What does Mistress Ashley have to say of it? Knowing her, I would guess she'd have *much* to say."

"Well —" Elizabeth was growing nervous as more and more of the uncomfortable truth came to light. "Kat is at first outraged —"

"As well she should be," Robin interjected.

"But then . . . she takes his side, makes excuses for him."

"She couldn't," he exclaimed disbelievingly.

"But she does."

"Kat's lost her mind along with the Queen Dowager, then," he said.

Elizabeth was silent for a long moment, staring off in the direction of Chelsea House.

"What?" demanded Robin. "What are you thinking?"

"That I've lost my mind as well."

"Meaning . . . ?"

"I love Thomas Seymour," she said quietly. "He dominates my dreams and my senses. I love him and I believe he loves me."

Robin Dudley stared at Elizabeth in abashed silence, unable to form a thought or a question or even an outraged oath, as the gravity and danger of the Princess's situation seeped slowly into his mind.

"Has he . . . touched you, Elizabeth?"

"No. Well, in playful ways . . ."

"How, exactly?"

"And who are you? Señor Torquemada of the Spanish Inquisition?" She laughed unsteadily.

Robin Dudley forced himself to smile. If he frightened the Princess too badly, he reasoned, she might run from his confidence. On the other hand, this was a deadly serious matter. He knew enough to realize these were serious offences, but if he were entirely honest with himself, he would have to admit his feelings were tinged with jealousy. This final realization shook his confidence. He had to be objective if he was to help his friend.

"Elizabeth," he said carefully, "you are by blood a legitimate Tudor princess. Your mother's perfidy had you banished and bastardized. But the Fates had other things in store for you. 'Twas no mean feat that Catherine Parr saw you restored to your family, and, more important, to your place in the succession. Would you defy Fate, sacrifice your God-given rights for a noisy, reckless hooligan?"

She looked at him with desperate eyes and cried, "I might, I might!"

Silenced by her own irrationality, Elizabeth turned and faced her horse, waiting for Robin's leg up into the saddle. When she was seated, she looked down at him, her flawless face creased with agony.

Robin watched his beloved friend as she rode away toward Chelsea House, her back straight as a rod, her chin high and proud. He felt he could weep at the sight, but instead he mounted his horse and with great purpose rode home to Warwick Hall.

Hampton Court, thought Robin Dudley as he strode down the wide corridor to the Privy Council Chamber, was as much home to him as any of his father's great houses. He had, from the beginning of Prince Edward's education, been playmate and schoolmate of the pampered boy — had been known, in fact, as "one of the King's children." Robin was four years older than Edward and, if not his favorite, was his boon companion in riding, hawking, and archery, and in secret played with him at cards and chess although their tutor, Master Cheke, had consistently frowned upon these as frivolity.

Robin paused for the briefest moment before the imposing portrait of Henry the Eighth before continuing — for the young man was on a mission — but the sight of Great Harry, his magnificent and bejeweled bulk balanced astride two shapely calves, renewed painful memories of the King as he'd been near his end. He had quashed civil rebellions at home and had finally returned from the French wars. Bloated and ill, he'd had to be carried about from room to room on a contraption, his ulcerous leg unable to support his bulk. He had ceased doting upon his only son, Edward, "His Majesty's most noble jewel." Instead, angry at his people's perceived betrayal of him, Henry had become peevish and wildly bad-tempered, bitter in his disappointment that he could not live to see Edward in his maturity. The vast power that Henry had accumulated — first personal and later semi-divine after he had usurped the riches and the reach of the monasteries — had corrupted him immeasurably. The once brilliant administrator and intellectual genius had given way to a cruel and capricious despot.

But Edward, like all of Henry's children, had been utterly blind to his father's shortcomings. The boy had been told that he should imitate the King, who was the greatest man in the world, and had come to believe that if he surpassed his father, none could ever surpass him. Now the only son of Henry the Eighth, himself a king, had been reduced to a helpless pawn in the Seymour brothers' Machiavellian games.

It was this thought, and fear for his dear friend Elizabeth's safety, that now animated young Dudley. The doors to the Council Chamber swung open as he approached. The Duke of Somerset was conspicuously absent, away, Robin knew, overseeing troop movements into Scotland. Lords Clinton and Arundel, Norfolk and Rutland drifted from the chamber, faces grim and strained. John Dudley's expression brightened at the surprise sight of his son, whom he embraced heartily. Robin nodded respectfully to the Privy Councillors before pulling his father aside with restrained urgency.

"May we go to the family apartments or some place of privacy, Father?"

John Dudley regarded his fourteen-year-old son's request with bemused indulgence and together, careful to speak only of frivolous matters in the public halls and corridors that were rife with eavesdroppers, the two repaired to the Dudleys' comfortable rooms.

Over a simple repast of cold meat pies and crisp ale Robin felt himself relax and soften, his father's presence so reassuring and comforting. It troubled him to think of revealing what had been a most private confidence between two friends. But Elizabeth's very life was at stake, he was sure of this, and he believed he was acting in her best interests. Taking several deep breaths to steady himself, Robin Dudley related to his father the treachery of Thomas Seymour and, more recently, the Queen Dowager, forcing himself to refrain from exaggeration or excess passion in his telling. For in truth, though he was entirely unaware of it, he wished as much for his father's good opinion as for the Princess's well-being.

John Dudley listened intently, closing his eyes as if to exclude all other thoughts and senses, and concentrated on the boy's telling. Occasionally he would shake his head with disgust and disbelief and occasionally require Robin to elucidate a point or clarify a statement.

"Are his actions treasonable, Father?" asked Robin finally, relieved to have finished his litany of offences.

"In and of themselves? I think not. However, a pattern begins to emerge here."

"A pattern?"

"Thomas Seymour has always been arrogant and foolishly reckless, but he seems now to be somehow *directed*. As you know, he has shirked his admiralty entirely and lent no support to his brother's efforts in the Scottish campaign. This is outrageous in itself, but word has come that the Lord High Admiral is dealing directly with pirates, using his position to buy them safety in return for a piece of their profits. We understand that he has placed a man, William Fowler, in Edward's privy service for easy access to the King, and has begun bribing the boy with gifts of money."

"I do see what you're saying, Father. He is taking all of his actions several steps further."

"Indeed. And now his resentment and jealousy of his brother have recently turned virulent. He pulls aside members of the Council one by one, trying to convince them that *he* is a more fit protector than Somerset. Christ knows what he has Fowler whispering in the King's ear."

"So what do you make of what I've told you this afternoon?" asked Robin.

"It appears that all of the Admiral's connivances on behalf of Edward and Lady Jane to see them married are insufficient," replied John Dudley. "This outrageous interference with the Princess is further proof of his grandiose intentions. He must believe in some twisted way that if he compromises her, defiles her, the Council will have to give her to him."

"You believe he means to go that far?"

"After what you've told me, son, I believe the man capable of any-thing." John Dudley fell into a prolonged silence. Fingers absently brushing his lips, downcast eyes fixed on a silver flagon, he seemed to be concocting a plan. After what seemed to Robin an eternity, the elder Dudley looked up.

"How does your orchard grow, Father?" Robin Dudley inquired with a sly smile.

"Very well, though the fruit is not yet ripe for plucking. Some tending is still required. Do you wish to help the princess Elizabeth?"

"You know I do, my lord, else I would never have breached my friend's confidence."

"Very well," said John Dudley, standing and moving to the win-dow and gazing down at the river below. "We shall move slowly and cautiously with regard to the Lord High Admiral —"

"But he mustn't be allowed to lay hands on Elizabeth again," Robin objected.

"It seems from your telling," said John Dudley, "that you invoked the wrath of the Privy Council, if not God, in your warnings to the Princess about jeopardizing her place in the succession by encouraging such behavior."

Robin thought for a long moment, trying to recall with exactness Elizabeth's response to his admonitions. "I worry," he said slowly, "that her heart rules her mind in this." He joined his father at the window. "That the man should wield such power over a woman of Lady Cather-ine's strength makes me wonder at Elizabeth's ability to withstand him."

"He does seem to hold some strange power over women's hearts," said the elder Dudley, then added thoughtfully, "and men's too. But I think he will not go the full distance with Elizabeth until he is free of his wife. In the meantime his scheming will no doubt continue. But we shall be watching him, waiting for a false move, and it will come. With men like Thomas Seymour it always comes. And then he will fall." John Dudley smiled warmly and threw an arm around his son's shoul-der. "You've done well in coming to me, son. This is one harvest that we shall enjoy together."

Chapter Seven

I despise the smell of salt air, admitted Thomas Seymour. Bracing himself against the rail of the *Princess Mary* as she rocked and bobbed in the choppy water, he enjoyed the irony of the thought. High commander of the King's Navy, and he loathed the sea. On land he'd been a brave and lucky soldier, but force him onto a boat of any nature and he was altogether lost. He had never attained a sailor's balance on the ever-tilting decks nor lost the green-faced nausea he experienced with virtually every ocean voyage or channel crossing. In his fighting days he'd been fortunate never to have overseen a water battle. The sight of a heaving commander would have been death to his dignity and probably to his command over the men.

The appointment to the Admiralty, he'd immediately understood, had been his elder brother's private and very nasty prank on Thomas, whom he knew to grow seasick playing with toy boats in a pond. Today, however, Seymour had braved the waters, reminding himself as he boarded the English flagship that it was but a short trip from England's southern coast to the Scilly Isles, and that the rewards of the jaunt would be well worth his discomfort. He'd stayed most of the rough journey in his cabin below decks, but now the island's shore was in sight, and he comforted himself with the thought that his feet would soon be on dry land.

"M'lord, will you board the dinghy now?"

Seymour was startled by the voice and turned to see Captain Broward, a rough man from Devon whose appearance was softened very little by the crisp blue and white uniform of the King's Navy. Thomas nodded his assent and made to follow the captain. But the moment he let go the railing, the sharply tilting boards under his feet sent him careening across the decks into the ropes and rigging. This, to Seymour's horror, elicited poorly disguised snickers of contempt from the sailors at their posts. Furious, he shoved away the arm Captain Broward offered for support. Then Seymour staggered to the rail and, steeling himself for the ordeal, heaved himself over the side to struggle down the rope net and into the small wooden dinghy.

The two-man crew kept their eyes respectfully downcast as they rowed staunchly through the chop, ignoring the ship they knew to be a pirate vessel anchored in the harbor not a mile's distance from the *Princess Mary*. At least the forward movement of the small boat relieved Thomas's nausea, but he found himself cringing at every large swell that approached, and he was therefore unable to muster the hoped-for swaggering attitude with which he'd hoped to greet his partners on landing. It would not do, he thought peevishly, to rendezvous with pirates wearing a sea-bilious face.

Before the dinghy's bottom scraped the sandy seabed and lurched to a stop, one of the seamen had jumped out and, grabbing the rope, towed the boat to shore. Waiting there was a tangle of rough men, their gaudy outfits a hodgepodge of rich booty, not the dirty and sea-worn rags most people imagined them to be. All but one were bearded and moustached, and that one, the pirate captain, stood in their protected center — Black Jack Thompson. He was an Englishman, handsome and sinewy, and so swarthy from the sun as to be mistaken for a Moor. A diagonal slash cut across his jutting chin, a scar still so angry that Thompson looked to have almost lost that piece of his face not many months before. Seymour thought to ignore it was best, and instead mustered his wits to confront the rogue, but Black Jack spoke first.

"The High Admiral of the Boy King's Navy," he said impertinently, eyeing Seymour from foot to head. "And green round the gills to boot."

The men laughed and Thomas stifled his outrage.

"You may call me Tom if I may call you Jack," he replied, managing to sound pleasant. He wished more than anything to be comfortable with these men, a third of whose stolen goods were now his own.

"What, just 'Tom'?" said Black Jack. "Naa, we all have a pet name 'ere." He turned to his mates. "What shall it be then, lads, Tom what?"

"Tom the Scum!" cried a patch-eyed pirate, asserting with his flagrant disrespect that these men did not abide by the laws of any king or country and that a nobleman such as Seymour was no better than Black Jack's ruffians.

"Green Tom," called another, alluding to his nauseous face.

"Tom Goldpockets," cried a wretched man whose face was gouged, chin and cheeks and forehead, with pockmarks.

"Perhaps that's closest to the truth," said Seymour with a look meant to be mischievous.

"And why is that?" asked Jack Thompson suspiciously. "Have you come bearin' gifts?"

"You could say that," replied Seymour. "Have you not wondered why I've asked for this meeting in the Scilly Isles and most particularly on the shore?"

"On shore for yer seasickness," Black Jack shot back. "And the Scillies? As good a place as any."

"Take a walk with me . . . Jack," Seymour said, holding the pirate's eye. "The two of us alone."

Thompson shot glances at his men that said, Back off, I'll handle him, and followed Thomas inland to where a green fringe of forest rimmed the beach in a near perfect semicircle.

"What think you of this isle?" asked Seymour.

"For a piece o' land, 'tis good as the next," replied the pirate.

"And this harbor?" Seymour persisted.

"Plenty deep, a narrow channel for its inlet, good protection from foul weather," Thompson said as he gazed out over the harbor for a spell. "A heavy chain across the neck and we've protection from any botherin' sons o' bitches who might want to have at us. And why do ye want to know my opinions . . . My lord Admiral?" he added warily and with something of a sneer in his voice.

"Because I've *bought* it for you, Jack. For us. A safe haven."

A smile crept over Thompson's dark face, pulling at the seam in his torn chin. "Goldpockets indeed," he said.

"I must protect my partners," said Seymour, "protect my investments."

Black Jack gazed landward along the rocky shoreline. "Mayhap I'll build me a house here, then."

"Mayhap a castle," added Seymour. "That is, if you've a mind for some grandiose booty taking."

"Such as . . . ?"

"That which the Holy Roman Emperor is plundering from the New World." Seymour replied.

"Charles's Gold?"

"By the ton."

"A good idea," Thompson said, his mind already beginning to work. "But I'll need a second ship."

"Done," said Seymour.

The pirate eyed the Admiral, studying him intently. "You've a rich wife, 'aven't ye?"

"Very rich," replied Seymour.

"But not so rich for yer needs, it appears."

Seymour's eyes narrowed. Black Jack was treading on dangerous ground, knew it, but seemed to care very little about the High Admiral's displeasure.

"And what *are* yer needs, Tom Goldpockets?" Thompson needled.

Seymour had no wish to discuss his planned rebellion with the pirate captain. "Do you want your island? Your second ship?" Seymour inquired with more than a hint of a threat.

"I could do with them things," answered Black Jack in a chilly tone, "and I could do without 'em."

Thomas Seymour regarded the swarthy criminal with impatience. "Find the ship you want and send me the bill. I'll send you a purse . . . and intelligence of the Spanish galleons' movements into Corunna."

Black Jack Thompson's eyebrows rose into an arch of surprise, impressed with his partner's resourcefulness.

"You see," said Thomas Seymour haughtily, "the Admiralty is worth something, after all."

It was much the same with William Sherrington as it had been with Thompson, thought Seymour as he sat at Sherrington's table drumming his fingers in nervous anticipation of his return. They were — as he and Black Jack were — partners in a crime against the

Crown for the purpose of moneymaking. But in this case, Seymour knew Sherrington was entirely his creature. He could lord it over the employee of the Royal Mint, secure in his knowledge that the man was entirely under his control. Sherrington, already a thief and a scoundrel before Thomas made his acquaintance, had long been shaving and clipping the edges off gold crowns — the minutest amount per coin but, when gathered from every piece that came through his counting room, an admirable bounty.

Seymour was proud of how he had lured the man into his own schemes, getting the money embezzled from the mint directed to his rebellion, with Sherrington oblivious that he was the victim of Thomas's blackmail. Instead, his new conspirator believed that he had taken up the cause of his own volition. By a happy coincidence the clerk distrusted the Duke of Somerset. Thomas had reinforced those sentiments with several diatribes against his brother. The Protector, he declaimed, had stolen the regency from King Henry's hand-picked council for his son. Somerset had perhaps not *caused* the debasing of the English currency, Thomas Seymour liked to say, but since Somerset's ascendancy, he had stood by and watched it being debased even further. With such seeds planted in Sherrington's mind, the man had become convinced that Somerset and his wife, grasping and nefarious as they were, were planning to do away with the King using slow poison so that they could take the throne for themselves. By contrast Thomas Seymour was, despite his noble airs, an honest man who wished to restore the worth of an English coin and restore control to the true king. So Sherrington had decided to help Thomas gain control of the government and become the new Protector. Thomas would require money to lead his revolt, and in this Sherrington could, happily, be of assistance. The High Admiral would of course protect him if his embezzlement were ever discovered.

The situation presented itself perfectly, Sherrington had explained. His office at the mint lay at the end of a long corridor with floors of raw wood, recently laid. Any footfall could be heard in sufficient time to cease his clipping and shaving and hide his tools, and never a coin was found missing to cause suspicion.

In just a moment, when Sherrington returned from his bedchamber, Seymour would get an accounting of his earnings, would see for himself the pile of gold that the man had smuggled out of the mint day after day in the secret lining of his jerkin. All employees were searched for filched coins before leaving, but the fine shavings had been unpalpable in his clothing, so no one was the wiser and Thomas Seymour was the richer. He smiled, mightily pleased with himself.

Sherrington returned lugging a studded wood and gilt chest and placed it carefully on the table in front of Seymour. "The fruits of my labor, my lord," he announced proudly. He pushed back the heavy domed lid to reveal a tray in which lay what Seymour supposed was the whole of the clerk's personal fortune. Then Sherrington carefully lifted the tray from the chest, uncovering a piece of oilcloth folded over itself. His spindly fingers peeled back the cloth, and there before Seymour's eyes was a huge pile of yellow shavings, so thick as to be a solid mass. It filled completely the compartment of the box.

"How much is there?" Seymour demanded.

"It's hard to say, my lord. With any exactness, I mean. I've not been able to smuggle a scale from the mint and I —"

"A guess, then," snapped the High Admiral impatiently.

"Well, I've kept count of every coin I've shaved — twelve thousand, two hundred and thirty-three of them — and the amount taken from each one is approximately six one hundredths of —"

"Spare me your innumerable calculations. How much have we got?"

"Slightly more than two thousand pounds."

"That's all?" Seymour's face darkened with anger.

"I've only been taking the shavings for six months," Sherrington offered meekly.

"I have arms to buy, man. A revolt to finance. Two thousand pounds . . ." Seymour snorted with contempt.

Seymour saw Sherrington's eyes darting every which way in his head, as though an idea were taking shape. He therefore remained quiet, allowing the man to conceive of further ways to please the one he believed would soon, next to King Edward, be the highest lord in the land. Finally, with a smile, Sherrington said, "If I were to be very, very careful, my lord, I believe I could take slightly more from each coin."

"Excellent!"

Sherrington smiled broadly, pleased that his solution had met with Seymour's approval.

"Then all that is left is to increase the number of coins coming through your hands."

Sherrington's smile faded. "That I cannot do," he murmured regretfully. "Surely someone will come to suspect —"

"There are other counters besides yourself, are there not?" interrupted Seymour, an idea forming.

"Yes."

"What are their names?"

"Oh, but, my lord, I should not trust them with such —"

"I do not mean to *trust* them, Sherrington. I trust only you." Seymour knew the words men longed to hear. Words that made them cleave heart and soul to his causes. He saw the set of Sherrington's shoulders relax almost imperceptibly. "If any of them were to be 'indisposed' for a time," Seymour went on, "would a share of their work fall to you?"

"Yes, it has happened before. A man in the office next door was ill for a month. I was altogether swamped until his return." Sherrington thought for a moment. "But you do not mean to harm one of the other clerks?"

"Only incapacitate him for a while. Don't you see, Sherrington? With his absence, he will be assisting the rebellion, helping his country, and never be the wiser."

"But these men have families and —"

"I will *see* to their families," Seymour snapped impatiently. "Just make me more money. England is depending on you."

Seymour watched as Sherrington puffed with pride at the thought.

"Have you many guns put by, my lord — for the rebellion, I mean?"

"My armory at Holt Castle has indeed begun to fill. I've plenty of arquebuses, muskets, and shot, and half a dozen large cannon soon to be shipped from the foundry."

Sherrington grew visibly aroused at the talk of artillery, and so Seymour embellished his description of the armory the clerk was responsible for having financed. He was a man who had never known war, never held a weapon in his hand, and was bewitched by the masculine allure of the gun.

"Powder is our next purchase," said Seymour, placing a congenial arm round the clerk's shoulder. "You can see why more money must be made, and you must know, William, how important your work is."

Tears sprung unbidden into the clerk's eyes. "You know I'll do everything I can, my lord."

Seymour rose to go.

"My lord?"

"Yes?"

"Is it true" — Sherrington became shy — "that you mean to marry the princess Elizabeth?"

Seymour was taken altogether off his guard. He'd not known how far and wide the rumors had traveled. If Sherrington had heard such gossip, the talk must have made it clear into taverns and inns, into sculleries and kitchens and backstairs of houses all over England. But he was not displeased. Clearly Sherrington saw him as a man fit to marry royalty.

"You must understand, my friend, that I cannot divulge such sensitive information." He leaned close to whisper, as if they were in the halls of Hampton Court with countless eager ears straining to hear his words. "But I can tell you that she is the loveliest virgin ever to walk God's earth, and if He wills it, the Princess and I shall marry."

An involuntary sigh escaped Sherrington's lips.

"Now, get some sleep," said Seymour with a conspiratorial smile. "You are going to be a very busy man."

God blast John Dudley! thought Thomas Seymour as he slammed out the double doors of the Privy Council Chamber. Blast him to hell! How dare the man defy his authority as Lord High Admiral? If he wished to oversee naval operations for his brother's Scottish campaign from his base in London, that was *his* affair, not John Dudley's — he of the deviously reserved manner that won over even his bitterest and most jealous rivals. Seymour's fist tightened around the hilt of his sword hanging at his side as he strode down the broad stair into the ground floor of Hampton Court, and he realized he wished that the fingers were gripped round Dudley's throat instead.

The man had goaded him in the Council meeting, flaunting his own long experience as High Admiral and parading his administrative genius, insinuating to the others that Thomas was incompetent. Incompetent! And this on the very day he had planned important inroads against the Protector, planting seeds of doubt within the Council members' minds about his *brother's* competence. But Dudley had very slyly taken control of the meeting in Somerset's absence, exuding a maddening confidence that had, since the last days of Henry's reign, inspired Thomas's jealous hatred of him. The man was too popular. Even courtiers who complained about Dudley jumped at the chance to ally themselves with him. And soldiers and sailors who had served under him were unerringly loyal. God blast him! Thomas would have to think hard about it, devise a clever plan to rid himself of John Dudley — but not now.

As he passed the huge subterranean kitchen of Hampton Court where hundreds of cooks and bakers and roasters sweated over the midday meal, he resolved to put his nemesis out of his mind, for he had far more important business to which he must attend. His bootsteps on the brickwork floors echoed down the long corridor that needed the light of torches, even on the brightest day. Finally he approached the door he sought and knocked twice, then once. A moment later a key turned and the door opened enough for the man inside, thrusting a candle through the crack, to recognize his caller.

Thomas was admitted into the locksmith's workroom. Peter Highsmith was a skinny fellow who resembled, with streaks of oil in his shaggy hair, the long-haired dog who slept on the stone floor and had not awoken at Thomas's arrival. He was dreaming, the dog was, his legs twitching as he ran in an imaginary field. The locksmith's tools were neatly arranged on benches and shelves about the tiny windowless cell that smelled of sweat and burnt metal. There were countless long iron keys, one for each chamber of the thousand-room palace, hung in their places on nails.

"My lord," Highsmith muttered as he made room for the admiral in his humble workplace.

There was nowhere to sit, but Thomas had not come for a pleasant visit, rather to conclude a vital piece of business. Without a word he plunked a plain leather purse down in the center of the man's workbench.

The locksmith stared at it warily, then glanced up. "I've thought about this, and I've thought about it some more."

"And what did you think, Highsmith?" Seymour said, trying to keep contempt from creeping into his voice, furious that yet a second man in one day might attempt to thwart his well-laid plans.

"I thought, my lord," Highsmith replied slowly, "that me makin' you a duplicate set of keys to the King's apartments is, uhm, shall we say . . . suspect? Shall we say, illegal? Shall we say . . . treasonable?"

"We've discussed this, Highsmith, and I've explained my need for them. I *am* the King's uncle and, if not his Protector in name, certainly his protector in principle."

"And if you're caught with these keys," Highsmith said, bending down to rub his sleeping dog's belly, "you are the King's uncle and protector and, might we say, 'protected.' But I, who made the keys for you, *illegally,* am just a lowly locksmith and *un*protected."

Thomas considered the man's objections. They were, truthfully, not unexpected, and after a moment he produced another leather purse from his doublet. This one was fancier, worked in colors and gilt and tied with braided strings. Seymour opened the purse and fished out three gold pieces, throwing them down on the table next to the promised purse. Highsmith's eyes flashed hungrily — a year's wages in addition to the small fortune in the purse. He could afford to leave the King's service with so much money to his name, move to Maidstone and start a business there. Afford to marry. Leave behind this underground dungeon and all the corrupted nobles, their arrogant ways, their condescending treatment of tradesmen like himself. He reached for the purse and the coins, stowing them on a shelf under his workbench. Then he lifted a nondescript set of keys off a nail and handed them to Seymour.

"There are your keys, my lord," he said. Highsmith could not miss the fire that flashed in Seymour's eyes as his fingers tightened round them. "You be sure you use those in His Majesty's best interests," he added, unable to hide the impertinence in his voice.

Outraged, Seymour leaned across the table and snatched Highsmith by the throat and shook him, his long, lanky hair flopping about his face. "How dare you!" Seymour cried.

The locksmith remained calm but the dog, sleeping no longer, had suddenly sprung to his feet and was baring his teeth, growling at the Admiral. Highsmith smiled a smug smile and Seymour thrust him away in disgust. Then the nobleman wiped the hand on his breeches as if to cleanse it from the touch of so lowly a creature and, sidestepping the threatening dog, left the room, slamming the door hard behind him.

He breathed to calm himself as he retraced his steps past the kitchen, from which an endless stream of servants were now carefully carrying steaming tureens and platters up the stairs to the dining hall. He must restore a good-natured visage at once, he told himself, appear solid and confident in purpose. There was yet so much to be accomplished if his scheme was to work. There was the small matter of acquiring a stamp of the King's signature. And he still had not secured young Edward's assistance in returning Catherine's jewels to her.

It was a blessing that his brother was gone away to his ridiculous war. It laid the field wide open for himself to play. At dinner, seated next to the King, he would reveal his most charming self, then afterwards, alone with the boy, he would begin to pull the strings that bound them tighter, and little Edward would come to understand which of his two uncles was the one he should trust with his life.

"All right, you've hacked off my right arm and I'm using my left. See if you can cut me now."

The boy king, wooden broadsword in hand, was so flushed with exertion that his normally paper-white skin was red as a Tudor rose. Perspiration dripped from his temples as he tightly clenched his two-handed weapon and swiped impotently at his uncle Thomas, similarly armed but with his right arm held behind his back. They fought alone together in one of Edward's private gardens under a dark, threatening sky. The pretty purse of red and silver, shy three gold crowns, lay on a bench nearby.

"If I teach you one thing today, Your Majesty, let it be the importance of aggression."

The words seemed to spur the boy on. His next cuts were well aimed and powerful, though Thomas's sword warded them off with expert ease.

"My swordmaster teaches me that *defense* is best," said Edward breathlessly.

"Be on the defensive always, but follow up defense with aggression. Most men, if they should cut to your head, would parry and then back away." Thomas demonstrated on the boy who was, ears and eyes and senses, fixed on this heroic swordsman. "I tell you now to parry your head, but follow it with a slash across the belly." His final cut sliced within an inch of the child's midsection. "Now you try."

Edward was proficient with the broadsword, but his masters had always during Henry's reign been cautioned to be exceedingly careful with the King's precious son. Now under his uncle's tutelage he threw himself into the manly art with unbridled fervor. The thrusts and parries came fast and furious, surprising Seymour into a good-natured laugh.

"Excellent, excellent," he cried.

But there was to be no respite.

Thomas continued the fight as he talked. "Your young cousin Mary Queen of Scots has been smuggled out of Scotland to France."

"What!?" Edward stopped dead in his tracks, and even Thomas's mock stroke that would have swiped off his head did not perturb him as much as the Admiral's news.

"I wondered if you'd been told," said Seymour, then urged the boy to continue fighting. They began again. "I know you're given very little intelligence. 'Tis unconscionable. You are the King, after all."

"My father meant for me to be as much a king at four as at forty."

"Indeed he did."

"And now something as vital as my bride-to-be being spirited off to the land of our enemies —"

"And betrothed to the Dauphin."

Edward's cuts flew at Seymour even more violently.

"Good, good, Edward."

"'Twas my father's greatest wish that I should marry with Mary of Scots and end the hostilities between our countries."

"*And* the threat of France's invasion from the north."

"How could my uncle have allowed such a thing to happen?"

"It pains me to say it, Your Majesty, but the Protector . . . and his wife . . . have more interest in growing rich than they have in your welfare, or, for that matter, the welfare of England."

The boy's cuts and thrusts had become instinctively exacting. His uncle Thomas was using mind and body with equal precision to forward the sword lesson *and* the political one. "Do you remember hearing tell of your father's chancellor, Cardinal Wolsey?"

"Of course."

"Why did he fall from Henry's good graces?"

"He was grasping and greedy . . ."

"And became the richest man in England next to Henry. And powerful. So powerful they called him the King of Europe."

After a final cracking overhead parry, Edward chopped his sword point to the ground and leaned on the jeweled hilt.

"Is that what my other uncle is up to?" demanded Edward.

"I cannot say for sure, Your Majesty," said Thomas as he laid down his broadsword. "But it is being said around the court that you" — he hesitated — "that you are king in name only."

Edward's posture slumped visibly and he blinked back angry tears.

"There is something else, nephew, though I do not like to say it."

"But you must. I command you."

"Your uncle, the Duke of Somerset, has begun referring to himself . . . as your brother."

The wooden broadsword in Edward's hands flew up above his head and, as he swung around in fury, came crashing down on a stone bench. The wood splintered and the shaft broke in two.

Thomas Seymour's heart swelled. It was all going the way he had planned it. "Perhaps," he said carefully, "'twould be better if my lord Somerset were dead."

"Perhaps it would," agreed Edward angrily. With that the boy king threw down the useless sword hilt and marched away into the palace without another word. But his uncle was anything but offended. He had given young Edward something to think about. He had given the child a great sword with which to kill Thomas Seymour's dragon — as well as a reason to do so.

Chapter Eight

Elizabeth's arrow sprang clean off her taut bowstring and, flying swift and straight, thwacked neatly into the bull's-eye's red center. Robin Dudley, Jane Grey, and Master Roger Ascham loudly applauded the Princess's efforts, and she, with a well-satisfied grin, curtsied playfully in their direction.

"Well done, Princess!" called Ascham. Elizabeth watched him nudge Lady Jane off the bench to take her turn. Her cousin smiled warmly at the sweet-faced man whose hair was a mass of dark curly ringlets, and Elizabeth realized with some surprise how much affection she herself already bore for her new tutor. For a young man he was very wise, very learned, and altogether patient. Most of all he loved his profession passionately and could do naught but instill that passion in his students, who now included Jane and Robin besides herself. The Cambridge scholar, she'd discovered very soon after his arrival at Chelsea, believed true education could only be achieved through an equal balance of fervent study and relaxation. Music was of course encouraged, but archery, said Ascham, when practiced properly, had the effect of strengthening and focusing the mind. It had therefore become as much an aspect of the curriculum as Greek translation. He devised games for learning as well, round-robins for the memorization of ports and capitals, mnemonic devices for the remembering of the names of all the heads of state on the Continent.

Lady Jane's aim proved true. Everyone clapped for the girl, who flushed with as much pleasure as Elizabeth remembered her demonstrating since her arrival at Chelsea House. She too was flowering under the tutelage of Roger Ascham. Even Robin Dudley's running debate, concerning his love for mathematics and Ascham's disparagement of the same, diminished their affection for one another not at all.

Since his arrival — and Thomas Seymour's departure from the household almost two months before — Elizabeth had regained a measure of composure and at least the outward illusion of normalcy. She was no longer harassed by the early morning romps, or plagued with their associated guilty pleasures. Plunging enthusiastically into Master Ascham's educational program, she could forget for many hours at a time the terrible emotions that had racked her mind, and the untoward sensations that beset her body.

Still, there was Queen Catherine to attend, and the woman was clearly not herself. Her once sweet compassion and utterly sensible demeanor had transmogrified into vagueness and distracted irritability. Clearly Catherine missed Thomas's presence, though she was not at liberty to express such sentiment. Ladies such as herself were trained from an early age to withstand their husbands' long absences — in wars, at court, traveling to their distant properties. But far from the strong resiliency that Catherine had once exuded, she had become so fragile as to seem brittle, her eyes shining with such extreme brightness that one felt if she were lightly struck she might shatter into a thousand shards of glittering glass.

Elizabeth, therefore, whilst paying the Queen Dowager all due respect — taking the required meals and walks and prayers with her — maintained a certain distance in feeling. It distressed the Princess, confused her, and she believed it pained her stepmother equally. But there was nothing else to be done. Perhaps, thought Elizabeth, when Thomas Seymour returned, the Queen's good humor would be restored and the Admiral would discontinue his advances toward her.

If only Kat Ashley would leave off her incessant reminders of Seymour, Elizabeth mused, she might be able to forget him altogether. But the waiting lady missed no opportunity to call up his name, remark on his handsomeness or other fine qualities, say how she missed his booming good-natured voice, lament that the house seemed empty without his presence. How many times had Kat repeated her outrageous suggestion that Elizabeth and Thomas made so much prettier a couple than he and the Queen Dowager? Elizabeth steeled herself as best she was able, but the statements were nothing less than an assault on her already tumultuous emotions.

Now Robin took his place before the target and Elizabeth found herself silently admiring his handsomeness and effortless grace as he set the shaft into the bow and took aim. At that moment she heard Catherine's voice on the far side of the hedge behind the archery range. It was difficult to make out the words, but the Queen Dowager's tone, while conversational, was loud and passionate. All in Elizabeth's party became aware of Catherine's approach and Robin held his shot, lowering bow and arrow to wait respectfully for the Queen and her companion to appear at the end of the hedge. But when she did appear, the shock of the moment riveted Robin, Jane, Ascham, and Elizabeth with equally ferocity. For the lady was altogether alone, talking only to herself or, worse still, to an invisible companion. So engrossed in the solitary conversation was the Queen Dowager that she never even looked toward the archery range nor saw the small party that, with unspeakable horror and pity, watched as she walked on and disappeared behind the castle wall.

Jane Grey burst into tears and, brushing off her tutor's comforting arms, ran for the house.

Robin, Elizabeth, and Ascham exchanged a silent and entirely helpless look. Elizabeth's chin began to quiver and tears blinded her. So engulfed in misery was the Princess that it came as a surprise when she felt a strong hand clasping her own. She blinked away the tears to find Robin Dudley standing before her, the boy's face a mask of such complete and sincere compassion that her composure broke. She wept and he held her as Roger Ascham turned and left them to their private grief.

"'Tis no one's fault exactly," said the Queen Dowager insistently. Walking alone, she had already completed her first full circuit of the castle grounds and was beginning her second. "'Tis no one's fault except my own," she added. "Or perhaps Elizabeth's. I think Elizabeth is to blame at times. The way the girl *looks* at him or does *not* look at him. I see her attempting many times to avoid looking at him, but she *wants* to look at him. Undresses him with her eyes. I see her undressing him. But that she *does* harbor such lewd fantasies, well, that must be *my* fault entirely. She is just a girl, after all . . . but not so much younger than I when I took my first husband," Catherine amended indignantly. She rubbed a spot on the back of her left hand, a spot she had rubbed so incessantly that the skin was raw almost to bleeding. She was altogether unaware of the damage or the pain. "Thomas," she went on, her voice rising shrilly, "has no defenses against such a nubile young virgin, a virgin with the heart of a whore!" The sound of her own strident voice so surprised the Queen Dowager that she stopped her forward movement and fell silent.

To her surprise she found herself in the rose garden, the balmy afternoon around her soft and benign. But she felt cold, her head spinning, frenzied. . . .

She had been talking aloud again, talking to her dear mother, Maud, dead for more than ten years. She sought a stone bench and lowered her body onto it. Though she had told no one, for they would surely think her insane, her mother did speak to her. It had been comforting to hear Maud's voice again, soothing her daughter's fears, reminding Catherine how much Thomas loved her. Maud knew the truth. She swore that Elizabeth did not matter to Thomas, that he loved Catherine and Catherine alone.

The Queen Dowager looked down at her hands and saw the spot she had rubbed raw. "He has been gone for so long," she moaned to her mother. "So long . . ."

"But when he returns, my dear," said the voice inside the Queen Dowager's head, "he will be yours, all yours — your much-deserved beloved. Have no fear, have no fear."

He had returned to Chelsea in spirits so unnaturally high, it seemed to Elizabeth, that the house and the gardens and the wood could not contain all of Thomas Seymour. His boisterousness and constant booming laughter alarmed almost everyone except the Queen Dowager, who once again blossomed pink with love. Her mad monologue had never been repeated — at least in the presence of others —

and whilst she was perhaps more demonstrative with her husband than thought seemly by most, she did appear sane enough. Kat Ashley was another who had nothing but praise for the man who, she insisted, looked handsomer and more virile than ever. Occasionally the Princess would overhear John Ashley speak sternly to his wife about her dangerous, perhaps treasonous ideas about her charge and the Admiral.

Every day Elizabeth warred with her own divergent passions, praying for peace of mind and even for a modicum of daughterly affection for Thomas Seymour, whose behavior toward herself since his return had been unimpeachable. But with his homecoming Elizabeth's torrid dreams of him had returned to haunt her nights.

She would awaken in the half light of morning bathed in guilt, feeling so unclean that she would dress hurriedly and hie to the chapel to pray for her sins. On her knees, fingers tightly intertwined, she cursed her mother and the wanton Boleyn blood that ran in her veins. And she prayed for Queen Catherine, for though the madness was no longer clearly apparent, Elizabeth knew that something inside the woman must be festering. Catherine, Elizabeth had come to realize, *loved Thomas too fervently,* was sick with loving him. The woman had to know he did not return that affection in kind, and she must know, too, that he felt an unholy lust for his stepdaughter. Worse still, thought Elizabeth, the Queen Dowager must be aware the Princess, despite her outwardly proper behavior, was seething with love for her husband.

How would it all end? Her mind's torture ebbed and flowed like a treacherous tide. Sometimes — as when she put her mind to studying, immersing herself in Plato's *Republic* or struggling joyfully for just the right word in a difficult translation — she found respite from all feeling. Then without warning the terrible thoughts would strike her, a great black wave that engulfed her, drowned her, till she gasped for her very life.

Perhaps, she prayed, perhaps it *was* over. Thomas had not come to her rooms since his return, had not gazed at her longingly, had barely spoken to her in private. Perhaps his love for the Queen Dowager would return to what it had been at the start of their courtship. Perhaps Seymour had never thought of herself in the way Kat insisted he did, in the way she dreamt he did.

Perhaps life would resume as it had been before Catherine's marriage to Thomas. Grace, peace, and sanity would again descend on all those who resided in Chelsea House. That was Elizabeth's sometimes prayer kneeling in the chapel as the morning sun finally found its way through the narrow windows and bathed her with light.

Other times, God help her miserable soul, she prayed for Queen Catherine's death so that Thomas Seymour could once and forever be her own.

Master Ascham had been unwell with the flux in the morning, and Elizabeth had gone alone to the south garden to read the assigned chapter of Plutarch's *Lives*. Her eyes had begun to trouble her, especially in the dim of the schoolroom, and the light in this hedge- and stone-walled garden was clear and strong. Farther from the house than the other yards, it was infrequently visited and altogether quiet. Elizabeth had brought a meat pie still warm from the baker's oven and a flask of light ale for her lunch. There were fruit trees — plums, apples, cherries, pears — from which to pluck her dessert. She had chosen for her seat a bench that lined one of the garden walls, so with the two cushions she had brought along and the empty box she had overturned, draped with a shawl and placed in front of the bench, Elizabeth had fashioned for herself a comfortable rest, one in which she could prop up her legs and lean back in relaxation. She was glad she had insisted to Kat that she not be laced into the stiff stomacher which held her torso rigid and perfectly erect, making free breathing difficult. Certainly the undergarment shaped the female body into its most perfect form, but this was to be a day of sweet and solitary pleasure, and the simple gray silk gown felt as comfortable as a nightdress. Now, as the sun illuminated the Greek words on the vellum page, Elizabeth reveled in the feel of her natural body and the unhindered flow of her breathing.

She heard voices outside the garden walls. Muffled though they were, Elizabeth recognized Lord Thomas and Lady Seymour at once. Her body stiffened instantly, for although the Queen Dowager was laughing, the sound was anything but gay. It was, Elizabeth sensed with alarm, tinged with hysteria.

As their voices grew closer, Elizabeth leapt from the cushioned seat and began self-consciously straightening and rearranging her loose gown. Suddenly the wooden gate flew open, and with a cry Catherine came flying through it as if she'd been propelled violently from behind. Elizabeth dashed instinctively for the Queen Dowager to steady her, lest she fall. The Princess caught her stepmother up in her arms and heard the gasping laughter, felt the perspiration-damp fabric of her gown.

"Madame!" was all Elizabeth had time to utter before the force that had propelled the Queen into the garden followed her in. Thomas Seymour, in a loose lawn shirt clinging to the lines of his muscular torso, was laughing and altogether nonchalant. His face was newly tanned and his red hair and beard flared with golden fire in the sun.

A man has no right, thought Elizabeth in that moment, to be so painfully handsome, no right . . .

"Come here, wife," Seymour cried. Snatching Catherine from Elizabeth's arms, he turned her to face him, kissing her full on the mouth. Elizabeth could see Catherine's body fall limp under the passionate assault, and the Princess was forced to avert her eyes. Some inner voice called out to Elizabeth, Run, run from this place! But she was paralyzed, as rooted to the ground as the pear or cherry tree was.

The kiss finished, Thomas disengaged his wife's body from his own and held her to his side, one arm round her waist. Catherine was flushed, dazed, eyes glassy, as if caught in a spell the magician Seymour had cast upon her.

"Lady Princess," he said in four clipped syllables. Unheeding of his wife's presence, Seymour devoured Elizabeth with his eyes, feasting on her soft unfettered curves, staring unabashedly at her with a gaze that began to unhinge her.

"My lord," she muttered so faintly she was herself unsure if she had spoken.

"You are alone?" he asked rhetorically.

Something in his eyes flashed dangerously and the voice came again into Elizabeth's head that she should flee. But why run from her beloved stepmother and stepfather? she reasoned with the voice. They could not possibly harm her. They were her protectors. This was a *queen of England* standing before her and she was a *princess.* No harm could come to her in this garden. Her imagination had simply run away with her . . .

"*Now,* Catherine," Seymour suddenly commanded his wife.

Her eyes darted sideways to her husband's face and his expression seconded his words. But Catherine was clearly panicking and did not move from her spot. Nor did Elizabeth, who by now knew something frightful was about to happen but had no more power to move than her stepmother.

"Catherine! Now!" Seymour shouted.

Inertia defeated, the Queen Dowager's hands sprang forward like two striking snakes, but Elizabeth had in that moment turned to run. She felt Catherine's hand clamp viselike round her right arm.

"Majesty!" cried Elizabeth, turning sharply back to confront the woman, but the eyes she found staring at her were mad eyes with nothing behind them with which to reason.

"The other, Catherine!" Elizabeth heard Seymour urging. "Grab the other."

Now both of Elizabeth's arms were pinioned behind her back by Catherine. The girl's outward struggle diminished. If I lash out, she thought wildly, I might hurt the Queen. Confusion muddled her thinking, and something else — a morbid curiosity to know the meaning and outcome of this outlandish display orchestrated by Thomas — caused her to cease her struggling altogether.

She was entirely still as Seymour came round to face her, his powerful body towering over hers. He was so close she could feel the heat rising off him, imagined she could hear the heart thumping in his chest. He smiled impishly at her, and in that moment she believed the silly prank was over, finished. No harm done to anyone.

Suddenly Thomas Seymour grasped the collar of Elizabeth's gown and ripped downward. As the dress tore away, revealing flesh, Elizabeth screamed and tried to escape Catherine's grasp. But the older woman was stronger than Elizabeth had imagined her to be and nothing she did could free the pinioned arms.

It was then Elizabeth saw the dagger in Seymour's hand.

Even her terrible nakedness before this man's eyes paled against the fear of the raised blade glinting in the sun as it descended toward her body. A shriek of unreasoning terror had already escaped her as the dagger found its mark — the front of her voluminous gown. It slashed the fabric down the middle between her legs. At the sight of the rent gown Thomas laughed aloud and with many shorter stabs began shredding the skirt into pieces. Elizabeth, dumbfounded by the mad hilarity, watched helplessly as her dress, skirt and bodice both, was reduced to ribbons.

Finally she found her voice. "Stop!" she cried. Seymour's movements slowed — as much, Elizabeth thought, because there was no more cloth to shred as because of her command. "My lord, stop this please, please stop."

Finally the assault ceased altogether. Catherine, silent throughout the entire episode, released Elizabeth's arms. Thomas's laughter died. And Elizabeth — a princess of England — stood cowering between the Queen Dowager and the High Admiral of the King's Navy, trying desperately to cover her nakedness with her hands. In the next moment she darted away and, grabbing her shawl to throw around her, ran through the south garden gate. It hung open for a long moment before a gust of wind slammed it shut with a resounding crash.

Kat Ashley and Thomas Parry marched side by side down the long first-floor corridor of Chelsea House toward Thomas Seymour's study. Though they appeared grim as two soldiers united in a sacred cause, inwardly they were, each of them, floundering confusedly. Both bore the Admiral a great deal of affection. Kat, if truth be told, dreamt of him at night in ways that made her blush to even remember. Parry, his whole life spent in service to royalty, had been drawn by Seymour's comfortable common touch and invigorated by his bold audacity. But the man had finally gone too far, Parry had to admit, with this outrage against a princess of England, against their Elizabeth.

They knocked on Seymour's door and were bade to enter. Seymour sat behind his desk poring importantly over a stack of documents, a uniformed naval officer standing at attention beside him.

"Kat, Thomas." He gave them a cheery smile, no hint of remorse or, it appeared, even memory of this morning's assault on their charge.

102

"Will you sit?" Seymour indicated a pair of benches in the corner of the room. "I'll only be a bit longer with Captain —"

"No, my lord," said Parry. "This cannot wait."

"Not a moment longer," Kat added threateningly.

They both took another step closer to the desk as if to insist that the officer should take his leave. In fact, the man looked questioningly at the Admiral, and with a small nod Seymour sent the captain from his study.

The door had barely closed when Kat began. "How do you sit there, my lord, as though nothing at all had happened?"

"Happened? What has happened?" he asked, sincerely perplexed.

"Your assault on the Princess," replied Thomas Parry. Seymour's calm so unnerved the servant that he doubted Elizabeth's story for a moment. Certainly she had been attacked, but perhaps she had been mistaken about the identity of her attackers.

"An assault on the Princess?" Seymour said incredulously. "As I recall, 'twas an assault on a *dress*." He smiled a fool's smile.

But Kat's face remained hard and Thomas Parry continued. "My lord, your behavior and the behavior of the Queen Dowager was — "

"'Twas a prank, Thomas, Kat. The Princess was done no harm."

"Only to frighten her half to death," replied Parry.

"She will recover," said Seymour lightly.

"The dress was cut to ribbons," insisted Kat, "her bodice ripped off her altogether. She was *naked* from the waist up. 'Twas a disgrace."

"How were we to know she wore no undergarments? *That* is the disgrace, Mistress Ashley."

"Oh!" cried Kat infuriated. "Well, if that is your answer, Thomas Seymour, then I think we shall be taking our leave. Come, Parry, we'll see the Queen."

"No, no, wait!" Seymour had come to his feet at the mention of his wife. His voice became suddenly placating. "We mustn't bother Catherine."

"As she bothered Princess Elizabeth?" Kat Ashley was not to be placated.

"Perhaps we were too rough in our little game," offered Seymour, moving round the desk. "But you must know we meant Elizabeth no harm. And she was *done* no harm."

Though Parry was starting to waver, Seymour was making no headway with Kat. He changed his tack. "You may have noticed the Queen has not been herself for some time. . . ."

Kat was silent, unyielding.

"Her moods have been incontinent since my return. I hardly know her myself."

"So, you blame your wife for your outlandish behavior?" Kat persisted.

"More to the point," he said, looking down at his feet almost shyly, "I blame our child, the one she carries within her."

"The Queen Dowager is pregnant?" said Parry, taken entirely by surprise. A much-believed rumor had it that after three childless marriages, the woman was altogether incapable of conceiving.

Kat Ashley's eyes were saucers. She was wholly silent as this intelligence pervaded all previous notions of Catherine, and every romantic fantasy she had held for Elizabeth and the High Admiral. All of them collapsed in that moment like a house of cards.

"Like all pregnant women, she has odd cravings. Sardines and marchpane — together." He gave a sweet indulgent smile as if remembering. "But Catherine has become in her pregnancy a slave to several strange, extravagant, even . . . unnatural desires, whims. She is my wife and so I try to oblige her." He held up his hands in a supplicating gesture. "Perhaps I should not have spoken so openly of the Queen's most intimate —"

"No, no, you were quite right to tell us," said Parry quickly. He seemed wholly relieved by Seymour's explanation, though Kat was much less convinced.

"Will you convey our apologies to the Princess," Seymour said, finally contrite. "We meant to cause her no distress. . . ." Then he chuckled at his own unintended pun.

Parry laughed, but Kat puckered her mouth in disgust. No man could possibly understand Elizabeth's terror and humiliation in that morning's violation of her.

"Shame on you, Admiral," she said and, turning on her heel, stormed out the study door.

"Women," said Seymour simply, and placed a friendly arm around Thomas Parry.

"Women," Parry intoned in agreement, all vestiges of disapproval having vanished.

Then the two men laughed.

Elizabeth's head hurt. She had stayed behind in the classroom long after Master Ascham and Jane Grey had gone for the afternoon, trying to finish a particularly difficult translation. As the day had faded her eyes began to burn and she realized she was lightheaded, probably from hunger. She'd again been unable to stomach any food at the midday meal. Perhaps she should write to her brother and ask if she might come to court for a visit. The pain of staying here at Chelsea House had become overwhelming. News of Catherine's pregnancy had been the worst of it for Elizabeth, worse even than the horrifying scene in the south garden that had left the Princess so shattered that she had cried herself to sleep every night since, and had so disordered her digestion that eating had become impossible.

The Queen Dowager had, since the episode, kept to her apartments. A blessing, thought Elizabeth, for what on earth would the two of them say to one another? Whose shame would be the greater?

Kat, who had finally regained a sense of propriety toward the Admiral — after all, he was to be a father — had assured Elizabeth that none of the servants knew the sordid details of that morning. But the Princess could not fail to notice the sideways glances, the whispering and giggling as she passed, that gave lie to Kat's assurances.

Only Jane Grey seemed altogether oblivious. She had been in a state of frenzied excitement and joy that her beloved Catherine and adored Lord Seymour were expecting a child. She had even taken time from her studies to work on a wardrobe of tiny embroidered caps and smocks and blankets for the babe, and glowed with so much happiness one would have thought it was *Jane* that was with child.

"Elizabeth."

The shock of Thomas Seymour's voice, soft as it was spoken from across the room, paralyzed her. Back to him, she did not turn her body nor even her head, but knew all the same that he stood in the schoolroom doorway.

"Elizabeth," he repeated, and the sound as he spoke her name was sweet as a prayer. "There are some things I must say to you, things that cannot wait another day, another hour."

Still she did not move. She felt, rather than heard, him moving closer to her chair. She stiffened at his approach and suddenly sensed that he had stopped in place, careful not to frighten her further.

The scrape of a bench on the floor announced that he'd taken a seat behind her, and when he began to speak again Elizabeth sighed heavily, relieved and thankful that she would not have to meet his eyes.

"First," he began after a long and painful silence, "I beg you to forgive me. There is no good excuse for what was done to you. But there is an explanation. If you bear with me, I will offer it to you."

The paralysis had extended to Elizabeth's organs of speech so she could neither encourage nor question Seymour. No dialogue this, but a solitary litany of contrition. He spoke softly and humbly with no trace of his usual boisterousness or arrogance.

"I have made a horrible mistake in my life, and only now are its consequences making themselves clear to me. You see, I have married the wrong woman. I was a younger son and therefore never constrained to take a wife for the furtherance of our family's fortunes. I could," he went on, his voice cracking with emotion, "I could have married for love."

But you did! cried Elizabeth silently, the words echoing inside her head. You married Catherine for love!

As if he had heard those words, Seymour answered. "I had befriended Catherine before your father married her. Widow to two toothless old men she was by then, and starved for true manly affection. That is why she fell in love with me. I cared for her very deeply, but I did not love her in the same way, so that when the King summoned her for his wife I was honestly relieved. And happy for her, of course. She was, after all, queen of England. When Henry died five years later, it became clear Catherine had her sights set on me still. You must have heard, Princess, that I, in those months after your father's

106

death, approached the Council to ask for the hand of the woman with whom *I* was in love. That woman was you."

Elizabeth's body began to tremble so violently that she was forced to clutch the desk to steady herself. Thomas could not help but see her shaking, but he went on with his story.

"You may have heard rumors that I asked for Princess Mary's hand, or the German cow of Cleves, but those rumors were nonsense. I had been watching you since your childhood, Elizabeth, had seen you buffeted about in the political winds and fearful turmoil of court. Seen you thrown away and ignored by your father, and finally returned to the fold by Catherine. And always, *always* you retained a grace and" — he groped for the words — "beauty in spirit that was matched only by the beauty of your form and face. Elizabeth, look at me," he commanded.

Silent tears were streaming down her face, tears she did not wish him to see. She did not move except for her trembling.

"Elizabeth . . ." Now he was pleading. "Please, look at me."

Slowly she turned in her chair and saw his face. It, too, was wet with tears. A sob caught in her throat.

"You are the most ravishing creature I have ever in my life known. You are brilliant of mind and sweet of heart. When I realized that I could not have you, something inside me withered and died. I was once a man of courage and dignity and pride. But I admit to you now that I" — he seemed unable to go on, overcome with shame — "I married Catherine because I knew you were living under her roof. I had to be near you, Elizabeth. I had no choice. But of course you were unreachable, a virgin princess, and I was a married man. My thinking grew perverse. My mind *snapped.* I began the morning visits. I could not help myself, I swear. I had to be near you! 'Twas unconscionable behavior and I apologize with all my heart." He paused as if to fortify himself to continue. "Catherine is, of course, an intelligent woman. She could not fail to see what was happening to me. But nothing was ever said, and so she grew more and more desperate. I think she believed that if she joined me in those romps I would somehow come to love her. But when I did not . . . she began to go mad."

The tragedy of the story filled Elizabeth with the most grievous pain she had ever known, but still she had no words to utter, no comforting sentiments to extend to this broken man before her.

"Then she became pregnant and I was forced by the responsibilities of the Admiralty to leave Chelsea House for many weeks. By the time I returned, well, *you* could not fail to see her deterioration. What happened in the south garden was — God help me — inspired by *Catherine,* and I, crazed with guilt and grief at this prison that is my marriage, allowed myself to be drawn into it. As I said, I'm not excusing myself, Elizabeth. I just wish your forgiveness. And I want you to know what I feel for you. My heart" — he touched his chest gently with his fingers, the gesture unbearably melancholic — "is broken. For I love you *passionately,* Elizabeth, and I know I can never, ever have you."

He uttered a short rueful laugh, then stood and moved for the door. Before he departed the classroom he touched his heart once again and was gone.

Elizabeth, stunned by her beloved's terrible confession, laid her head in her arms and wept.

Never before had Thomas Seymour acted so much the kind and reserved gentleman, and never had Elizabeth succumbed to such unutterable despair. He was doting and devoted to his wife, who every day grew more plump and healthy, and charming and generous to his ward Jane Grey. Thomas seemed to Elizabeth the perfect figure of a man — an ideal husband and father brimming with the qualities every girl in her dreams of marriage imagined, and in true life rarely found. But here he was, flesh and blood, respected head of a great household, High Admiral of the King's Navy — and he loved her. Pined for her. And she could never have him.

Elizabeth was not alone in her improved estimation of the man. There was great whispering at Chelsea House that Lord Seymour had come to see the error of his ways and reformed himself. He went frequently with Catherine to the chapel. They walked slowly together, her small hand tucked in his arm, she smiling up at him with unabashed adoration, all transgressions forgotten. Her madness was a fading memory.

With Elizabeth, Thomas was painfully restrained and correct. He was careful never to encounter her in private, and in public studiously refrained from meeting her eye. But when they chanced to be in one another's presence — at mealtimes, at prayers, or on a family occasion — he would never fail to make the most subtle but telling of gestures. He would, so she could see it, slightly and briefly touch his fingers to his heart. This signal of his ever faithful love tore at her soul. Sometimes she thought him cruel for the small act of constancy, but more often she found herself waiting breathlessly for it to come. When it did, she was forced to control her sigh of relief that he had not forgotten, and still loved her. Sometimes she worried that she had never in the schoolroom that afternoon admitted to him the reciprocity of her love. Every night as she lay in her bed, sleep evading her, she found eloquent words to voice those feelings. But they would never be spoken aloud. He was Catherine's, now and forever. Elizabeth had, truthfully, never been devout — nothing like her sister Mary or even Jane Grey. Prayers for her heart's guidance had gone unanswered and there seemed to be no help coming from God. Nights were the worst, for her dreams were filled with Thomas, the ones in which he was sweet and kindly, more painful to remember than those in which the pair of them practiced all manner of lewd and sinful behavior. When she believed her suffering could become no greater, Elizabeth dreamt a dream that saved her.

Walking alone in the south garden she came upon Jesus, barefoot, with birds playing fearlessly at his feet. There was no heavenly light surrounding him, no halo round his head. He was, strangely, just a man in the south garden, albeit one who exuded a blessed peace. As Elizabeth came closer, even knowing he was the Lord, Son of God, she was altogether unafraid. Jesus held out his hand to her, and Elizabeth's heart burst with joy and relief that her sins had not debased her, that Jesus loved her still. His comfort flowed freely into her. He fixed her with his piercing eyes and in a voice deep and mellifluous said, "Have no fear, for where there is love, there is no sin."

Elizabeth woke then, the words echoing in her head. She felt altogether refreshed and purified. Her breath, previously sour, was suddenly sweet. As the face of Jesus faded slowly in her memory, she seemed to float in bed. Daylight flooded her bedchamber, and she felt the first happiness she had known in many months.

She had not sinned for loving Thomas, nor had he for her.

She must tell him this, free him from his pain!

Elizabeth slipped silently from her bed and, leaving Kat to sleep on, dressed herself. Then she went out into the quiet halls of Chelsea House to search for Thomas Seymour.

She knew she must speak to him alone, and so Elizabeth was forced to stalk him for the better part of that day. Several times she was frustrated, for he was a gregarious man, seeming more comfortable in the company of others than in his own. People, she noticed, were somehow drawn to him like flies to honey, and as he moved through the day she saw that he would naturally gravitate to others — for a brief conversation with a laundress or a lengthy one with the chaplain, lending his opinion on a stone wall being mended or a horse being shod. Elizabeth had, all of the morning, stayed a discreet distance from Seymour, but only when midafternoon had passed did he make for the river and the boathouse in which Catherine's barge was housed.

Allowing him first to disappear into the wooden structure and careful that no one was watching her, Elizabeth, book in hand, pretended to stroll across the broad lawn to a bench near the boathouse and the water's edge. She sat to steady herself before entering, then realized suddenly that she was strangely calm. But of course she would be. She had a message of peace and comfort to deliver from Jesus himself! Perhaps she and Thomas would even pray together. Elizabeth laid down her book and, pulling herself proud and tall, entered the boathouse.

The dim light of the place after the full sun of the afternoon blinded her almost completely. She stood, therefore, quite still while she slowly regained her sight, listening to the creak of the wooden deck underfoot and the slapping of the water on the sides of the barge.

The hand, laid lightly on her shoulder, caused Elizabeth to start violently, though she knew immediately it was Thomas. When she turned to face him she wore a serene smile, and was therefore entirely unprepared for the visage that greeted her. Savage desire distorted Thomas Seymour's normally handsome features. Gone was the constrained gentleman signaling his affection for her with the subtlest of gestures. Elizabeth had only heard about the passion of lust, but now she could see it blazing in Seymour's eyes — blazing for *herself.*

Without a word he seized Elizabeth. No thoughts of struggle restrained her. Instantly lost, she went willingly into his rough embrace. Her arms flew up to encircle his neck. His hard mouth found her lips and crushed them in a bruising kiss. Never in her wickedest dreams had love felt so raw or cruel or beautiful. Elizabeth clung to Thomas as if her very life might be extinguished were they to part, and so his hands, free to explore, boldly sought all of her — long slender neck, the flesh of a breast, delicate save the hardened nipple, slender waist straining against the stays. The kisses never ceased, nor did his moving hands. The skirt lifted, a creamy thigh caressed. Elizabeth's gasp as fingers found her cleft's soft wetness. Groans of delight. Ecstatic dreams come real —

No! A voice commanding him to stop. But not her voice, not *her* voice. She wished him to continue the pleasure forever —

"No!"

Thomas stiffened, arms dropping to his sides. His head whipped behind him.

Senses returning, Elizabeth peered round the firm trunk of Seymour's body, saw a specter so terrible her knees jellied.

Catherine! One arm clutching the boathouse wall to keep the high-bellied figure from crumpling. Face ravaged with pain and defeat. Lips moving, but no sound emerging.

Thomas gazed down at Elizabeth for the space of time needed to say a silent good-bye and then was gone, pulling his wife from the wreckage of this moment. With his going, all light and heat, all life receded from the boathouse.

Elizabeth was alone, bereft, drowning in the horror of what she, in her reckless passion, had done to beloved Catherine — the only woman she had ever called mother. And Thomas, hers for the briefest moment in time, was now gone without a word. Gone forever.

Elizabeth's legs failed her then and she crumpled to the boathouse floor. She was altogether dazed, bewildered, knew the furor that would shortly erupt all round her, shatter the existence she had known for these last years, known and cherished.

She was a wicked girl, she decided, wicked and deserving of whatever punishment was forthcoming. She must steel herself to face the storm of scandal and gossip, anger, derision, and richly justified scorn that was her future. There was much to do, thought Elizabeth, a cloud of weariness beginning to settle over her. Much to think about and plan. But for now, for just a few moments longer, she would stay where she was, in the cool dark of the boathouse, and remember the taste of Thomas Seymour's lips, and the feel of his hands on her delicate flesh.

Thomas.

Chapter Nine

It should be raining, thought Elizabeth grimly, pissing down cold, hard rain for this monstrous occasion. But it was, in fact, an exquisite day, the air soft and warmed by the sun in a rare cloudless sky. Twelve carts and carriages had been loaded with the belongings of her household in embarrassed silence by the Princess's staff.

Neither Catherine nor Thomas had shown their faces since the day of the boathouse debacle, though a message had been delivered to Elizabeth's door that very evening. It had been a brief and dignified epistle requesting that the Princess and the whole of her household remove themselves from Chelsea House at their earliest possible convenience. Arrangements had been made for their extended stay at Cheshunt under the patronage of Sir Anthony Denny.

When she'd returned from the boathouse Elizabeth had prepared Kat and the Parrys as best as she'd been able, choked with uncontrollable sobs that at times grew so hysterical her servants worried for the girl's sanity. Kat had at first been outraged at the scene described by Elizabeth, believing that Seymour had forced himself on her, but the waiting woman was tearfully disabused of that notion by her mortified charge.

"I allowed it, Kat. I *encouraged* it," Elizabeth had cried. "I love him," she wailed, "and he loves me. He does love me. . . ."

"Our fault," Kat had muttered to Thomas Parry as she passed him on the way from Elizabeth's room. She'd put the girl to bed, though it was clear that there would be sleep for none of them that night.

Parry was silent, knowing that Kat had spoken truthfully, that all their encouragement of the flirtation had rendered the soil too fertile for *something* not to grow from it. The calm, responsible behavior of the last months since the scene in the south garden had been no more than a sham. Emotions had been growing rampantly, fulminating, festering. Those close to Elizabeth should have known, should have seen the inevitable coming. Done something to stop it.

Now Elizabeth had disgraced herself, alienated the most powerful woman in England, one who had adored the Princess as if she'd been her own child.

It had been decided that something had to be done to salvage Elizabeth's reputation. Kat and Parry sat together by candlelight that whole night and composed a letter to the Queen Dowager, begging her forgiveness for Elizabeth's aberrant behavior. Try as they might, they found neither explanation nor excuse for it, but they hoped Catherine could find it in her heart to help minimize the scandal, to speak of the reason for Elizabeth's sudden expulsion from Chelsea House to no one, so that gossip would not spread like a plague through the countryside, the court, and all of England.

With unbelievable grace Catherine had complied, and in the days following, as preparations were made for the Princess's hasty departure, the rumors flying rampant round the manor never lit upon the exact details of Elizabeth and Seymour's sordid tryst.

This blessing, however, gave the Princess no joy, for she believed herself worthy of the greatest scorn. Catherine's kindness made her misery all the more poignant.

Now the members of Elizabeth's household were themselves piling into the carriages as Elizabeth and the Ashleys and Parrys vacated the Princess's lodgings for the last time. The girl's eyes were red-rimmed, her face puffed from sleepless nights and days of crying. She kept her gaze full forward, refusing — as if punishment for her actions — to look round her and gather pleasant memories of the place she had called home for the past two years. She took the stairs stiffly and carefully, and when she passed through the front door she did not turn back. Elizabeth allowed herself to be helped into a conveyance, and waited while the Ashleys and Parrys took their places beside her. Signal was given to the driver and the carriage lurched forward.

She was dry-eyed now. Perhaps, thought Elizabeth, if it were raining she would be able to weep, but the sun was bright and warm, giving lie to the tragedy of the day. Nothing, she thought as the carriage passed through the gates of Chelsea House, would ever be the same. And even Jesus would be unable to forgive her most heinous sins.

Chapter Ten

"'Tis a clever ruse, my lord Admiral," said Lord Rutland as he followed Thomas Seymour by torchlight through the basement doors of Holt Castle, "to use the dungeons here for your armory. 'Tis so pretty a palace, no one would guess at its real content."

Seymour smiled at the compliment. Rutland, a fat and pompous nobleman of ancient heritage, was one of the growing number of Council members whom he was confident to have won over to his cause. It had taken little argument to convince the man, irritated by the Protector's ruthless and domineering personality and disgusted by his poor showing in Scotland, that the harsh, overly ambitious Somerset should be overthrown and replaced by his younger brother. Thomas and the much-beloved Queen Dowager would make a far more congenial joint protectorate for the boy king who, according to the Admiral's glowing reports, had already thrown his support behind them.

Thomas fixed his and Rutland's torches in the stone sconces and with a triumphant smile swung open the tall cabinets that had been specially built along the walls of the musty dungeon. They were already half filled with firearms and well-made halberds, pikes, and swords. A corner of the flickering chamber boasted a dozen cannon and neat piles of shot.

"We have a way to go with the arms and ammunition," said Seymour, "but our forces are growing with every passing day." He cleared a wooden trestle with a heedless sweep of his arm and unrolled a large parchment map of England before them. His eyes gleamed with firelight and genuine excitement as he began poring over it. England was to Seymour nothing more or less than a great campaigning ground, filled with potential soldiers who were either for him or against him in his cause.

"See here, Rutland, in the West Country," he said, indicating the counties surrounding his family's estates. "All that be in these parts be my friends. But here" — he stabbed with his forefinger several counties south and east of London — "men are loyal to John Dudley, and others to Lord Somerset." With a dismissive gesture he added, "The northern parts are Catholic, of course, and no good to any of us."

"How many do you count in your favor then?" asked Rutland, studying the map intently. Certainly the nobleman's own interests came first. He would never be so stupid as to back a rebel leader short of troops.

"Ten thousand of my own servants and tenants alone," answered Seymour with obvious pride. "This counts neither my other supporters nor the French."

"The French!" cried Rutland disbelievingly.

"I have the word of a high duke in Orléans that two thousand armed soldiers are at my disposal. My brother's Scottish campaign sits poorly with the Frogs."

"They'll cause us problems later," warned Rutland.

"And we will deal with them later," replied Thomas with a confident grin. "By my calculations, I have twice the forces that both my brother and Dudley have combined. In the meantime, we shall gather our loyal men to us. I say we recruit the gentlemen, but more importantly the wealthy yeomen in larger towns. *They* are the true ringleaders. A gentleman may waver once he's fallen in behind you, but never a yeoman."

"You're right about that, my lord," Rutland agreed, a touch of admiration creeping into his voice. Seymour might be a reckless man on a dangerous errand, but he did seem to know men's hearts.

"We should go out amongst the small landholders where they live," Seymour went on, "and make much of them. Dine with them in their modest homes like friendly fellows. In this way we will gain their goodwill once and forever, I promise you. And what loyalty we cannot curry with our fellowship," he added archly, "we shall buy with gold."

"Money does speak sweetly," agreed Rutland. "Have you enough put by for bribery *and* arms? By the look of this," said the nobleman, suddenly skeptical, sweeping his hand round at the gun closets, "you're short many weapons and much ordnance."

"Come back in one month's time and see how short I am," challenged Thomas with more than a touch of bravado. "For I have everything I need for this rebellion, and more. Keep your eyes open and watch one Seymour fall, my lord Rutland, and the other rise to glory."

His business completed at Holt Castle, and satisfied that his preparations were moving apace, Thomas Seymour rode for London. The weather was unusually fine. With the sun and wind on his face all his hopes flowered, and he strolled blissfully in the warm garden of his dreams.

His brother and sister-in-law were disappeared. Where, he knew not and cared not. But he and Catherine, ensconced where they belonged in the royal chambers, frolicked with young Edward, who showered them with favor as they embraced him with familial affection. All was light and happiness. His own son by Catherine was as near to Edward as if he were the King's own brother, and of course his wife had forgiven him his indiscretion with Elizabeth. Marriages for the two princesses had been arranged at the highest levels — Elizabeth to a French dauphin, Mary to her Spanish cousin. These matches had strengthened England's alliances with their enemies, and both the nobility and the common people rejoiced in the country's leadership.

All of it was possible, thought Thomas as he spurred his horse to pass a fine coach on its way to London — his destiny!

Beyond the carriage he discovered the road crowded with riders and was forced to rein his mount to a complete halt. He saw, to his delight, that the crush was a gaggle of Privy Councillors who had, each for his own reason this day, taken the road and not the river back to London for the opening of Parliament.

Riding boldly into their midst, he was glad to find his friend Dorset, who rode next to Lords Clinton and Wriothesley. The trio were embroiled in an earnest conversation regarding the Protector's policy toward the unrest brewing in Devonshire and Cornwall and, after a brief but cordial greeting to the High Admiral, resumed their discussion. Thomas found that both the content of their conversation and their rude dismissal annoyed him. He listened, occasionally interjecting an opinion, but he was having little impact on the course of their argument. He felt the bile rise in his throat and the blood to his cheeks. Finally he could stand it no longer.

"It is wrong that I should not share the protectorate with my brother!" he blurted.

Dorset, Clinton, and Wriothesley were instantly silenced, and the rest of the men in the party looked up from their divers conversations in surprise at the outburst.

"Thomas . . ." said Lord Dorset, trying to hide his alarm. His outward tone was placating, for he did not wish to give away his own part in Seymour's schemes. "The Protector's policies may not be perfect, but for now they will suffice."

But the words seemed only to enflame Seymour further.

"If this is how I am to be treated by you all . . ." Thomas paused as if gathering the furious force of his malevolence. "They speak of a black Parliament," he declared passionately. "Well, by God's precious soul, I will make the blackest Parliament that ever was in England!"

"My lord Admiral!" exclaimed Wriothesley, appalled at such an oath. "This is a rash threat!"

There were shocked mutterings all round. Lord Dorset had gone quite pale. He spoke quietly but firmly to Seymour.

"Quiet yourself, my lord, for you will antagonize your brother."

"My brother!" He spat. "I tell you now, I can better live without my brother than he can without me!"

At that Seymour spurred his horse with a vicious kick and sped off, leaving the Privy Councillors in slack-jawed dismay.

"They have been told," Thomas said to himself as he rode away, kicking up dust he hoped would envelop the noblemen in a choking cloud. "'Tis time they heard the truth, time they learned the future of England!"

Chapter Eleven

The hinges on John Cheke's door creaked so loudly as he pulled it open that he winced, vowing once again to petition the palace carpenter for a dab of oil on its hinges. He was altogether startled to see his royal charge standing outside waiting impatiently to be admitted, the boy's pale face even more somber than usual.

"Your Majesty, come in!" said Cheke, genuinely pleased if somewhat bemused to see young Edward. "You've not seen my quarters before."

"I haven't," said Edward, entering the room tentatively, as if it were a sacred temple. Indeed it was a sanctuary of erudition. All the walls had been lined with specially built shelves, and the shelves were overbrimming with books and manuscripts of every shape, age, and description. More volumes were piled on the floor, and the small table was littered with the implements of writing. There was hardly space for the simple cot, table, and domed chest that held the tutor's scant belongings other than his books. Edward's eyes were wide as he moved slowly and reverently past the shelves, perusing their bounty. Cheke watched as the child tilted his head to read the title on a spine and saw his face illuminate with quiet joy.

"You've an original Theocritus," whispered Edward, "and a Livy as well."

"Have a look, Your Majesty," said Cheke with gentle amusement.

"May I?" asked the boy as if he were being given permission to handle a nail from Jesus' cross.

"Please." Cheke observed Edward as he paged carefully through the leather-bound Greek text and wondered if he should ask outright why the child had come, or wait for the King's explanation in the time he chose to give it. When Edward replaced the Theocritus and began thumbing through the Livy, Cheke spoke up.

"While my library is certainly fascinating, Your Majesty, I think perhaps you've another reason for gracing me in my humble quarters with your presence this evening."

"I do, sir," the child admitted quickly and with obvious relief, but then was silent while he collected his thoughts before explaining himself. "My uncle —" he finally began, but Cheke interrupted him.

"Which uncle would that be? You've three of them."

"Not my *honest* uncle," replied the King ruefully.

The tutor chuckled at the child's cleverness. "By that, I take you to mean the Queen Dowager's brother, Lord Parr?"

Edward nodded.

"Then, we are speaking of a Seymour uncle," said Cheke.

"The Lord High Admiral."

"Aha."

"He wants a favor of me," said Edward carefully.

"You mean *another* favor," Cheke corrected.

"So it would seem."

"You wrote to the Protector on behalf of Thomas Seymour's secret marriage to your stepmother," said Cheke, "and later at their behest you requested the crown jewels be returned to her."

"But they were *not* returned to her, at least not yet."

"And you feel you owe your uncle Thomas another favor?" Cheke insisted gently.

"He's lent me a great deal of money, you know," said Edward, looking sheepish.

Cheke turned away to minimize the King's humiliation at such an admission before he inquired, "What has Seymour asked you to do this time?"

"He wants me to write to the Privy Council" — the boy hesitated as if unwilling to speak the words — "and tell them that I wish him to replace my lord Somerset."

"Thomas Seymour wishes to become the Protector in his brother's place, and he wishes *you* to speak for him," asked Cheke rhetorically.

121

The tutor was not altogether ignorant of Thomas Seymour's outrageous machinations, for news of his "black Parliament" oath had circulated very quickly to all corners of the court. But Cheke had not counted on the Admiral trying to use the King in quite so boldfaced a manner. He and his pupil had, in addition to the classics, been studying moral philosophy and rhetoric, and now Cheke wished to observe these practices in the context of kingship. He therefore refrained from jumping immediately to conclusions for the boy.

"What are your thoughts on this, Your Majesty?" said Cheke with gravity and respect.

The ten-year-old, momentarily startled — for he had indeed come here for guidance — began to speak, slowly at first but with great clarity. "First I should say that I love my stepmother very dearly and wish to do nothing to hurt or anger her. So many times I've wished that it was Catherine who still mothered me" — Edward's lip quivered — "instead of that old witch, Lady Somerset. My uncle the Protector . . ." Edward paused again. To be saying aloud such unutterable thoughts was as terrifying as it was exhilarating. "The Protector is a cruel and noxious man. He does not love me, and yet though Thomas showers me with gifts of money and good fellowship and all the rest, I feel he loves me no better."

"But is there not more at issue here than love, Your Majesty?" inquired Cheke evenly.

Edward thought very seriously on this, then answered, "Yes. There is the question of England's best interests. Who is the better protector?"

"And . . . ?"

"Lord Somerset makes so little of me. I hear he has begun signing dispatches without reference to myself. He takes more power for himself and away from me every day."

"But?"

"But what is to say that the Admiral would not do the same were he to hold the same office?"

Cheke smiled broadly at this last. The boy's mind was clear and moved in logical ways. He was able in great matters, despite deep and confusing emotions, to retain a levelheaded demeanor and arrive at a sensible conclusion. Edward would in his majority, thought John Cheke, be a formidable king. He had done his job well. Now it was time to lift some of the burden from this sweet boy.

"So you think to deny the Admiral your support in his petition?" asked Cheke.

Edward took a deep breath as if to ready himself, like Atlas, for taking the weight of the world on his shoulders.

"I think that would be best."

Cheke stroked his beard solemnly as if he were just now formulating the thought. "Perhaps, Your Majesty, 'twould be more politic if *I* were to take the blame for this decision."

"Oh, Master Cheke, the Admiral will be very angry, and I think it safer that he be angry with me. I am, after all, the King. He can do me no harm, but you are only a tutor." Edward stopped, silenced by the irony of his own words. Here was a man so lowly in title, but more courageous and honorable than two of the realm's highest peers, who did not hesitate to fight like vultures over a piece of carrion flesh. Cheke was ready to take the blows meant for Edward himself. The King fought back tears. "I cannot let you . . ."

Cheke put an arm around Edward's small shoulder and said very soothingly, "Then I shall have to insist, Your Majesty. 'Tis the best thing. Put your trust in me."

Edward laid his head against Master Cheke's chest and felt for the first time in a very long while a sweet and blessed sense of relief.

Chapter Twelve

I should have known, thought Thomas Seymour as he stomped round the kitchen garden behind Hampton Court kicking at turnip and pea plants with the toe of his boot — should have known that great evil was afoot when I was denied entrance to the King's privy and bedchambers. What paltry excuses they offered — His Majesty is unwell, His Majesty is resting, His Majesty's engagements prevent him . . . My brother's orders, no doubt. I should throttle him, nay, rip the throat from his skinny neck. Terrified, he is terrified of me. Knows what power I hold over the King's heart — what power I *did* hold, Seymour corrected himself irritably. Even the boy has deserted me. That lowly schoolmaster — wretched man. They think they have beaten me, think I'll slink away devastated by humiliation.

Thomas cringed at the memory of approaching the King's bedchamber that morning only to be denied entrance by Fowler — *his man* Fowler! — and for the most transparent of excuses. Two times before it had been Master Cheke. The tutor had actually answered the request Thomas had made to the boy for his help himself. How *dare* he speak for the King of England on a matter of such import! Cheeky Cheke. He will feel my wrath, Thomas vowed, when my time comes. My time indeed! Well, they have shamed me, but for that they will pay tenfold. There must be more than one way to the throne.

For a brief moment Thomas found himself free of anger and his mind suddenly cleared. He stopped in his tracks and just stood, breathing in the fragrance of the herbs lying in low bushes at his feet — rosemary, marjoram, thyme.

Why, he asked himself, should he settle merely for the role of Protector? When King Edward reached his majority, all control of him would vanish. In Thomas's mind a new idea, huge and grandiose, had begun to take form. *I could be king of England.* The thought transfixed him and he was momentarily paralyzed. Then he moved, propelled as though by a great force pushing him from behind. He moved from the modest kitchen gardens out into the paths of Hampton Court's formal flower garden, walking in great energetic strides as his mind spun and unthinkable thoughts dazzled him. He could be king! But how? His eyes devoured the masses of summer roses, pinks, and daffodils. Fresh young flower heads . . . *like maidenheads.* Yes, yes! The answer lay within the succession — a succession all of virgin girls, all in line for the throne. Marry a queen and be the king!

His mind darted from one possibility to the next. Princess Mary was first in line for the succession, but she was already old and peevish. A Catholic, too, whose pious ways would cause her husband as much trouble as her hair-shirted Spanish mother had caused Great Harry.

Little Jane. His ward certainly stood in line for the crown. She was meek and malleable as a lamb. Her father, Dorset, was his pawn. Something could be arranged.

Elizabeth . . . A lazy smile creased Seymour's face at the thought of the girl, sweet and juicy as a peach. A princess of the blood, and all of it English. The people would see Henry in her. And she loves me, thought Seymour; more important, she *wants* me. She'd thought nothing of betraying her beloved stepmother to have him. *Elizabeth.* Marry her and be king. Thomas was walking quickly, nearly running, but he knew not where he was in body, for his mind had taken him far, far away. *To Winchester for his coronation, to a festive New Year's Day feast at which he presided, to the great Bed of State where he . . .*

No, he must steady himself. 'Twas a brilliant scheme, but there was much to be done. Many obstacles to be swept away. Catherine, King Edward, Princess Mary, his brother. He would need permission for the marriage from a majority of the Council. Formidable obstacles, but certainly not impossible. Yes, it could be done! True, more money than he now had was needed for his army that would support the palace coup. He would begin taking a greater share of the pirates' booty. Suddenly Black Jack Thompson's words played again in his head. "You've a rich wife . . ."

Aye, thought Seymour, *the richest wife in England.*

In that moment Thomas grew calm. All was feasible, and the pieces of the grand plan were coming together in his head. He would be king of England, and there was no one in the wide world who could stop him.

Chapter Thirteen

Dr. Huick held two fingers over the pulse in Catherine's wrist. "And your appetite, Your Majesty, have you been eating well?"

The Queen Dowager, staring out the large leaded bedchamber window, seemed not to hear her physician's question, and when it was clear she would not answer, Lady Tyrwhitt said, "Her appetite is much improved of late, Doctor."

"Indeed it has," Catherine chimed in, as if suddenly awakened from a daydream. She smiled then, and if her expression could not be described as enthusiastic, it appeared sincere enough. The too bright eyes and the shrillness of voice that had recently afflicted her were gone, though what replaced them was a kind of sad resignation. Catherine placed a hand on her great belly and patted it affectionately. "The child is strong and very healthy inside me," she said. "I can feel it."

"You are remarkably well for a first-time pregnant woman of your advanced age," said Huick.

"And you are remarkably direct for a court physician," was Catherine's retort. "You're lucky I'm not more vain or I might have snapped your head right off." She gave him an even warmer smile and added, "'Tis the main reason I like you, Dr. Huick."

The sober expression on the man's long, angular face brightened at the compliment. "Your mind, too, seems much more at ease, if I may say so, madame."

Lady Tyrwhitt and Catherine exchanged a meaningful glance.

"I survived a great crisis, Doctor, and emerged on the other side bloodied though not defeated, with the help of my friends." Catherine gazed fondly at Lady Tyrwhitt. "I've regained much of my former strength and see no reason why my lying-in and delivery of this child should not be altogether successful."

Dr. Huick stood to leave. "It will indeed be successful, Your Majesty. Now I pray you call for me the moment the midwives have finished with their work. There are potions for strengthening those humors in your body which have been depleted that I shall want to administer, and another which several women have lately employed to ward off childbed fever."

"I'll call for you then with pleasure, Doctor, and we'll celebrate the birth of my son or daughter, whichever God wills. Lady Tyrwhitt, show the good doctor out, if you please."

The waiting lady accompanied Doctor Huick through the door, leaving Catherine to herself. She stood, with some difficulty due to her bulk, and gazed about her chamber. The bed beckoned to her, and she wished for nothing more than to lie back and sleep, but she fought the urge, knowing there was much to do.

First and foremost, she must write back to Elizabeth, whose most tender letter she had received almost a week before. Hearing that Catherine suffered a sometimes uncomfortable pregnancy, the Princess had declared that if she were allowed to be present at the delivery, she would beat the child for the trouble it had put her stepmother through. Catherine had laughed aloud at these words and realized that in the weeks since that terrible discovery in the boathouse, not only had she regained her sanity, but she had fully forgiven her stepdaughter's betrayal. It was as though the sight of Elizabeth in Thomas's arms had shaken her from a grave stupor, and from that time on, anger — like a stiff wind from the western sea — had blown the cobwebs from her eyes, allowing her for the first time to see her husband for the man he was. She had, in the beginning, chided herself unmercifully for having been so blinded to his unscrupulousness, but eventually she realized that *everyone* had been duped by his bonhomie and great good-natured charm — men, women, servants, nobles, and royals. 'Twas some sick part of him she understood not at all, but now could observe quite clearly with her new vision. He was not an evil man, she concluded, and meant no harm, but was simply incapable of true love or honesty of any kind.

After the incident in the boathouse Thomas had never left her side for weeks. He had wept and beat his chest in apologies and obeisances so extravagant she was embarrassed by them. His excuses, all of which rang false, ranged from a bout of temporary lunacy to Elizabeth's having stalked him for an entire day before *molesting him* in the boathouse. He had covered Catherine with kisses and caresses — feet, hands, neck, lips, and belly — swearing with God as his witness that no such madness or weakness (depending upon his current excuse) would ever overtake him again. Then there would be more weeping. The spectacle had been so overwhelming that it simply shocked Catherine into sanity. She was England's queen dowager, carrying her first child. Surely she must still contain enough sense to go on with her life.

When she had finally had enough of his histrionics, she allowed Thomas to believe she'd forgiven him, if only to quell the untoward outbursts. Once convinced of her sincerity, he'd left suddenly for London, claiming Admiralty business there and promising to be back in a fortnight. The two weeks without him, as well as the absence of Elizabeth and her household from Chelsea, had allowed for a timely repair of Catherine's soul.

Lady Tyrwhitt, stepdaughter from a previous marriage, had welcomed her mistress back to levelheaded normality from a pendulum swing between mania and melancholy, punctuated by behavior suited more to a common slut than a queen of England. The two women had shared the secrets of their hearts, and the younger had provided the elder with a calm sensibility that had nourished Catherine's spirit back to good health. Now the child thrived within her once again and she was fully prepared for her husband's return.

She would be kind to him, allow him to shower her with affection. She would go to her lying-in and have the child. And when her strength had returned, she would speak to her dear friend Archbishop Cranmer and begin proceedings for a divorce. It would prove difficult, of this she was certain, but he had once helped extricate a king of England from his lawful marriage to a queen of England. Surely he would find a way to help her divorce Thomas.

The Queen Dowager lowered herself into her desk chair and dipped a new quill into the inkpot. *Dear Elizabeth,* she wrote, then hesitated. She could only guess at her stepdaughter's frame of mind at this moment, and knew that her tone must be altogether kindly. If someone of her own intellect, maturity, and worldly wisdom could have been lured into idiocy by the charismatic Lord High Admiral, then what terrible state of mind, she wondered, must the fourteen-year-old be suffering? Once Thomas was out of her life, thought Catherine, Elizabeth and she would be reunited. She loved the girl deeply, and no real damage had been done. Perhaps one day, she mused, they would even laugh about it.

Chapter Fourteen

The sound of Elizabeth's piteous moan was too much to bear, thought Kat Ashley as she hurried into the Princess's bedchamber carrying a potion given her by the local apothecary. Ever since their arrival at Cheshunt, Elizabeth had been unwell with a seemingly endless string of rheums which kept her nose running and her lungs inflamed. Worse, however, were these headaches that prostrated the poor girl with agonizing pain for days at a time, and nausea which made eating impossible. Already slender as a reed, Elizabeth had grown dangerously thin, and her monthly courses, which had just begun the year before, had ceased.

She had only herself to blame, Kat knew. She had done nothing but encourage Thomas Seymour's flirtation with Elizabeth, seeming to forget that he was a married man. Frequently she asked herself how she could have been so stupid, but each time the excuse was repeated: because she herself adored the Admiral to distraction, despite his obvious weaknesses. And if truth be told, she still believed that if somehow the Princess and he could be married, his only fault would be that he would make *too much* of Elizabeth. Perhaps she was mad, but it seemed to her a match made in Heaven.

Coming into the bedchamber, she saw Blanche Parry standing over the bed and placing a cool compress on Elizabeth's forehead. Blanche had insisted that the sudden change in living arrangements had caused Elizabeth's ill health, as Cheshunt was near a large marsh, and its rooms therefore more dank than Chelsea House. But Kat knew the truth. These illnesses were simply the Princess's terrible emotions displayed in bodily form. She mourned for Seymour's loss as much as she suffered for her disgrace. Though Catherine had written kind letters to Elizabeth, and replies had been sent the Queen Dowager, the girl believed that all trust between them had been irrevocably lost.

The Princess had, in the first weeks under Sir Anthony and Lady Denny's sympathetic hospitality, attempted good cheer. Roger Ascham and his wife had, of course, joined them in their new home and he'd immediately set up his schoolroom to continue Elizabeth's education. Always cheerful and mellow in demeanor, he pronounced the new atmosphere far more conducive to study than the old, and silently gave thanks for the absence of Elizabeth's untoward preoccupation with Seymour.

Of late, with the Princess's illnesses, there had proven to be too much free time at Cheshunt for Ascham's taste. However, in Elizabeth's household he had found not only a most brilliant pupil but a congenial family of friends in the Ashleys. John Ashley was himself a scholar, and the two couples spent many happy hours in discussion and argument over the classics, punctuated by much laughter and merriment. The only bone of contention that marred the friends' congeniality was the subject of Thomas Seymour.

Ascham's Cambridge colleague, John Cheke, had written to him of the Admiral's alarming schemes and his desire to draw the young King into them. But the normally levelheaded Kat, perfectly named for her feline protectiveness of Elizabeth, never listened to reason on the subject of the Admiral, to the extreme annoyance of her husband and the exasperation of Ascham. The tutor had, from the beginning, done his best to warn the Ashleys of Seymour's villainy, and been forced to watch helplessly as the disastrous events at Chelsea House had unfolded. Now all he could do was lend his optimism to Elizabeth's new circumstances. Soon the Princess would be well enough to continue her studies and forget about Seymour. Though love had confounded and blinded Elizabeth's wit and reason, there was no reason she should not now revert to the modest and virtuous young woman she had been before Thomas Seymour had exploded into her life.

With a nod to Blanche Parry, Kat closed the door quietly and moved to the bowl and pitcher on the table beneath the window. Into a glass flagon she poured some water and half of the new powdered potion she'd been given by the apothecary, the foul odor of it twitching her nose. The taste of it, she reckoned, would likely turn Elizabeth's stomach, but something needed to be done about the pain in the girl's head, and the man had promised relief with his "special powder."

As Kat approached the bed with the medicine Elizabeth moaned again, and Blanche Parry shook her head somberly. One look at the Princess told the story. She had again lapsed into delirium. Her normally milk-white skin shone with a sick gray pallor, and there were rust-red circles under her closed eyes.

"I came as fast as I could," Kat said quietly.

"She's been in this state since you left," murmured Blanche. "Just dead to the world and moaning like a sick cow." She looked at Kat with terror in her eyes. "She cannot die of it, can she, Kat?"

"I think not, but then, I've never seen a headache so dire before, either. We shan't think such things, Blanche. We'll just get this down her throat. Come now, lift her head."

Just then Elizabeth uttered a sound, urgent in tone, that was something more than a moan, though less than a word. The women leaned forward, for she was about to utter it again. This time, however, her lips moved and no sound came out of them at all.

"Say again, Elizabeth," urged Kat. "Say again, dear girl. We cannot understand you."

"Thomas," she uttered feebly but clearly.

The ladies Ashley and Parry stiffened and could not bear to meet each other's eyes.

"Thomas," Elizabeth cried louder now, her strength fueled by delirium. "Thomas, Thomas!"

Kat's eyes filled with tears, and she turned away so quickly that the foul liquid sloshed over the top of the container and soiled Elizabeth's coverlet. Irritated, Blanche snatched the flagon from Mistress Ashley's hand, and as Kat fled the room, Blanche dribbled some of the potion between Elizabeth's parched lips.

At the door Kat, blinded by tears, ran headlong into Roger Ascham.

"Kat?" he said, taking in the waiting woman's appearance. "The Princess . . . ?"

"My fault!" wailed Kat Ashley. "My fault!" She rushed past the tutor and down the corridor.

Greatly alarmed, Ascham pushed open the bedchamber door just enough to convince himself that Elizabeth had not died of her infirmities. He sank back against the door frame heaving a sigh of relief, but wondered in that moment if the Princess or her retainers would ever recover from the misdeeds at Chelsea House. Despite his displays of optimism, Roger Ascham was anything but sure that they would. In fact, where Thomas Seymour was concerned, it was probable that the worst was yet to come.

Chapter Fifteen

Catherine lay in her great bed gazing mildly at the women who stood in small whispering knots round her room. She had not felt mild an hour before when, at the advanced age of thirty-six, she had successfully pushed her first child into the world. She had been altogether undignified, she remembered. Her ladies had certainly never heard such colorful oaths emanating from the mouth of the Queen Dowager before, and the thought of their shocked faces strangely pleased her.

But then, everything pleased her at this moment. She had a healthy daughter, and though the nearly two-day labor had proven exhausting and had left her achy and raw, *she had survived.* The child was beautiful — a perfectly shaped head, deep pink bud lips, and long dark curling eyelashes. If she were lucky, thought Catherine, little Mary would look like her father.

The sudden memory of Thomas forced a short stabbing pain through Catherine's chest. *Thomas.* He had afforded her her wildest unspoken dreams — a young, handsome husband, virile and exciting. A man that had loved her as much as she had loved him. And he had given her a child, one whom she would live to see grow into a magnificent woman. Mary would have all of her mother's worldly wealth and the finest humanist education, and she would certainly bring her mother great joy. But now Thomas must needs depart their lives. His darker gifts had nearly stolen her sanity, and she flatly refused to end her brilliant life a beaten shell of a woman, slave to her misguided passions. She was more than that, deserved more. As soon as she'd regained her strength, she would speak to Cranmer about the divorce. Word had come down to her of Thomas's outrageous and highly treasonous plots against the Crown. Somerset, too, had learned that his brother was working against the government and called Thomas before the Council to explain himself. He had stunned them by refusing to attend, and only when threatened with imprisonment had he apologized for his behavior. The Protector might have taken harsher measures against his next of kin, but had chosen to be lenient — some said because of the Queen Dowager's pregnancy. In any event, Catherine knew that she and little Mary must separate from Thomas soon, or when he fell from grace, they would fall along with him.

Catherine lifted a hand and beckoned to Elizabeth Tyrwhitt.

Her stepdaughter approached the bed with an expression of the sweetest delight. "Do you wish to hold Mary again, Your Majesty?"

"In just a moment, Elizabeth. What I do wish is for you to call my physician, Doctor Huick."

"Of course, madame. Are you sure you wouldn't like a sip of wine first?"

"Perhaps in a while. Just go now, my dear." Then Catherine grabbed Lady Tyrwhitt's hand. "Thank you kindly for your help in my great hour."

"Oh, you're welcome, Majesty. And it *was* a great hour! We were all so heartened by your courage."

"And by my fine oaths," added Catherine with a smile.

"And your fine oaths indeed," said Lady Tyrwhitt.

Catherine's happy expression was a sun that warmed her stepdaughter's heart. She moved from the bed and had just placed her hand on the door when it was thrown open with such force that she jumped back to avoid being knocked over. Thomas Seymour blew into the room like a gale.

"By God's precious soul!" he fairly shouted. "I've a daughter!" He strode to the cradle where the rocker rocked the infant girl lying in milky sleep.

"I will not disturb her," he said, and gave the babe a brief pat. "She's a beauty, my little girl. Looks like her mother." But Seymour's jolly bluster did little to hide the bitter disappointment he clearly felt for his wrong-sexed child. As he moved to the great bed and gave Catherine a smacking kiss, nearly a dozen people pushed into the room — the Lords Dorset, Sommers, and Blaylock, and several ladies of the household who, Catherine knew, were deeply besotted by her husband. These were "Thomas's people."

"And where are you off to in such a hurry, Lady Tyrwhitt?" Thomas said. "I've brought wine for us all. A celebration! Just stay for a moment while we drink a toast to my daughter and my beautiful wife."

Sommers and Blaylock were filling the cups they'd brought with them from a wineskin and handing them out to the ladies and gentlemen, the wet nurse, and even the midwives who had finally packed up their instruments and were making to go.

"To the great health of Lady Catherine and Mary Seymour," Thomas said, holding up his cup.

He was very good at deceit, thought Catherine, watching him from her bed. It came naturally to him, like a fish swimming. He seemed to fear nothing, perhaps had no clue what danger he was concocting for himself, and though he had made great shows of shame and remorse for his most appalling behavior with Princess Elizabeth, Catherine was sure he never did *feel* it. Thomas fooled everyone with displays of wild emotions but, she realized in retrospect, the emotions had nothing whatsoever to do with anyone but himself. It pained her to think that the love he had shown her was pretended, but she was determined to remember it as she had believed it to be then, and not in bitterness. It was over now with her and Thomas. But she would not have changed her time with him for all the world.

"Good ladies," Seymour announced, waving his cup of wine toward the women who had attended Catherine at the birth, "I thank you one and all for your service, but now I perceive you are well and truly exhausted by *your* labors and deserve some rest."

Her ladies, laughing and glad to be relieved of their chores, came one at a time to Catherine's bed to kiss her hand or cheek and wish her well before slipping out the door. It was only when Elizabeth Tyrwhitt came forward that Catherine realized that with her stepdaughter's departure she would be quite alone with Thomas and his people. The thought gave Catherine pause. She clutched Lady Tyrwhitt's hand and pulled her down so she could whisper, "Hold and stay with me now, my dear. The doctor can wait for an hour."

Without questioning, Lady Tyrwhitt retired to a stool in the corner near Catherine's bed. Thomas shot the woman a strange look as he approached his wife and sat beside her. He picked up her hand and kissed it with a dazzling boyish grin.

"You amaze me, Catherine. You're so . . . well."

"Did you think your aged wife would wither and die in child-birth?" she asked impishly.

"Of course not, sweetheart, but you look as if you could rise from your bed and run a race."

In spite of herself she laughed, seduced by his utter good humor and devastating charm.

"But you know," he went on, becoming suddenly serious, "you *might* have died, Catherine. So many women do. And we've never discussed your will."

"My will?" Despite Catherine's new and intimate understanding of her husband's true nature, Thomas's words and the complicated tapestry of meaning that lay behind them were like a hard fist to her belly.

He saw her recoil, but he persisted. "Surely you must wish me . . . and your daughter . . . and any subsequent children we might have, to inherit . . ."

"My considerable fortune," she finished for him.

She saw all the charm drain suddenly from his expression, boyish no longer.

"You *shall* have a will, Catherine." He spoke to her as he would a child. "Any sensible person of means has a will." He was not bothering to lower his voice, and all in the room, save Lady Tyrwhitt, were beginning to titter nervously.

Catherine grew enflamed. She swept the room with her gaze. "You would laugh at me?" she said sharply to the assembled group.

There was silence, and now Thomas's minions squirmed with discomfort. But Catherine's ire had been roused. Before this she had comforted herself with the notion that Seymour had no evil intentions, meant her no harm. But suddenly it was clear. He wished her dead! He needed her fortune for his plans.

She found her voice and it was indignant. "You come to me demanding a will, do you?" His silence was stony. "Well, I tell you *my* demand. I wish my physician be called."

"He's already been summoned," said Thomas coldly. "I sent word to him myself. I think he may be away."

"I wish my lady Tyrwhitt to fetch him *now*," said Catherine, shrill panic beginning to rise like bile in her throat.

"You're getting overwrought, sweetheart," said Thomas, reacquiring a soothing tone. He then moved quietly to Lady Tyrwhitt on her bench. She, confused and undone by her mistress's discomfiture, became more so when Seymour leaned down and whispered, "May I lie beside Catherine on her bed? She clearly needs comforting."

"I . . . I . . ." Elizabeth Tyrwhitt was lost for a sensible reply. Here was the lord of the manor asking permission to lie down with his own wife.

"Of course you must comfort her, my lord," she finally stammered, and was instantly heartsore to see the look of horror that passed across Catherine's face.

His people, thought the Queen Dowager as Thomas gently laid himself full length beside her, carefully tucking her head in the crook of his right shoulder — his people are enjoying the sight of my humiliation. They're laughing at me, *laughing.*

As Thomas kissed her cheek, Catherine realized with a shudder of fear how completely Thomas had her under his control.

This is not safe! she wished to cry out to her only ally, but Elizabeth Tyrwhitt, sitting stone still on her bench, was paralyzed by her own mortification. There was nothing to be done now, thought Catherine, but wait for the arrival of Dr. Huick, and pray that Thomas Seymour's evil intentions were simply a measure of her overzealous imagination.

Thomas could see that Catherine believed the physician was on his way. He perceived this flicker of hope in her eyes as clearly as her knowledge of his immoral design. Of course Huick was not coming. At least not now. He had been paid well enough to keep him away forever, though that, Thomas mused, was unnecessary. If the salve worked as well and quickly as it was meant to, Catherine would have no memory of the good doctor's presence at all. "Good" indeed. The man had been bought much more cheaply than Thomas had ever dreamed — he who had been Catherine's personal physician for eleven years. It had not mattered to Seymour if the doctor's motives were corrupt or, as he suspected, selfless. It was whispered that Huick's family had fallen on hard times, and that twenty gold crowns would keep his old father out of debtor's prison. It mattered only that the physician remain unreachable until Seymour sent word that he might finally attend the Queen Dowager.

The services of Thomas's other confederate in this scheme had been even cheaper to purchase. John Meaken had served under his command in France during the skirmish at Montreuil. When a French cavalryman had come from behind wielding a battle-axe at the helpless sixteen-year-old standard-bearer's head, Thomas had taken the Frog down with a well-aimed slice of his broadsword and saved the soldier's neck. Meaken's outpourings of gratitude to his savior knew no bounds, and he'd made a heartfelt pledge to return the favor in kind one day.

It would be foolhardy, Thomas knew, to visit an apothecary himself, especially to acquire so questionable a potion. "Flying salve" it was called, and was reputedly used by witches in their black ceremonies. Delusions were the result of rubbing the concoction of henbane, datura, and belladonna into the skin, and wild visions were said to be produced. Some even believed they could fly whilst under its influence — hence its name. Overuse of the concoction caused death. So he'd sent Meaken to fetch it. The young man, already in Seymour's debt, was overawed that the commander who had once saved his life — now High Admiral of the King's Navy — should come to him for the returned favor. He had fallen over himself to comply, and had never asked for a reason nor questioned the motives of his hero. He was told the name of the apothecary and of the ointment, and given a purse to pay for the stuff. He had, as honor demanded, refused to be paid for the mission.

As Seymour bent his head to nuzzle his wife — who, he noticed, cringed visibly at his gesture — he made sure the sheep-gut finger cot was firmly in place on the middle finger of his free hand. Then quietly he slipped his hand into a pouch at his waist, dipped the protected finger in the tiny jar of flying salve, and lightly coated it with the ointment.

"We've had a fine letter of congratulations from the Protector," announced Seymour loudly and sarcastically. This served to set his friends in the room agog and made his gesture of grasping Catherine's wrist seem most natural. The salve-anointed finger was thus hidden from view, and as he continued his boasting talk, quoting liberally from the letter signed "your loving brother," Seymour began slowly massaging the tender flesh of her wrist with the odorless ointment. She seemed altogether unaware of her poisoning. Poor Catherine, Seymour mused. What a pity that a woman should be worth more dead than alive. And she *had* been good to him. Had loved him. Provided him with a child, albeit a girl.

"Did I say," said Thomas jovially, "that the Protector called Catherine my 'bedfellow' and not my wife? I think that insulting, do you not, sweetheart?"

"Think what?" said Catherine, her eyes bright but ill-focused.

"My brother calling you my bedfellow. Think you this a proper title for a once queen of England?"

She did not answer, just closed her eyes. He could see the eyeballs beneath the lids jumping round in their sockets. A soft groan that no one but himself heard escaped her lips. How quickly the potion was working! He wondered if in her mind she was flying through the night sky on her witch's broomstick. He released her hand in order to replenish his finger with the salve, and resumed its application at once.

"Oh my . . . oh no, no, no!" cried Catherine, and suddenly all attention was upon her.

Lady Tyrwhitt jumped up from her bench and with a troubled expression placed a hand on her stepmother's forehead. "Madame? Madame!" She stared at Thomas in alarm. "I feel no fever, but Her Majesty seems to be in great distress."

"She does indeed, Elizabeth," said Seymour. "Perhaps you should go and find Doctor Huick after all." He was much concerned that Catherine's stepdaughter might try to grasp Catherine's hand, the wrist of which was now greasy with the ointment.

"Why are you laughing at me?" Catherine suddenly roared. "I have no friends." Her eyes opened but they were wild and panicked.

"All of you stand there laughing at my grief." There was dead silence in the room. "The more good I give to you, the less you give to me!"

"Catherine, my darling," crooned Seymour comfortingly. "These *are* our friends. They love you."

"No, no, they are hideous creatures, demons!" She was becoming more and more distraught. Thomas ceased his application of the flying salve, for he did not wish to kill her — not just yet. Now he simply wished for these witnesses to observe her delirium. The wilder her utterances and accusations, the better. And it would surely be attributed to her difficult lying-in and delivery, perhaps even to a fever. Catherine's condition and outbursts would first be spoken of in hushed tones in the kitchens, laundries, and stables of Chelsea House, then spread more vocally in local taverns and churchyards, and finally take the form of self-important gossip amongst the nobles in St. Paul's and the London court. It was perfect.

In a few moments Thomas would beg everyone to leave, saying it hurt him to have them see the Queen Dowager in such dire extremities. In privacy he would then import two chosen representatives who would bear witness to the drawing up of her will, have her sign it — and it would be done. Catherine's great fortune would be his. It was all so simple.

"Good friends," he said to those assembled in the bedchamber with so perfect a feigned sadness that not one of them ever suspected the cold avarice of Thomas Seymour's heart, "I think my dear wife, proud as she is, would not wish you to witness her suffering, so I will ask you to leave us now."

In respectful silence Thomas Seymour's people removed themselves from Catherine's bedchamber.

How were they to know they had left the Queen Dowager lying in the devil's embrace?

The gibbering demons were finally receding from the cavities of Catherine's mind, the frantic waves of color and the fearful sensation of soaring and falling from great heights were gone as well. But as she regained her senses she realized with growing horror that she was ill, very ill indeed. She burned, as though the blood was boiling in her veins, and in the next moment she shook with the most fearsome chills.

"Childbed fever," she heard Doctor Huick say with the utmost gravity, giving a name to her fearful symptoms. He had finally come to attend her, she realized. "It grieves me to say," he went on, " that having escaped danger for three days —"

Three days? thought Catherine. I have been lost in those netherworlds for three days.

"— the Queen has fallen victim to this terrible sickness."

Catherine forced open her crusted eyelids in time to see Thomas cover his mouth with a hand, hiding what she knew to be a smile. She understood in that moment, with the greatest clarity, the cause of his amusement. He would not, after all, have to kill her as he had planned. He would allow the puerperal fever to do the deed for him.

"Catherine . . ." Thomas stepped forward to the bedside and took her hand in his. "I am sorry."

She managed a cold smile. "I think not, sir. I think you wish me very ill."

"Not true, my love."

"Too true, Thomas. I would have given a thousand marks to have had Doctor Huick brought to me that first day I delivered, but you saw to it that he did not come."

"Her mind is very clear, Doctor," insisted Elizabeth Tyrwhitt from her place behind the three men now crowding Catherine's bed — Thomas and Doctor Huick and a local pastor, a young man whose dark robes hung like loose flesh on his skeletal frame. "Clearer than it has been these three days past."

"Catherine was clear enough when she dictated her will to us," said Thomas, unable to hide the triumph in his voice.

"Will? What will, my lord?" demanded Catherine, struggling to retain her dignity as a sudden chill racked her body with shuddering.

"This one," he replied simply, dangling a parchment between his fingers, "witnessed by Dr. Huick and Reverend Blackwell here."

She tried to grab the single sheet from Thomas's hand but he snatched it from her reach.

"Allow me to refresh you as to the contents of the document that you dictated to us several hours ago." He began to read. "'I, Catherine, Lady Seymour and Queen Dowager of England, lying on my deathbed, sick of body but of good mind, give all of my estate to my married spouse and husband, wishing my fortune to be a thousand times more in value than it was or had ever been.'" He looked up and added, "Simple and to the point, I think."

"I bequeathed nothing to our daughter, then? Nor to the princesses Elizabeth and Mary, nor to Jane Grey, nor my lady Tyrwhitt?" demanded Catherine, ice crisping her voice.

"All of your wishes have been faithfully rendered in this document, sweetheart. Just the way you told it to us."

"Were you witness to this, Elizabeth?" Catherine asked of her waiting woman, her voice barely a croak.

"No, madame, I was not," her stepdaughter answered sheepishly.

"Lady Tyrwhitt was so unnerved by your ravings," said Thomas, clearly enjoying the lady's embarrassment, "that she fled from your room for a time. But of course you were attended, and this will was witnessed by two men of the highest moral character. Now you have naught but to sign it with your own hand."

Catherine managed a feeble smile. "I would sooner ride to Hell on Lucifer's stallion than sign your paper of lies," she said, wholly gratified by the expressions on the three men's faces. For a moment she felt almost well, as though her strength of will alone could drag her from the arms of the Reaper.

Then Thomas leaned down and whispered in her ear so that no one else could hear him. "With these men as my witnesses I have no need of your signature."

Catherine's skin began to crawl, horribly, knowing his words were true.

"I win, sweetheart," he said even more quietly, "for you are already dead." He kissed her mouth, more sweetly and tenderly than so filthy a monster had a right to do, then stood and turned to Doctor Huick. "You will see to it my wife does not suffer in her final hours."

Catherine heard Elizabeth Tyrwhitt's sobs and watched as Thomas Seymour turned and disappeared out her door for the last time. She would never lay eyes on him again, of this she was sure.

Indeed, she thought as the next surge of heat swept over her like a wave of fire, Thomas *has* won and Mary, my daughter, is soon to be motherless, friendless, and altogether lost. The Old Testament speaks of a cruel, vengeful God, Catherine mused as consciousness began to slowly slip away, and today he has shown his terrible face in England.

Chapter Sixteen

Thomas Seymour wished to God he did not have to see the whimpering little brat Jane Grey. She would, he supposed, be prostrate with grief for her beloved Catherine, and dripping with compassion for the grieving widower she supposed him to be. He wondered, as he made for Jane's apartments the day after Catherine's agonizing death, if he should bother pretending some sadness for the girl's benefit. For *his,* really. Should he appear too cold-blooded, he knew, she might judge him unworthy of her loyalty, which till this time had been complete. But Jane was necessary to his plans now, and he would soon be forced to the unpleasant task — aside from all the others — of informing her that she was to return to her father's house quietly after the funeral. She would probably cry and carry on at the news, for Lord and Lady Dorset were appallingly cruel parents, even by his undemanding standards. But what was he to do with a prissy virgin in this household without a wife? He had much to do and no time to worry about her, for he had completely abandoned his plans to marry Jane off to King Edward. Well, he would send her home for now. Perhaps his aging mother, who was coming to look after his baby daughter, would look after Jane too. Something to think about.

The moment Seymour was admitted into Lady Jane's room the girl flung herself at him weeping, but with far more passion than he believed she possessed.

"Oh, my lord, my lord!" she cried through muffled sobs.

"There, there," he muttered, attempting some semblance of comfort. "She's gone to a better place, child. She's with Jesus now."

"But *you,* my lord. It is you who are all alone."

Yes, said Thomas to himself, but not for long if I have my way. He said aloud, "I do find much comfort from dear friends like you, sweet Jane."

"You do?" she sniffled, gratified by such a sentiment.

"But of course," he said, then cursed himself, thinking, Idiot! Now I cannot tell her she must leave my house.

"I want you to know, Admiral, that I am entirely at your service. So many plans must be looming for Catherine's funeral, and the household is in terrible disarray. None of us expected her to die." With this the girl fell into even more uncontrollable weeping.

"Jane, Jane, you must gather your wits, do you hear me?" Seymour pushed her to arm's length and gave her tiny shoulders a shake. "If you're going to be of help to me, you cannot be carrying on like this."

"You're right," she said and, straightening her spine, pressed her lips tightly together, forcibly holding back any further vocalization.

"Good," he said. "Much better. Now listen carefully. I'll be leaving here in two days' time."

He could see her silently calculating and was prepared for her next outburst. "But the funeral is not for four days yet!"

He forcibly restrained himself from any sarcastic retorts about her mathematical skills and only said, "I'm afraid I've urgent business to attend to in the West Country. In fact, I'll be seeing your father there."

"But, my lord —"

"You will therefore," he interrupted, "at my express command, be Lady Catherine's chief mourner. I know you will execute the task with the utmost reserve and perfect dignity."

Jane's eyes were dark pools of confusion. She whined, "You will not stay to see your wife buried?"

At her words, the doors to Seymour's patience slammed shut.

"I will do what I will, my lady," he answered coldly. "I will do as many a loving husband in these circumstances does, and absent myself from the ordeal of his wife's funeral. And I will furthermore tolerate no judgment from a —" Seymour was seized at that moment by a rare fit of restraint, for he wished to use one of the many epithets with which he had come to think of the gnomelike Jane Grey, any one of which would have lost him her adoration forever. So he chose his words with care — enough venom to properly chastise her for her impudence, and enough compassion to retain her love. He continued, "— from an hysterical if well-meaning child."

He saw, with pleasure, the color of humiliation rise in the girl's cheeks. He had chosen precisely the description of Jane that she herself most feared.

"Forgive me, Admiral, I had no right —"

"Jane, Jane," he crooned, pulling her to him. "There is nothing to forgive. I know you're up to this most daunting task. 'Tis not every day a young lady is named chief mourner to a queen of England."

Seymour realized with irritation that he had lost any possible opportunity to break the news of Jane's own departure for her father's house. He would simply leave it to Dorset, and consequences be damned. He'd spent too much time on this silly girl and unpleasant task already — he, one of the wealthiest and most powerful men in England. Indeed, he'd made quick work of having Catherine's will, still unsigned at the time of her death, deemed good in law. There was a rebellion to be raised and a princess to be wooed. The memory of Elizabeth's white velvet skin and powdery fragrance buoyed him suddenly, and his good humor returned.

"You are the dearest of all girls, Jane," he said, lifting her chin so she could meet his eyes. "And I will be eternally in your debt if you will do me this —"

"Honor!" she finished for him. "Yes, it would be my greatest honor, my lord. I will make you proud."

"Excellent, excellent," Seymour said with finality and relief. "Now, dry your eyes and go downstairs. There's much to be done before my departure."

"Yes, my lord," she said somberly and turned away. But a moment later Jane had turned back and thrown her arms about Seymour's neck in order to reach his cheek, upon which she planted a wet-faced kiss. "You are so good, my lord Admiral. So very, very good."

I am indeed, thought Thomas Seymour with a self-satisfied smile. I am all that and more.

Chapter Seventeen

When first the rider appeared at the end of the long rutted road he was no more than a tiny bobbing speck against the browning autumn fields, but in that moment when he'd appeared, Elizabeth's heart fairly leapt from her chest. She was, as she'd done every day since Thomas Seymour's first letter had been secretly delivered to her, waiting on horseback for his courier, several discreet miles from Cheshunt. Their clandestine correspondence was the only thing keeping her alive in this dreadful season since her enforced exile from Chelsea House and Catherine's untimely death, just two days before Elizabeth's fifteenth birthday.

Catherine. Just the remembrance of her name sickened Elizabeth with shame and pity. That she'd died before there had been full reconciliation between them would plague Elizabeth, she was sure, for the rest of her life. Catherine's letters after the Princess's hasty departure had been altogether kind, with scant reference to the terrible betrayal she'd suffered, but Elizabeth had expected that after the baby's birth she would visit the Queen Dowager in person and beg her forgiveness for her miserable behavior. She had played the scene over in her mind dozens of times and could almost feel Catherine's loving arms around her, a hand stroking her hair, the motherly voice allaying Elizabeth's guilty confessions.

But that day would never come. Catherine was in her grave and her widower, free of his bondage — as Thomas liked to call it — had begun pursuing Elizabeth with a fervor that reignited her desire for the man she had sworn vehemently to forget. Whilst he had begun meeting frequently with Thomas Parry to discuss the Princess's land holdings, patents, and the costs of her household — even suggesting an exchange of their properties and making very clear his intentions to marry her as soon as he'd received the Council's permission — Elizabeth and Thomas's correspondence was an altogether secret affair. Their letters, exchanged every day via his courier, spoke of their most torrid passions each for the other and would, if uncovered, be so damaging to them that a promise had been made on both their parts that the pages, once committed to memory, must be immediately destroyed. For the most part, Elizabeth had eagerly complied, as many of Thomas's letters made her blush just to read them, but there were several of late whose sentiments describing a state of eternal marital bliss were so tenderly and lovingly couched that she had hesitated, even procrastinated, before consigning them to the flames.

Thomas had traveled far in the West Country for many weeks after Catherine's death and then had gone on to London. It was there that Parry had met with him, and Thomas had been attempting to lure Elizabeth to the city for some time. Her brother Edward had, in his letters, also been pressing her to attend him at court, and she truly wished to leave the unpleasant memories of Chelsea and Cheshunt behind. But Elizabeth's own establishment in London, Durham House, had been turned into a mint. Seymour had invited the Princess and her household to take up residence at his London home, Seymour House, on the Strand overlooking the Thames. But even Kat, beside herself with joy at the prospect of Elizabeth's love match with the Admiral — now a legally available suitor — believed the plan unseemly. As far as Kat and Parry knew, however, Elizabeth had not, since leaving Chelsea House, corresponded with Seymour even once. The waiting lady had nagged the Princess incessantly about writing her condolences to the Admiral, conveying her great respect for him and her desire for the Council to grant them the needed permission to marry. But Elizabeth had demurred, pretending little interest in the man. When asked by Parry if she liked Seymour's pursuit of her and if she would consent to such a marriage, she had simply replied that if the time came she would do "as God put in her mind to do," exasperating him thoroughly.

Elizabeth had not laid eyes on Thomas since the day in the boathouse, and of late all their letters had been consumed with plans and preparations for their first clandestine meeting. Delays and complica-

tions had frustrated them, however, until the lovers were nearly un-
strung with desire. If they did not soon meet, thought Elizabeth as the
rider came galloping toward her at breakneck speed, she would surely
die of love's terrible fever.

Unable to wait any longer, Elizabeth spurred her horse and raced
to meet the courier. She was shocked therefore, as they came within
sight of one another, to discover the rider was not the man sent by
Thomas Seymour at all. It was, in fact, Robin Dudley.

She had hardly the time to gather her wits about her before they
were face to face, their reined-in horses snorting and dancing in place.
'Twas odd, thought Elizabeth in the moment before she spoke, how
very pleased she was to see her friend, even as much as she had suffered
disappointment in not receiving news of her love.

"What brings you this way, Robin?" she said striving to catch her
breath.

"What brings me this way?" he repeated incredulously. "What
else would bring me this way but *you,* or are we so estranged that you
would never expect a visit from your old friend?"

"I — I —" she stuttered.

"You haven't replied to my two last letters," he said. "I'd begun to
worry."

Elizabeth felt the heat rising in her face. So preoccupied had she
been with her secret correspondence that all else had fallen away. She
had simply forgotten to write back to Robin.

"I've been ill," she offered, glad that this was not a lie. She had always been entirely honest with her childhood friend.

"You seem well enough now," he said, examining her face and
form astride the horse. "Maybe a little peaked, but well enough to hold
a quill, I daresay."

"If you mean to shame me, you have," said Elizabeth with a contrite smile. "Tell me, how is your family?"

"Everyone is very well. Father's been away at court, and he tells
me that your brother wishes my presence back in his schoolroom, so
perhaps I'll go to London soon and see what Master Cheke is teaching
these days."

"I may go to London as well," said Elizabeth. "Poor Edward's been despondent since Catherine's death. She was the only mother he ever knew. Perhaps that is why he calls us all back to him."

" 'Twill be fun," Robin said. "Masques, revels, tilts. And your favorite — bearbaitings." He was teasing her now.

"Robin!" Elizabeth laughed delightedly, forgetting for a moment her obsession. Then she looked up to see Thomas's rider almost upon them. An expression of panic swept across her features, instantly obliterating her joy.

The courier, a new man that Thomas had sent for the first time this day, was not well enough acquainted with their secretive procedures to realize his gaffe. He reined to a halt and, taking no notice of the stranger, handed Elizabeth the sealed letter. Without a word, he turned his horse and galloped back the way he'd come.

There was a terrible moment of silence as Robin Dudley strove to make sense of what had just happened and Elizabeth fumbled for sensible excuses.

It took Robin little time to guess what was afoot. "Please, tell me you're not seeing him, Elizabeth," he said.

"I haven't seen him since I left Chelsea," she said. "At least not yet."

"Then you plan to?" he demanded.

"He's no longer a married man, Robin. He's free to pay court to whomever he pleases."

"Then why the secret courier? Elizabeth, what are you planning?"

"I've got to see him, Robin, at least the first time alone. No one understands what is between us. Kat and Parry have their plans for a public courtship, and Thomas plays along with them. But we *will* see each other, just the two of us, if only to pledge our true love to one another."

Robin's mind worked furiously. He wished to shout at Elizabeth that such madness would bring utter ruin down on her head and those around her, that she should think carefully before she acted. But the young man knew that such vehement protestations could, in a person of such strong will, precipitate the opposite effect. Elizabeth might hie to her secret tryst even more quickly. Time was what he needed now to find a solution to this dilemma.

Elizabeth reached across and grabbed Robin's hand, fixing him with her eyes. "If you're my friend, you will tell no one of these plans," she said urgently.

"I am your friend, you know that."

"Then promise me."

He held her gaze steadily and replied, "I promise you, your secret is safe with me."

It was the first time Robin Dudley had ever lied to Elizabeth. As he rode by her side back to Cheshunt, he prayed fervently that it would be the last.

It was several days before Robin Dudley was meant to ride for London, but after he'd left Cheshunt, the news of Elizabeth's disastrous plans haunting his every thought, he accelerated his schedule for the journey and now found himself being shown into his father's new offices at Hampton Court.

They embraced warmly and the boy excitedly launched into an explanation of his reason for the visit.

"Does the Princess have no conception of the danger she is in?" asked John Dudley with keen interest.

"I think she must, but I fear her passions have begun overruling her intellect, much as happened with the Queen Dowager. What can we do, Father? We cannot allow Elizabeth to compromise herself."

"Let me think a moment, son. Let me just think."

John Dudley clasped his hands behind his back and began to pace before his large window looking out into the palace's great square courtyard. He appeared to be formulating a plan on the spot, but in truth his intricate plot had been in place for some time. His importance and prestige had been growing in the last months, and he'd slowly begun acquiring power over the Council as well.

In contrast, more grumbling was heard every day over the Protector's handling of the government. Somerset was perhaps well-meaning, but his policies pleased no one. By tearing down six acres of buildings on the Strand — primarily churches and monasteries — to build himself a magnificent new home worthy of his exalted position, the Protector had infuriated many Catholics. Conversely, his tolerance of Catholic doctrine had enflamed the radical Protestant faction. And whilst many of Somerset's policies were simply a broad continuation of Henry's — the debasement of the currency, the enclosure of once-public land to provide private grazing for sheep — they engendered gross poverty and served to weaken and discredit the Protector. Rebellions were brewing in the West Country and in East Anglia. But Somerset, content with the high station he had procured for himself and his family, seemed strangely oblivious to the trouble that was bubbling all around him.

Not so John Dudley. His orchard had finally come into flower and the first fruits of his labor were about to be plucked. The friendship and cooperation he had shown Somerset in the final years of Henry's life had, in the first months of King Edward's reign, given way to loathing and jealousy, emotions that Dudley had managed to hide. Lord Somerset had moved with the speed of lightning to grasp complete power for himself, and the rest of the Council be damned. The Protector had proven himself despotic and insufferable — but these defects, thought John Dudley, were all the better for *his* purposes.

In Thomas Seymour, John Dudley had discovered the proverbial crack in the foundation, the means by which to bring the wall, and finally the palace, tumbling down on the Duke of Somerset's head. It would happen, he knew, in stages. It was incumbent upon him to continue moving carefully and patiently toward his goal — the wresting of power away from the Protector and into his own hands. Henry's grandfather Owen Tudor, a wardrobe master to royalty, had been no more noble than himself, thought John Dudley. His own family, he reasoned, had as much right as any Tudor to aspire to such exalted heights. He would, he had decided, climb to the throne on the crumbled walls of the Seymour family fortunes.

His son must not know of his plans. Not yet, for the boy was still too loyal to the princess Elizabeth. Thankfully she was a Protestant, on the right side of things. And perhaps when the power was in his hands she could be of some use. For now, Robert must know only that he was saving his friend from a terrible fiend and ultimately from a traitor's death. But his dear son had brought him the very tool he needed for the breaching of the heretofore impregnable Seymour edifice.

"I think luck is with us," said John Dudley, finally continuing the conversation with Robin. "I've heard that Thomas Seymour has lately returned to London. Clearly he is fomenting a rebellion against his brother, but we have no proof of it. He may be a fool, but he knows enough to watch his back in this. He'll be suspicious of any man trailing him. But I'd wager he'll not be alert to a *boy* on his trail." John Dudley was not so ruthlessly driven as to miss, alongside the excitement and pride at his father's suggestion, the look of hurt in his son's eye. He added, "I am sending you on a man's errand, Robert, remember that. Your tender age *particularly* makes you suitable for the task, so be thankful for it."

"Yes, my lord, I will," said Robin humbly. "When and where should I begin?"

"Tomorrow. I think he will be working every moment toward his end. Begin with St. Paul's Cathedral. 'Tis the meeting place of beggars and kings and everyone in between. He will like to go there for recruitment of men and procurement of weapons, ordnance, and supplies. And he must be raising money for the rebellion, though I've not yet proven his sources. I think, with his wife dead and his eye on Elizabeth, he will begin to work more quickly, and he is therefore bound by his nature to make more mistakes. Follow him, but discreetly, wherever he goes, and bring me back evidence of his wrongdoing. *Hard* evidence, Robert, for if we falter now he may, with the devil's help, succeed. Not only will your princess be lost, but all of England." John Dudley regarded his glowing boy, who seemed to have grown several inches taller in the past hour. "So go now, son. This will be the first service you'll do your country, though certainly not your last." He clapped a hearty arm round the boy's shoulder. "You're more of a man than many who should be so," he said. "I know you're going to make me very proud."

Dearest Princess,

Whilst pressing responsibilities have kept me from writing you these past several days, nothing has alleviated the pain in my heart caused by our enforced absence one from another. Every waking moment is consumed by thoughts of you, and it is only with the strictest self enforcement that I can attend to my divers duties, not the least of which is procuring a majority of the Privy Councillors' support for our marriage.

Touching this most important task, I have lately conceived of a notion that may forward its achievement substantially. Your own dealings with my brother the Protector and his wife, the Duchess of Somerset, are cordial, are they not? If so, perhaps you might petition that lady in some personal fashion and see if you might obtain her support for our marriage. Truly she abhors me as deeply as I do her, but she may wish to curry favor with a Princess of the Blood, and would therefore speak in our favor to her husband, my brother.

Will you consider it?

In the meanwhile I pine every day more pathetically for the sight of you, the feel of you in my arms once again, though I have promised you before and promise you again that when we do meet, it will be under the most chaste of circumstances. The loss of our senses in the boathouse, whilst a memory I cannot but cherish, was a regrettable lapse in restraint and conscionable behavior. If you can see clear to come to me without chaperone, I promise that the time will be spent in complete decorum, making plans for our legal marriage, perhaps allowing ourselves some time to dream dreams of our future happiness, and many healthy sons.

I pray you trust your lady, Kat Ashley's, good opinion of myself, for it is surely deserved, Elizabeth. Your friend and cofferer Thomas Parry, too, is confident that I will make you a good husband. My heart tells me that you yourself believe it, and love me with the same fervor that I do you.

I will wait, fighting impatience, to hear when you can slip away from your retainers and see me. Until then I will remain

Your faithful servant and future husband,

T. Seymour

Admiral,

You and I have opened our hearts to one another in these months since the death of your good wife and my beloved stepmother, Catherine, and I have no doubt that you are sincere in your protestations of love and devotion to myself and your desire to see us married. I share that desire, deeply, but I must admit shock and a certain peevishness at your request that I approach the Duchess of Somerset to gain support for our marriage. You are wrong to think our relations cordial. I loathe her quite as much as you do. Recently she chastised Kat Ashley rudely and publicly for simply allowing me to travel to London on a barge. Ridiculous! Therefore, to grovel and seek that lady's approval would prove nothing short of humiliation. We shall simply have to find other sources of help in our cause.

Touching on your request for a private meeting with myself, I have only these words of reply. Yes! Yes! Yes! Nothing would do us better than to be in one another's company again, but finally without fear or guilt or remorse, but filled with joy and hope for our future together, though not with obstacles. Our marriage is in my mind a certainty, for your will and desire are as strong as my own. I await your instructions as to the time and place of our meeting. Till then I remain

Your Dearest Friend and Future Wife

Chapter Eighteen

Robin Dudley had presented himself at King Edward's court only long enough to reacquire his modest quarters in the palace. He went directly to Master Cheke, explaining that family business would keep him from the classroom for perhaps a week, but that he looked forward to resuming his studies with the King.

He then promptly began a program of intelligence gathering. Using casual conversation and a gentleman's favorite pastime, gossip-mongering, he informed himself of Thomas Seymour's day-to-day activities — how often he appeared at court, how he traveled, whom he visited, how long he stayed, where he dined and drank and whored. Robin schooled himself till he had memorized lists of both the Admiral's supporters and his enemies. Only then did he feel ready to follow the man and move close enough to begin spying.

Two hours before dawn on the fifteenth day of January he rode to Seymour House, and from across the way in the shadows of another great house began his vigil, certain that Seymour had gone home the previous night, late, after an evening of gambling in Lord Monroe's house. There was small chance that the subject of his investigation would use a barge or boat for his conveyance to the day's destination, for Robin had learned that the man was not fond of water travel of any kind — a strange dislike for the High Admiral of the King's Navy. Happily it meant that following Seymour would be easier, comfortable, as Robin was on horseback.

Young Dudley was forced to wait for hours. His thoughts, normally precise and straightforward as the mathematical problems he so enjoyed solving, now veered and collided inside his head. With the commencement of this mission he felt no longer a boy but a grown man with the fate of a princess and perhaps a kingdom on his broadening shoulders. Yet in his heart he felt fallible and frightened of failure. He wondered if his father, in his plan to bring about the Seymour family's demise, had backed his son's covert operation with other spies and functionaries, or if John Dudley in fact trusted Robin enough to act alone in this. He prayed for the latter, and prayed too for success in his assignment. As much as he wished to serve England, he longed even more fervently to please his father.

And then there was Elizabeth. Her behavior of late and her turn of mind had become irrational, altogether unfathomable. Ever since they'd been children she had bested him in the power and precise composition of her thoughts, the rational and preternaturally adult grace with which she deported herself. Her course, he mused, had been inconceivably difficult from the start — a royal princess whose mother had been disgraced and beheaded. Had Elizabeth failed to learn early the lessons of caution and restraint, of invisibility from her father's furious eye one moment and abject groveling the next, she would never have survived Henry's reign.

Elizabeth had teased Robin unmercifully about his betrothal to Amy Robsart, claimed that he'd lost all his good sense over the girl. She was right. Amy was a beautiful girl and possessed a sweetness, like rose milk, that both softened him and, admittedly, made him hard. Now Elizabeth had done more than lose *her* senses to love. She had placed her very life in jeopardy, betrayed Catherine, and for what? A singularly vile and dangerous scoundrel — a man who was plotting the overthrow of her brother's kingdom! What on earth could she be thinking? What power did Thomas Seymour possess, Robin asked himself time and time again, to cause so violent a passion in his dear friend? And why, he finally wondered with red-faced shame, did their too obvious lust for one another arouse his own jealousy? He was betrothed to Amy Robsart and he looked forward to their marriage. Elizabeth, a royal princess, was too far above him in rank for even a fantasy of marriage. And they were friends of the heart, she more dear to him than any person outside his family. Did he love her? Did he lust for her as Seymour did? Certainly she was beautiful, but just yesterday, or so it seemed, she was a gangly girl who raced with him on horseback side by side as his brothers did — and sometimes won. If she *could* be his, he suddenly wondered, if all rank and title magically fell away, if Elizabeth were just a girl and he a boy (or, more precisely, woman and man) would he desire her for himself? This silent question disturbed young Dudley profoundly, but with his sharpest reason brought to bear, and an honesty allowed in his most private heart, the answer burst forth with strength and startling clarity. Yes! He loved Elizabeth, loved her deeply, and if the stars had not already sealed his fate, he would have her before any woman in the world!

The thought, once realized, plunged the boy into immediate despair. This was lunacy. He could never have Elizabeth. He was legally betrothed to Amy Robsart. Elizabeth was second in line for succession to the throne of England. A pig would fly before she would marry a man such as himself, and grandson of a traitor at that. He must put such insanity out of his mind. He was here this day on a sacred mission. He and his family owed their lives and their fortunes to the Tudors. It was his bounden duty to protect his sovereign's kin from all harm. This he would do as an upstanding and loyal servant of the Crown. He would. He would! If only, thought Robin Dudley morosely, he could banish Elizabeth's pale and splendid face from his mind's eye.

Amy. He would force himself to think of Amy.

The Admiral, some five hours after Robin had begun his vigil, finally rode out through his gates alone on horseback and clattered down the cobbled Strand, heading into the heart of London. Thomas rode well and knew his way through the winding, cluttered, and filthy streets of the city. He was, Robin learned as he followed, a popular figure in town, calling friendly greetings to men, women, and children of every rank and occupation. And as each of them called back to him, Seymour sat taller and prouder in the saddle, as though such fame and popularity enlarged him. Such support could, Dudley realized, mean the difference between the Admiral's rebellion succeeding and failing, and from the look of it, the common people were on his side.

Robin's quarry made directly for St. Paul's, riding into the cathedral's courtyard. Far from being a sedate cloister, the place was a seething marketplace of booksellers and peddlers, food stalls and auctions of horseflesh. Robin did as Seymour had done, paying a groom to take his mount, and followed the Admiral into the nave of the great cathedral, London's most outrageous meeting place. Here was a preacher in the pulpit shouting his sermon over a mass of Londoners engaged in anything but prayer. The aisles and pews teemed with courtiers, merchants, and prostitutes. Lovers shamelessly embraced in shadows along the walls, and victuals were hawked and purchased over the marble-topped tombs of England's kings and queens.

Robin watched Seymour as he moved through the crush, here attempting to appear less conspicuous than on the streets and clearly scanning the faces to find his assignation. Even before Seymour was aware, Robin Dudley noticed a small, rough man wearing a strange array of once fine but now filthy clothing making straight for the Admiral. To his surprise the man grabbed Seymour in midstride and whipped him round by the arm to face him. Instantly Seymour's hand found his blade and the blade found his attacker's throat, poised for the cut. Short though he was next to Seymour, the man bristled with contempt and showed no fear whatsoever. Some folks round the pair were momentarily taken aback by the sudden contretemps, but most, mired in their own business, ignored it altogether.

Robin pushed through the crowd to be privy to the next action. He arrived within earshot just as the stranger uttered the words "Black Jack" and Seymour, still bristling at the stranger's rude introduction, sheathed the dagger and released the man from his grip. Keeping well behind an effeminate courtier taking great pains to choose the perfect leather gauntlets from the dozen pairs spread out before him on the tomb of King Ethelred, Robin Dudley was able to hear Seymour's entire exchange with his companion, who, it was now apparent, was a pirate. The man was angry and spoke with surprising impudence, thought Robin, to so high a nobleman.

"I tell ye, they're harrying our bloody ships again, and me captain don't take it too kindly, what with yer fine promises of safe conduct an' all."

Seymour looked genuinely alarmed at the news. "You're sure they're naval vessels and not private ships?"

"D'ye think we're idiots, sir? We know a naval vessel when we sees it."

"And the names of the ships?" Seymour demanded.

"The *Princess Mary* and the *Avenger* were two that I remember."

Robin could see the Admiral's forehead crease as he strove to put a captain's name to a ship.

"I'll see to it," he said finally.

"And how'll ye 'see to it,' Admiral?"

The man's impertinence, Robin could see, was starting to grate on Seymour's implacable reserve. "I will have the captains arrested and replaced with more . . . tolerant men, men who know how to obey my orders. You tell your captain that."

"Aye."

The pirate abruptly turned to go but Seymour pulled him roughly back by the collar till they were nose to nose. The little man's feet dangled off the ground. "And you tell Captain Thompson I will not wait much longer for an accounting of what's mine. If it is short, God help him." He dropped the man's shirt and his feet hit the ground.

"I'll gladly tell him of yer threat, Admiral," was his derisive retort.

"Do that, you scurvy piece of scum."

The pirate spit dangerously close to Seymour's boot and, with a final defiant look, turned and disappeared into the throng. As soon as he was gone he was forgotten, and Thomas resumed his original search.

The man he sought waited half hidden behind one of the cathedral's massive columns, his eyes darting nervously from side to side. He was of middling age, florid faced, dressed in a doublet all black but of the richest fabric and finest cut. It was a man young Dudley did not readily recognize. The two men were quite apart from the crowd and, maddeningly, Robin could get no closer than twenty feet without appearing suspicious. He therefore was able to hear only snatches of their conversation. Fuses, artillery, light cannon — they were speaking of Thomas Seymour's armory!

Robin doubled back and disappeared into a nearby group of gossiping courtiers and emerged into the open space near Seymour and his conspirator as close as he dared. He walked slowly, as though he himself were looking for someone, and overheard Seymour in an urgent voice saying, "Half the purse now and the rest only if you take delivery on the powder before Wednesday next."

The next words were drowned out as a gentleman shouted loudly that a pickpocket had robbed him. A scrambling chase ensued down the central aisle, knocking over half a dozen clerics and a chestnut vendor. By the time Robin could resume his eavesdropping, Seymour was saying, "A penny a day per soldier, and ten thousand troops. Who knows how long —?"

The Admiral grew suddenly silent. Robin felt Seymour's eyes boring into the back of his head. He was forced to move on. Blast it! He had lost his opportunity to discover the armory's whereabouts. Robin lost himself in the crowd again but turned back in time to see Thomas placing a heavy purse in the gentleman's hand. The two men parted, leaving in separate directions.

Seymour, happily for Robin, did not leave the cathedral but joined a group of nobles engaged in a noisy debate about enclosures. Meanwhile, however, his coconspirator was heading for the door. Who was he? Robin had never seen the man at court, though that meant nothing. He could follow the stranger, but this meant losing the trail of Seymour today, and that would never do. By the sound of it, the rebellion was imminent. The man might or might not lead him to the armory. All he needed was a name.

Blessed Jesus! The black-suited gentleman had stopped to speak with a whore whom Robin estimated to be no older than Elizabeth. An idea struck him suddenly, and he moved directly to a trio of prostitutes sharing a bawdy laugh near the cathedral door. When they saw the tall, handsome boy approaching, they began to hoot and throw kisses his way. The prettiest one quite brazenly tugged at her bodice till a rosy nipple popped out. The sudden sight of it left him momentarily speechless before the women.

"Ew, such a pretty young gentleman," said one.

"Why, 'e's blushin'," said another.

"Makes 'im all the prettier, I think."

They cackled lasciviously.

"Well then, young gent," said the oldest of the whores, "what 'ave you in mind? All three of us at once?"

Robin was smiling now despite his urgent mission and said playfully, "I may look green to you, ladies —"

"Ew, now we're *ladies,* says 'e."

"— but I wager I'm man enough to take you on one after the other."

They shrieked with raucous delight.

"A letch at your age," said the youngest. "Why, good sir, you ought to be ashamed. Should 'e not be ashamed?" she asked her cohorts.

"Please, come close. I have a favor to ask," he whispered suddenly and pulled them round him. They were baffled but highly intrigued, and so they waited in silence to hear his request. "See that gentleman all in black with the sweet young woman by the door?"

"Slag Maggie, you mean?" asked the oldest whore, pointing with her chin at Seymour's liaison and his prostitute.

"The very one. I'll let you have everything in my purse if you tell me his name."

"'Ow do we know you've anything in your purse worth 'avin'?" asked the middle whore.

Robin removed the pouch from the waist of his doublet and discreetly displayed its contents.

"A rich young lad, as well as 'andsome," observed the youngest with growing interest.

"Why, that's Lord Brockhurst," announced the oldest whore with great authority.

"I know Lord Brockhurst," said Robin, withdrawing his purse, disappointed, "and that is not him. I thank you for your time, ladies," he said and turned to go.

"I ain't 'ad 'im," he heard the youngest say as he moved away.

"Nor I," added the middle whore.

Robin grew alarmed to see Slag Maggie taking the arm of the black-suited gentleman and the pair making for the door. Thankfully the crowd was slowing their progress, and the man would stop occasionally to greet someone he knew.

"Wait!" cried the middle prostitute to Robin. "We'll find out 'is name, just you wait." She pulled her friends to her and whispered to them. "Stay 'ere," she ordered Robin, "and don't spend the contents of that purse o' yours, y'ear."

A moment later the whores had dispersed into the crowd. He watched them assail, one by one, every unengaged prostitute under the roof, some that were in midtransaction, and even a few gentlemen who Robin supposed had at one time employed them, and point questioningly to the man in black. Sometimes the women would be forced to drag their source to a place from which they could see the gentleman better. Robin watched with amusement as the youngest girl hoisted herself up onto a pew seat for a better view. Within moments she had returned, breathless and bursting with her intelligence, but Robin put a finger to his lips to still her until the others had returned. They both did so a few minutes later, and none too soon. The man in black and Slag Maggie were disappearing out the great cathedral doors.

"All right, ladies, at the count of three. Pray for consensus or you'll not have your purse." They gave each other a hopeful look. "One, two, three," he counted.

"Lord Kendall!" they all cried at once, then screamed with delight, falling upon Robin with hugs and kisses.

Finally he pulled from their embraces smeared with face paint and dusted with powder. He smiled and held out his leather pouch. "That was a brilliant bit of espionage, ladies."

"Don't underestimate a whore who can make a week's wages without spreadin' 'er legs," said the middle girl, plucking the purse from Robin's hand.

"And what might our benefactor's name be, then?" asked the oldest prostitute.

"Robert Dudley, son of John Dudley, Lord Warwick."

"Warwick? Never 'eard of 'im, never 'ad 'im," she said. The other two concurred. "Must be a right upstandin' gent, 'cause between the three of us, we've 'ad all of 'em been 'ad."

"My mother will be very pleased to hear that," said Robin jovially, "but now I'm off. And thank you very kindly for your good work."

He turned and was instantly lost in the crowd, though for several moments more he could hear their laughter and the eldest whore crying out after him, "Don't be a stranger now, young Robert!"

Though previously Robin Dudley had dreaded the loss of daylight as he sought to tail Thomas Seymour — first from St. Paul's and

165

later from the Royal Mint accompanied by an employee who Robin supposed or *hoped* was his accomplice in treason — the young man now held it as his good fortune that the sun had finally set, the ever-darkening shadows shielding his espionage in the cloak of night.

Seymour had met the man briefly on the steps of the mint at closing time, pretending it a chance meeting with only a few words exchanged. They had parted and the unnamed employee had quickly hired a litter, disappearing into the slapdash web of London streets. Remounting his horse, Seymour had ridden off after him. Robin had followed both, careful to keep a discreet distance between himself and the men, who were already carrying on in a covert manner. He had every reason for suspicion and was frantic at the thought of losing them in the crush of the workday's end. More than once Robin Dudley found himself separated from Seymour and the litter by carts and carriages and masses of tradesmen leaving their home businesses and shops to make for the nearest tavern. Darkness came quickly to the narrow London streets and even tinier lanes, their houses' second and third stories jutting farther and farther into the street's midline.

But Robin was secretly pleased to find a fresh usefulness for his precise and subtle command of the horse beneath him. A quick swivel, delicate steps in place, even a graceful leap, avoided several mishaps and kept the objects of his pursuit always in his sight.

As young Dudley watched, the litter headed down a short dark lane whose end was the front of a three-story house covered in trellises and ancient vines of ivy. This, he assumed, was the mint employee's residence. The as yet unnamed man climbed out of the transport, and the two litter bearers, relieved of their load, trotted back up the street, passing Seymour as he clattered past them to his destination.

Now Robin paid a boy to guard his horse and peered round the corner to see the Admiral tie up his mount to the post in front of the man's house. The mint employee opened the front door, admitted Seymour, and closed it behind them. Only then did Robin steal furtively down the lane.

By the time he reached the house and took his place in the shadows beside the ground-floor window, the two men were already deep in conversation. Robin had no way of knowing what vital intelligence had already been lost to him. Further, the window was closed, and it was only by the grace of Thomas Seymour's booming voice that Robin could hear any part of their dealings.

"... delivery of powder ... Holt Castle ... gold shavings ... see the cache now ..."

To Robin's dismay, the mint employee began climbing his stairs, and Seymour followed till both men were out of sight. Hardly considering the consequences of his act, Robin moved to the front door and carefully tried the handle, but the old mechanism creaked loudly and set a dog inside to barking. In moments footsteps could be heard as the owner traipsed back down the stairs to learn the cause of the commotion.

Robin flattened himself against the front wall, losing himself entirely in a profusion of ivy. The door opened and the man peered out. Seeing nothing but a stray cat padding across the cobbles, he quickly shut the door.

Dudley slumped with relief, sure that the man would have heard his wildly pounding heart, and in the next moment was gifted with a most extraordinary bit of luck. Above his head Thomas Seymour threw open the window of the second-floor chamber and, leaning out over the sill, sucked in a lungful of air. Robin, still hidden in the ivy, remained still as a post. Now he could hear the other man return to the upstairs room and the conspirators' conversation begin again.

Quickly Dudley extricated himself from the leaves and stood back to survey the situation. The two men's voices were now too muted by distance to hear distinctly. He must get nearer to them. A full moon had just risen and the added light allowed Robin to make out the instrument of his success.

Beneath the thick curtain of ivy lay its age-old vines, some of which were thick as a boatman's arm.

He was unsure that the uppermost branches would support his weight, or if they grew close enough to the open window to give him access to the conversation. And in the moonlight anyone coming down the street would clearly see him in his clandestine pursuit. But there was no time to think. Now action was all that counted.

He began to climb.

He had to move with the utmost stealth, for the unnatural rustling of the leaves on this windless night would surely alert the two men of his approach. But speed was crucial as well. The incriminating words he needed desperately to hear might already have been spoken, and all of this would have been for naught. His sinewy muscles and youthful grace did not desert him as he placed each foot and hand higher on the vine and pulled himself up. Thankfully the distance to the second floor was none too great, and with a last blessed bit of luck he found a narrow foothold four feet below the window ledge.

"God's precious blood, Sherrington!" Robin heard the Admiral exclaim with disgust. "Is this piddling pile the best you could do after all this time?"

Finally, thought Robin, the mint worker had a name.

Hardly daring to breathe, he grasped the sill with both hands and hoisted himself just high enough to peer into the window. What he saw were the two men standing over an open wooden cask piled with what appeared in the candlelight to be a mound of gold shavings.

"Piddling pile, my lord?" spat Sherrington. "I've risked my neck every day for a year to shear those coins to pay for your bloody rebellion, and what thanks do I get?"

Robin ducked out of sight as Seymour swung round and began pacing the room.

"'Tis *your* rebellion too, sir," said Seymour, "or so you would have had me believe."

"You are dreaming, my lord Admiral," said Sherrington contemptuously. "If you search your memory for the truth, you'll remember our dealings were the result of blackmail, with me the victim."

"True," replied Seymour. "You'd already started your little 'shaving' operation, but I thought you agreed that there was no better use for it than removing that worm of a man from power."

"If you call your own brother a worm behind his back, my lord, I do wonder what you call me."

Robin took another furtive peek just in time to see Seymour wheel on Sherrington in fury.

"What I call you is an incompetent fool! How shall I pay for the powder on its delivery, and food for my men? Or would you have them eat dirt for their service in this righteous revolt?"

"Righteous!" shrieked Sherrington. "You call yourself righteous?

You are correct in one thing, Admiral. I am a fool. A fool to have taken up with the likes of you!"

"Just give me the gold," demanded Seymour, "what there is of it."

"No sir, I will not," cried Sherrington, slamming the chest shut and turning the key in its lock. "And if you try carrying it off by force I shall call 'thief,' *very loudly.*"

"Will you?" said Thomas Seymour, menacing the smaller man with his powerful body and the full force of his wrath. "And how will you say these four thousand pounds in gold shavings came into your possession, Master Sherrington of the Royal Mint?"

"At this moment I would rather stand in the Star Chamber on charges of treason than give you this gold."

To Robin's amazement, Sherrington produced a carefully planted pistol and leveled it at Seymour's chest. "Now if you would be so kind as to leave my house, sir." The smile that creased the man's face was perfectly smug — happy at least for this brief moment to have bested the Lord High Admiral of the King's Navy.

Seymour, red-faced and silenced by his own frustration and rage, wheeled about and headed for the door.

In the same instant, Robin Dudley scrambled down the vines with no thought to stealth or cunning, just the will to remove himself from his perch on the wall and out of sight before Thomas Seymour came through the front door. His feet hit the ground at the same moment the door flew open and Seymour exploded through the portal. Robin tried to disappear amidst the ivy but his efforts were, in the end, unnecessary, for Seymour, blind with fury, mounted his horse and without a backward glance rode off hell-bent down the cobbled lane.

Once Seymour had disappeared round the corner, young Dudley raced after him to retrieve his horse. He found the boy into whose keeping he had given his mount, still muttering oaths and nursing two bloodied knees sustained when the Admiral's horse had knocked him down. Robin paid the boy extra for his pain, then took his saddle and, with intelligence most vital to the kingdom, galloped off to Hampton Court and his father.

*

169

John Dudley, as he closed the door behind his son and sent Robert off for a well-deserved rest, smiled with the profoundest pleasure. The evidence of Seymour's rebellion — one that in the fullness of time would probably have emerged stillborn — was nevertheless more than sufficient to bring the High Admiral to justice. It was, thought the elder Dudley, difficult to concentrate his thoughts on Thomas Seymour alone, for he saw the man's downfall as only the first step in his own great design. And in the day's dealings with Robin — a show of enormous pride for his effort and achievement in bringing the damning evidence of Seymour's wrongdoing — it was incumbent upon him to hide the coming torment that the boy was likely to endure. For John Dudley knew full well that Princess Elizabeth, in the course of Seymour's fall, would herself suffer, though to what degree he did not know. His son would surely be heartsick with the knowledge that his actions had placed Elizabeth in danger, when his prime motive had been to protect her. Robin would — and John Dudley regretted this — feel betrayed by his own father.

But in the end he cared less for his son's hurt feelings than for the good of the kingdom. At least this is how he framed his actions. If he were perfectly honest he would have to admit that his plan to bring the brothers Seymour to ruin was simply a matter of personal ambition. Young Robin would one day forgive him. But, thought John Dudley as he settled himself at his table to write the Privy Council of this most momentous intelligence, if the boy did not, it was — in the greater scheme of things — all the same to him.

Dearest Princess,

I am at the end of my wits with longing for the sight of you. Can you come to my lodgings at Seymour House this evening? In disguise would be best, and with no one's knowledge, even dear Kat who wishes us well. I await you breathlessly.

Your friend and future husband,

T. Seymour

Chapter Nineteen

Elizabeth's plan had been in place for weeks. It was only the call to come that had been lacking and finally she had been summoned. With less trepidation than she'd imagined, the Princess had had delivered to her London residence, Crosby House, at four of the clock in the afternoon, a sealed letter to Kat — one that Elizabeth had paid very handsomely for a court scribe to write. It called her waiting lady to the bedside of a desperately sick aunt in Cheapside. Elizabeth knew she would in due time be forced to face Kat's prodigious wrath for the deed, but she felt equal to her nurse's most severe recriminations if it meant a meeting alone with Thomas.

With news of her aunt's illness, Kat became henlike, clucking importantly as she searched her private apothecary shelf for the needed remedies. She was ready by the time her conveyance, not half an hour later, pulled up to the front of the house. When Kat poked her head into Elizabeth's bedchamber to say good-bye, she found the Princess at the writing table immersed in a translation of Pliny with which she had been struggling for the last week.

"You'll stop when it begins to grow dark, Elizabeth," she cautioned. "Your eyes will suffer first if you do not, and then your head." It was the same warning she gave Elizabeth virtually every afternoon of her life.

This day, instead of the mild irritation with which the Princess normally answered her nagging, she mildly replied, "I will, Kat. And I do hope your poor aunt recovers quickly this time."

"Thank you, my dear. Blanche will be up to see you to bed. I'll return the soonest I can."

"Never you mind me. 'Tis your aunt who needs you now."

When the door shut behind Kat, Elizabeth slumped with relief and went quickly to lock and bolt it. There was a brief moment of remorse for such boldfaced lying to the one person in the world who had loved her the longest and the best, but Elizabeth had no time for anything now except the precise execution of her subterfuge.

From under her bed she pulled a shallow chest in which was stored a suit of men's clothing, a purchase she had made from Master Coke, one of King Edward's young wardrobesmen. She'd smoothly explained that the suit was one she'd be needing for a court masque.

The moment she received Thomas's letter Elizabeth had initiated her plan. She had already been dressed for the day in a stiff stomacher which corseted her into a wine-colored gown with separate laced sleeves and a hundred tiny buttons. She knew that without the normal help of one or two waiting ladies she could never possibly extricate herself from her garments, so she began complaining loudly to Kat about a pain in her belly. Pretending to swoon, she suggested that perhaps her condition was being made worse by the washboard-stiff stomacher. As she had no plans for going abroad this day, did not Kat think it wise to change into a simpler gown with no underpinnings? Kat had sniffed with minor disapproval, for she believed that a lady — and a princess in particular — should for modesty's sake be firmly encased and held upright by her rigid undergarments. But the woman's heart was altogether soft when it came to Elizabeth's health, and the girl's complaint had been authentically delivered.

Elizabeth had therefore been able, with hardly a struggle, to undress herself and don the young man's suit. It was not particularly fine, for when she rode out she did not wish to draw attention to herself, but hoped she would pass for a courier or page boy. She easily put on the hose, shirt, and doublet. But the breeches — two legs with a seam only at the back and tied round her waist — required her to carefully lace the front together with a codpiece. Elizabeth giggled at the absurdity of the contraption, then blushed at the thought of the male parts it was meant to cover.

Her hair presented the greatest problem, for when the mass of it was stowed under the boy's felt cap, her head appeared unnaturally large and lumpy. It would never do. She thought hard for a moment, then snatched up one of her own stockings and pulled it down over her head, tucking all the red curls underneath its edges. Now the cap fit her, but she looked bald beneath it. She tugged a few strands out from the stocking and placed them artfully round her hairline for a natural effect.

What stared out at her now from the mirror, however, startled and dismayed her. She was a perfect boy. Her tiny breasts, even unbound, would never give her sex away. Without her red-gold mane framing her pale face, she observed, she looked handsome enough, but not at all a beautiful woman. What would Thomas think? Would he be repulsed at the sight of her? Perhaps she should have disguised herself as a scullery maid or a laundress. What had possessed her to pose as a boy?

But it was too late for such thoughts. Thomas was waiting for her. And she — blessed Jesus, she was dying with anticipation to see his face again, to feel his arms round her, to breathe in the manly musk of him. But they would act with restraint, this they had in their letters promised one another. They had much to discuss, to plan. She would thrill him with news of the letter she had decided to write to the Privy Council, setting forth with bold dignity and Socratic logic her reasons for believing the match with Thomas Seymour a good one, as well as her passionate desire to become the High Admiral's wife.

It was time to leave. This was the most dangerous part of Elizabeth's escape from Crosby House — to get from her upstairs bedchamber, unseen and unrecognized, into the lower level of the house and then to steal away to the stables.

Elizabeth stood in place for perhaps the longest moment of her life. Nothing had prepared her for this. She was a princess of England, just fifteen years old, dressed as a boy and about to ride out into the night alone for an assignation with her love. Was she mad? she asked herself. Before she could draw another breath, the silent answer rolled over her like a wave. Yes, I am mad! Mad in love with Thomas Seymour!

To fortify herself she brought to mind again the story she'd heard about her aunt, Henry's youngest sister, the Princess Mary. Mary had fallen into passionate love with the King's dearest friend, Charles Brandon. But before they could wed, Henry promised Mary's hand in marriage to his craftiest enemy, the ancient and decrepit King Louis of France. The marriage was no more than a peace treaty signed in a virgin's blood, but that was the way of the great dynasties and the lot of royal princesses. Mary was sent from England — and her beloved Brandon — to be crowned queen of France. Ninety-two days later she found herself a widow. Henry thereupon sent his most trusted friend across the Channel to fetch his sister home. When Charles Brandon arrived in France, Mary acted with boldness so shocking that Brandon had no choice but to bend to her will, blown like a sapling in a gale. She had carried on for two weeks, alternating hysterical tears with cold-blooded remonstrances, proclaiming to him unequivocally that she meant to marry him, and marry him before they left France. She had, she insisted, struck a bargain with her brother before her departure from England, that when the old king of France died she would be free to marry for love. That King Henry had not confirmed his approval since that time meant nothing. He had promised, and she meant to hold him to that promise. If Charles Brandon did not marry her, she would kill herself. It was as simple as that.

Reckless? wondered Elizabeth. Dangerous? Outrageous behavior for a princess of England? Yes, all of these things! But what had been the outcome of such audacity and willfulness? Mary and Brandon had married in France. Henry had at first been livid with rage, thundering about betrayal and treason. But the lovers had held firm in their resolve, and in less than a year the King had forgiven them both and called them home. As Henry loved his sister and his friend Brandon, Elizabeth reasoned, King Edward similarly loved *his* sister and his uncle Thomas Seymour. If their own resolve could hold as faithfully as Mary and Charles Brandon's, Edward would surely come round. The Council, and even the Protector, would finally be compelled to relent in the light of the pair's sincere devotion and firm commitment.

Such a thought strengthened Elizabeth. She felt her back grow a little straighter, her chin harder. She was ready.

A sudden knock at the bedchamber door caused her heart to leap to her throat. Someone was jiggling the latch.

"Elizabeth! Are you in there? Why is the door locked?" It was Blanche Parry, sounding distinctly irritated.

"I'm lying down," called Elizabeth, collecting herself. "I've a headache, Blanche. I read too long by candlelight again."

"Silly child. Let me in and I'll fix you a poultice."

"Oh, Blanche," Elizabeth whined. "I'm too sore and weary to raise myself from the bed. I'll be all right, I promise you. I just need to rest undisturbed for a while."

"Let me at least bring you some broth."

"No please, I was almost asleep when you knocked. Soon as I wake, I promise I'll knock on your door and then you can put me to bed properly."

"Are you sure?" the waiting lady called in.

"Quite sure. Thank you, Blanche." Then she added, calling in a pathetic voice through the heavy wooden door, "Blanche, would you go to the kitchen and ask them to fix me a marchpane sweet for later?" The Parrys' bedchamber door was dangerously close to her own and she wanted the woman out of the way when she made her escape.

"Of course, dear. Rest well."

It was only after Elizabeth heard Blanche Parry's footsteps fading away down the corridor and main stairway that she exhaled with relief. Now was the time to hasten out, with Blanche occupied in the kitchen.

Elizabeth unlocked the door, peered in both directions, and slipped out. Down the servants' stairs she tiptoed to the laundry, which at this late hour was empty except for a sole laundress wearily folding and sorting linen by candlelight. The woman looked up briefly from her work to see a young man hurry by. She did not recognize him, but then, countless messengers and couriers regularly came and went from a royal household, so she thought nothing of it.

Out in the night air Elizabeth breathed more easily, but in the stable, she knew, she faced a greater hurdle. Every day she saw and spoke to the stable hands. All of them knew the princess Elizabeth. Now, she must pass herself off as a common boy and, without explanation of this unknown "courier's" presence at Crosby House, secure from the stablemen a mount on which to ride off to her rendezvous.

She'd planned for this by writing for the "courier" a note in her own hand, explaining simply that the boy should be given a horse. There was only one stable hand who could read, Geoff, and it was he that Elizabeth sought in the stables, now blessedly awash in shadows, lit only by a few lamps.

But Geoff was nowhere to be seen. Two of the other regular stable hands, Peter and Ned, were crouched together throwing dice against the rough wood wall, and hardly looked up when she entered. Realizing she would be forced to speak, Elizabeth fought panic, then cleared her throat and said in a tone she hoped sounded boyish, "Where is Geoff?"

"Gone for his supper," called Ned offhandedly as he threw the dice again, whooping with glee at the result.

"I've a note for him from the Princess," she mumbled at the men. "Need a horse."

"I'll 'ave a look this note," said Ned, rising and approaching Elizabeth.

Peter snorted. "And do what with it, ye little turd? Ye canna read."

"Shut yer face," replied Ned, snatching the note from Elizabeth's hand. He held it up to a lantern and squinted at the writing in the flickering light. "What's it say?" he finally demanded from the courier.

"Need a horse," muttered Elizabeth, her panic rising as the time in these men's company lengthened past the short, safe interlude she had imagined.

"And where's the one you rode in on, then?" Ned asked suspiciously.

"Well, just as I was —" Elizabeth suddenly coughed loudly in the stable hand's direction and pretended to be unable to stop. Ned backed away.

"Uugh," he cried disgustedly. "Back off, lad!"

"The note," Elizabeth continued through her hacking, "is in the Princess's own hand. See here —" She cleared her throat and pointed with her gloved finger at her own elegant signature, then turned and spat on the ground for good measure. She was, she realized perversely, beginning to enjoy herself. By the time Elizabeth turned back, Ned had already begun saddling a horse.

Peter was eyeing this strange messenger from the shadows, and Elizabeth pretended to be examining the horses in their stalls to keep their eyes from meeting.

A sudden hand on her shoulder caused her to jump.

"Easy, lad," said Ned. She half turned to face the stable hand, and he gave Elizabeth the reins to her mount.

"Take care of that chest, young fella," offered Ned as Elizabeth took the saddle, "or ye'll be a corpse before the week is out." With a final slap to the horse's rump the stable hand sent Elizabeth on her way. As she headed into the London streets the Princess thought she had never in her life been so relieved or so grateful for a misty, moonless night.

"Damn him!" shouted Thomas Seymour, pacing his bedchamber floor. "Damn him to Hell and may fire consume him eternally!" He swept the tray with the pitcher and Venetian glass goblets from his table and they crashed to the floor, the glass shattering and the red wine spraying about his room in a wild arc. He had not recovered from Sherrington's foul betrayal, indeed had grown more and more furious with every passing hour.

There came a tentative knock at the door.

"What is it!" he thundered. His servant, John Martin, asked through the door if all was well. "Bring me more wine and more glasses," Seymour growled. He had already drunk two pitcherfuls and was roaring drunk, his mind reeling. It was difficult to focus his thoughts, which had been all but overwhelmed by emotion.

This much he knew. The pirate Thompson's bounty had been disappointingly meager. And he should never have trusted Sherrington. Without the gold he could not pay for his shipment of powder. Without powder he had no rebellion. All of Catherine's monies were tied up in properties and probate. He would not see much of his inheritance for several months more. And the revolt must be now. Now! But that was impossible. Men and arms were at the ready, and he had no powder. He'd kill the blighted bastard Sherrington with his own two hands!

Suddenly, like the sun peeking out from behind a raft of storm clouds, Thomas beheld a calming light. He slumped heavily in his chair to contemplate it, allow himself to be soothed by it.

Elizabeth. She was on her way to him even now. If he could not have his rebellion, he would simply marry Elizabeth. True, there were obstacles. Though Kat Ashley and the Parrys were his allies, the Council was for the most part opposed to the match, and there was no time to win them over. Perhaps they would *never* change their minds about him — certainly for as long as that brother of his and his filthy cunt of a sister-in-law whispered behind his back.

But in no time at all Elizabeth would be here with him in his room. Elizabeth the Fair. She would, he realized, be expecting a gentleman this night, a perfectly mannered husband-to-be. But she wanted him, he knew that as well. Remembered her utter compliance to his will in the boathouse. He would lift her skirts and she would swoon in his arms. If she resisted, he thought suddenly, he would simply ravish her. Deflower her. Force their marriage on the Council, for a princess lacking her maidenhead was altogether useless to them.

The image of Elizabeth rose before his eyes, and suddenly the thought of her slender, powdery whiteness struggling under him made him hard, caused a pulse to thump in his throat. *Young royal flesh and the crown of England on his head . . .*

Another knock snatched him from his reverie, and he threw the door open. John Martin stood there with a new pitcher and goblets. Thomas turned away and gazed out at the foggy night as the man followed him inside.

"There is a messenger here from the princess Elizabeth," the manservant muttered, eyes downcast.

"Why did you not say so, man?" Seymour hissed. He wondered with irritation why she had sent a courier. Could she not come herself? Aloud he said, "Send him up."

"I am here already, my lord."

Still staring out the window, Thomas heard the messenger's words through the haze of drink. "Leave us," he told his servant. "I do not wish to be disturbed."

"Yes, my lord." John Martin backed out the door and closed it behind him.

"How does your lady this evening?" Thomas asked icily, assuming that his plans were already in tatters.

"Very well, my lord," he heard the messenger say.

Thomas found himself even angrier than before, furious that Elizabeth had sent a youngster on so important an errand — a boy whose voice had not yet broken.

"She sends you her most passionate love and undying devotion," continued the courier.

Seymour, confused by the intimacy of the spoken message, turned and saw the red-gold halo of curls, just now loosed from the felt cap, fall down around Elizabeth's shoulders.

"Princess!"

"My lord."

With the shock of so amazing and magnificent a sight, Thomas Seymour found himself suddenly and altogether sober. The look on Elizabeth's face was pure joy at the sight of her beloved, and pride for achieving such an astonishing masquerade.

"My lord, are you ill?" she inquired with sincere concern, for Thomas had never moved a muscle since his first sight of her, and he had indeed gone pale. He was silently working to quell a faltering of resolve in his planned rape of the Princess, who had by now taken a first tentative step in his direction.

"Not ill, no, Elizabeth. Not ill."

"Are you not pleased to see me, my lord?" she said, and moved even closer.

"More delighted than you could ever know," he said, emboldened by the nearness of her nubile body and the soft fragrance of her hair.

"I arrived here almost two hours ago but was afraid to come in," she said. "So I waited till I could gather my courage. I know it was silly —"

They stood inches apart now, she looking up into his eyes with great and earnest affection.

He was a lion waiting for the precise moment for the strike and kill.

"I have news that will please you, Thomas," she said, using his name almost shyly, for it was the first time she had done so in his presence.

"News?" Piqued with interest, Seymour momentarily retracted his claws.

Elizabeth was visibly discomfited by the man who now stood before her, her future husband whose many letters had warmed and excited her with their admiration and protestations of undying adoration. He had become strange and cold and reeked of wine. Still she went on.

"I am prepared to write to the Council on our behalf," she said with resolve. "And to the King. Edward loves you —"

"He hates me!" Seymour roared, startling her with the violence of his reaction. He turned away so he would not have to see her bruised expression.

"He does not hate you, Thomas," she cried, confused by his strange behavior.

"And you believe," he said scathingly, "that a letter from a fifteen-year-old *girl* will persuade a majority of the Privy Council to sanction our marriage?"

"I cannot be sure, but I —"

"You cannot be sure? You cannot be *sure!* What good is it, then?"

"Thomas —"

"They will never let us marry, Elizabeth. If you think they will, then you are a fool!"

She stood paralyzed, seared by the blast of his fury.

"There is no other way," he muttered, beginning to pace again like a great caged cat. "No other way . . ."

"But there is, love, there is," said Elizabeth. "I have been thinking long and hard on this. Do you know the story of my father's sister, Princess Mary, and Charles Brandon?"

Before Elizabeth could utter another word Seymour had turned and leapt at her, pulling her into a deathlike grip, covering her mouth with a desperate, crushing kiss. Though terrified, she at first succumbed, remembering their embrace in the boathouse and her many carnal dreams of him. But this was not the man she knew, nor the way it was meant to be. They'd agreed that the tryst, though secret, was to be *chaste and decorous.* But his hands were all over her now, pulling at the fabric of her doublet, groping between her legs.

"Stop, please stop!" With all her strength she pushed Seymour away from her. The look on his face was a mask of lust so violent that Elizabeth, instincts screaming, wrenched from his arms and fled for the door.

He seized her as her hand found the latch and snatched her off her feet. She struggled as he carried her across the room, but it was useless. He flung her down across his bed and she lay staring up at him horror-struck but altogether dry-eyed.

"No, my lord," she pleaded. "Think what you are doing."

"I *have* thought, Princess. And thought and thought. . . ."

His eyes were terrible, mad.

"Comply and make it easier on yourself," he commanded her, deftly unlacing his codpiece. Then he lowered himself, straddling her, and began to unlace her breeches, muttering curses at her difficult disguise.

She continued to gaze at him, but he did not notice, engaged as he was in his task. The enormity of this man's betrayal, and the horror of her predicament and fate, descended fully upon the Princess. She might have been smothered, incapacitated by it, but for the great upwelling of rage that suddenly took hold of her — anger not for Thomas Seymour's heinous actions but for her own fatal stupidity.

She slapped him a stinging blow across his face and began to struggle violently. He stopped, startled by her defense, then renewed his efforts to undress her, seeming untroubled by her squirming. The hail of fisted blows to his face and arms, indeed, enflamed him all the more.

Her breeches undone, he ripped them down off her narrow hips and pried open her legs with his knee.

"No, please, Thomas, please . . ." She was crying now, unhinged with loathing and fear.

"Come, Elizabeth," said Thomas Seymour, staring down at her with the eyes of a snake, "give your sweet husband a kiss." He leaned down, placing his lips ever so gently on hers.

She bit him hard.

He screamed in pain, pulling away, then slapped her. A trickle of blood dripped from his torn lip onto her doublet.

"You will pay for this, pay dearly," whispered Elizabeth.

"Oh, Princess, 'twill be well worth the price." As he lowered his body to hers, his mouth curled into a leering smile. In the very next moment the smile froze on his face. Someone was pounding on his door.

"Go away!" he shouted.

"My lord, my lord, open the door!"

"Go away, I tell you!"

The frantic banging continued.

"The Council Guard has searched William Sherrington's home!"

John Martin called through the door. "They've discovered the armory at Holt Castle!"

As if touched by a hot poker, Seymour leapt from the bed, a wild, animal look of terror in his eyes. Pulling his breeches together, he shouted through the door, "Are they coming here?"

"I do not know, my lord, but they may already be on their way!"

Thomas flung open the door, having altogether forgotten his victim cowering on the bed.

"Have my horse saddled immediately," he ordered the panicked servant.

"Already done, my lord."

Thomas was breathing hard, rubbing his forehead with his fingers, trying desperately to pull his thoughts together. What was he to do? *What was he to do!*

In this moment a slender figure dashed past the men and out the bedchamber door. Thomas Seymour made no move to stop Elizabeth. Indeed, he hardly realized that she had gone. His world, his schemes, the vision of the crown of England on his head, were crumbling, before his eyes, to dust.

Only one hope finally remained. He pushed past his servant and down the stairs of Seymour House. His horse was saddled and ready.

He rode for Hampton Court.

Never in all his thirty-six years had Thomas Seymour felt so unsettling a sensation. As he rode through chilly London in the dead of night, it seemed as if he were incapable of gathering his wits about him, unable to formulate a cohesive plan of action. His previous schemes, so brilliantly conceived, had now collapsed, each and every one. Before his eyes the darkened streets faded and he beheld a vision. *A rotting corpse on the ground, wolves tearing at it, carrying away pieces, and ravens plucking out eyes, pulling at the raw stringy sinews.* This, then, was all that was left of his master plan, and desperation was his new and unwelcome companion.

Before departing Seymour House, Thomas had directed his servants to alert his most trusted followers to meet him at the palace. Now he wondered bitterly if any of them would appear. News traveled fast in London, and they might be aware of the search and seizures at Sherrington's house and Holt Castle, might realize the nature of Seymour's summons — a final hopeless attempt to wrest control of what was now uncontrollable.

He argued silently with himself as he rode, succumbing one moment to despair, enflamed by arrogant confidence the next. He had not struggled and connived for all these months and years to be thwarted at the last moment by the Fates. No! His destiny was the English throne — if not to sit upon it, then to stand close beside. He would simply not be outdone by his brother, outsmarted by his enemies. And who *were* his enemies? How had his plans been uncovered? Who amongst the high nobles wished him the most harm? When he found out, thought Thomas furiously, he would take revenge on the man and his entire family. They would, indeed, know his wrath.

Stealth being essential this night, Seymour dismounted a hundred yards from the darkest and least heavily guarded entrance to Hampton Court. Several of his people lived within the environs of the palace and they, still unaware of the Admiral's approach, must be roused once he'd gone inside.

"My lord," came a harsh whisper from the shadows.

Seymour could see nothing in the darkness and fog. He stopped still and placed his hand on his sword in the event that the whisperer was not a friend.

"I'm here at your command, Admiral."

"Who is it?" Seymour whispered into the dark.

"Charles Belmont," the man replied.

Thomas followed the voice till he stood with Belmont, both of them shrouded in blackness. "Have Dorset or Carrington come?" he demanded.

"No one that I've seen. But Longly and Pierson should be easily rounded up inside."

The man's confidence fortified Seymour. Perhaps none of them had, in fact, heard of this evening's misfortunes. Perhaps they still believed that all was well with the rebellion.

"Come, let's begin," said Thomas commandingly as he moved toward the East Gate.

"Should we not wait for the others?" asked Belmont. "And why have we met here and not at Holt Castle to arm ourselves before assembling the troops?"

Good, thought Seymour. Belmont knows nothing. "Plans have changed," he muttered, "and if Lords Dorset and Carrington could not see fit to make haste, as you have, then they shall be left behind." He said no more, for he did not wish anyone to know what exactly he had in mind. It was clearly dangerous, and this was no time for disagreement or a lessening of confidence in his leadership.

Assuming his most commanding attitude, Seymour approached the East Gate with Belmont at his side, nodding to the two guards armed with halberds. Seymour knew one of them well. The man snapped to attention, returning the Admiral's good-natured smile as the noblemen entered the palace.

Once inside, the men's movements assumed an altogether secretive demeanor. The palace halls were quiet and deserted, the hour being late, and all but the guards and several whispering stewards were asleep in their beds. Thomas could not be sure if his brother was aware of the raids at Sherrington's house and Holt Castle, but a careful peek at the Privy Council chamber assured him that no all-night session was being held by his enemies there.

First he and Belmont must find the balance of their coconspirators in the enormous palace without alerting anyone who might be suspicious of their presence, their movements, or their motives. It would be best, explained the Admiral, if Belmont found the others and convened them in a prearranged location to wait for Thomas's return. Belmont agreed and stole off down the corridor that flickered eerily with torchlight.

Thomas moved swiftly now through the square palace to the southwest staircase. He climbed to the second floor, nodding offhandedly to the guards at the entrance to his brother and sister-in-law's apartments — the queen's chambers. Those were the rooms, he thought bitterly, that should rightly have been granted to him and Catherine. But all would be different after tonight.

Presently he reached an alcove where hung a long tapestry, which he pulled aside to reveal a little-known door. It was not guarded but it was tightly locked, for it was the entrance to a warren of secret rooms and winding passageways leading to the King's apartments.

Smiling to himself, Seymour withdrew from his doublet the set of keys he'd had Highsmith cut for him. Though it had never occurred to Thomas that the keys would have been needed for the precise purpose to which they'd be put this night, he had known that such a tool would be invaluable to his plans.

Confidence was surging back into his blood like a tonic. What had seemed, an hour before, a harebrained scheme — the kidnapping of the boy king — was now entirely plausible as the unguarded doors opened one after the other, and the object of his pursuit was nearly in his grasp. He imagined the surprised look on little Edward's face as Thomas roused him gently, the child rubbing sleep from his eyes, wondering why his uncle had come. He'd be quickly mollified by Seymour's smooth answer — that a dangerous rebellion was even now raging all round the palace, that the duke had been slaughtered by the rebels, and that the only safety Edward would know was in the arms of his uncle Thomas. Edward, terrified, would go willingly with Seymour, allow himself to be spirited out of the palace before he noticed that there *was* no armed revolt in progress within the palace walls.

But a shock awaited Thomas when he opened the final door leading to the back entrance of the King's bedchamber. There he saw his nephew's favorite dog, a normally sweet-faced brown-and-white hound, on its feet and, though still silent, entirely alert and watching the intruder with its hackles raised.

Thomas froze. Why was the dog not inside the bedchamber with the King as he always was? How was Thomas to get past the beast without its setting up a racket? He knew the dog, of course. Indeed, as all animals did, it liked Thomas. But here, late at night, the hound seemed confused by the presence of this stranger from the shadows. And whilst it had thus far refrained from barking — no doubt owing to Seymour's familiar scent — it was surely aroused and unpredictable.

Thomas went down on one knee and remained still as he clicked with his tongue, a signal for the hound to come to him. With only the briefest hesitation it did, and within moments the animal was licking Seymour's fingers and allowing itself to be patted and stroked by the familiar hand.

Then, still rattled by the unexpected complication, Thomas set about finding the correct key to the King's secret bedchamber door. His hands shook as he fingered the keys, and his fumbling irritated him. It was a sign of weakness to be frightened into tremors. He was stronger than this, Thomas told himself, and willed his hands to stop their shaking. He had previously marked the all-important key with a ring of red paint, and now, with the greatest care, he slipped it into the lock. He could hear the iron mechanism click and tumble gently. Once the door was unlocked, he sighed audibly with relief and blessed Highsmith for his good work. The dog, its head cocked slightly to one side, watched Thomas as he pushed against the door to open it.

It did not budge.

What was happening? Why was the unlocked door not opening? It was, it dawned on him then, bolted shut. Bolted on the inside! The dog had been left outside and the door bolted from within, clearly because the King feared for himself. Trusted no one.

An eleven-year-old boy had outsmarted them all!

Thomas flared with rage. He would not be thwarted by a child. He threw the key ring down and, without thought to consequences, began to kick the door in with his heavily booted foot. Instantly the hound began barking loudly. A commotion could be heard within the bedchamber, the voices of Edward and his keepers — amongst them Fowler, who Thomas assumed could be counted on to assist him in the kidnapping.

Suddenly the frantically barking dog lunged at Seymour and sank its teeth into the flesh on the back of his thigh. Thomas yelled in pain and whirled to face the beast, glaring at it in fury. He saw not a poor snarling hound protecting its master, but every villain that had conspired to undermine his glorious future.

He loosed the pistol from his waistband, aimed with precision, and fired once. The dog was propelled backwards by the force of the shot, its blood splattering the antechamber wall.

There was a child's cry of outrage from within — it was clear the intruder had shot his dog — and the sound of booted feet coming

186

from inside the bedchamber, no doubt Edward's front-door guards. Coming Seymour's way. With a curse and a final splintering kick at the secret door, Thomas fled back through the warren of rooms, never bothering to close or lock their many doors behind him.

Racing through the final door into the main corridor, he plowed directly into a patrol of palace guards. Standing white-faced and cringing behind the patrol was Belmont, and with him Longly and Pierson, the only conspirators he'd been able to rouse for the task.

Seymour wrenched himself free of the soldiers' arms and pulled himself up to his full towering height.

"Take me to my brother," he demanded of them icily.

"Our orders are to take you directly to the Tower," answered the head guard firmly but courteously.

"God blast your filthy orders, I will see my brother!"

"It will go better for you, Admiral, if you do not struggle. We prefer not to restrain you."

"I'll have your head for this," he snarled, then glanced at his cohorts and saw a look of such naked terror in their eyes that he was instantly silenced, himself seized by their unspeakable fears.

The four men were marched to the palace quay and placed aboard a rough barge — an ignominious conveyance for the High Admiral of the King's Navy — and on the ebb tide floated downriver through the Traitor's Gate of the Tower of London.

Edward, poor lost and friendless child, saw no sleep that night, just wailed and mourned the loss of his favorite hound. He cried too, and prayed fervently that even one nobleman lived in all of England who truly wished him well and might guide him with honesty and compassion into his majority.

King Edward the Sixth, heir to Great King Henry, eleven years and three months old, prayed in vain.

Another of Henry's children that night saw the death of hope and of love everlasting. As she rode through the bitter January night, Elizabeth's tears mingled with the thick London fog on cheeks that still burned with fresh humiliation and rage. Her mind had been no clearer than Thomas Seymour's when she'd fled his house moments before him. She could ill discern the source of her anger, for she was as furious with herself as she was with the faithless, betraying beast she had once called her beloved.

Thomas had attempted and almost succeeded in ravishing her — a princess of the blood — and she had, in a state of blind stupidity, walked naively into his trap. Only the Fates had saved her. What lucky star, Elizabeth wondered, had protected her tonight? She must, when she had recovered from the tragic affair — if that were even possible — consult an astrologer on this evening's portent.

Thomas, Thomas! she cried silently. She had been so sure he loved her. From the first moment, the first touch . . . Had this always been his plan? The idea further chilled her already icy body, the sweat of fear wetting her boy's disguise from within, the cold night air from without.

At least her journey home through the streets, thickly black except for the occasional point of lantern light hanging at the door of a late-night tavern, had thus far been easy. But that too was about to change.

"Hey, boy!" came a drunken voice from the cluster of ruffians loitering outside the Red Rooster Inn as she passed it. A beefy hand clamped around Elizabeth's ankle. Shocked by the suddenness, she let out a high-pitched shriek.

"'Tis no bloody boy!" cried another drunk. "Look at 'er 'air!"

Though the grabbing hand had not stopped her forward motion, and she spurred her horse faster, she could tell several of the men were chasing after her — and, to her horror, she heard the sound of at least one horse's hoofbeats echoing on the cobbled streets behind.

Elizabeth stifled panic. She must be close to home by now. Both Crosby House and Seymour House were located on the Strand, on the banks of the Thames. She had avoided using the river as a conveyance, for it was so public. Now, as she raced down the road to evade her drunken pursuer — perhaps another rapist — she mouthed foul oaths at herself for having gone into the strange and fabulously dangerous streets alone.

Were those the lights of Crosby House ahead? Elizabeth was suddenly aware that the clattering hoofbeats she heard were entirely those of her own horse. The ruffians had given up the chase. She slowed her mount to a trot and began to suck in great gulps of the dank river air to calm herself. It was indeed Crosby she now approached. She would have to present a collected appearance and demeanor to her retainers, who would, by now, be aware of not only her disappearance but her deceit. Kat Ashley would be livid to have been sent on a fool's errand.

Elizabeth knew that she could not conceal this night's doings — for she would never have risked her loved ones' wrath for less — but she had determined that she must never allow them to know of Thomas's appalling conduct toward her. She would simply pretend she had gone cold to the idea of the marriage to him, and none of their convincing or pleading would begin to change her mind.

She cared not at all that the stable hands knew her true identity now. She could see by their faces that Peter and Ned had already been roundly chastised for failing to notice that the "messenger" they had given a horse to had been the princess Elizabeth. As they helped her down from her mount, she muttered embarrassed apologies, wondering all the while how she could have thought so little of the consequences of her rash act.

The Ashleys and the Parrys were waiting grim-faced and fully dressed in her bedchamber when Elizabeth, disheveled and perspiring, opened the door. At least they had spared her the humiliation of a more public reprimand. No doubt the entire household had been sent into a frenzy when her disappearance had been noticed. Now it occurred to her how transparent her destination was, and she wondered if they had sent someone to Seymour House to fetch her home.

The four retainers stood silent, waiting for Elizabeth to speak. Only in that moment did she remember that a condition of urgency so terrible to Thomas Seymour had occurred that it had halted his ravishment of her, even allowed her to escape. If it had been so important, thought Elizabeth before she spoke the first word to her servants, perhaps it had some significance beyond this evening's debacle.

"Have you nothing to say for yourself?" asked Kat with more ice in her voice than Elizabeth had ever in her life heard.

"I have nothing but apologies," said Elizabeth, willing herself to be calm.

"No explanations?" said Thomas Parry.

"I think . . ." Elizabeth began, "that I have been temporarily mad." It was not enough. They stared at her, demanding more. "I went to see my lord Seymour . . . in his home."

"In his home," repeated Kat. "Dressed as a boy."

"I did not wish to have my movements known."

"We have guessed that, Princess," said Parry in a wry tone.

"What was the purpose of this assignation?" said Kat in the voice of an inquisitor.

"To discuss our marriage." Elizabeth's simple statement had the sound of a question.

"Your marriage?" said Kat. "Whilst we here have been advocating this match, you have been studiously naysaying it." Her voice had risen to a shrill pitch. "What perverse notion has you rejecting Thomas Seymour's suit on the one hand, and on the other sneaking off like a common slut to consummate it!"

"Kat!" John Ashley's hand went to his wife's arm to calm her.

"The visit was meant not to consummate our lust for one another," said Elizabeth, relieved to be speaking the truth before she began weaving her fabric of lies and omissions. "He was a gentleman —"

John Ashley snorted audibly. He was the one amongst them who had never hidden his distaste for the Admiral.

"And we were discussing the methods by which we might secure the Council's approval of our marriage." Elizabeth hesitated. What reason could she give to justify the change in feelings toward Thomas Seymour of which she must convince this trio?

"Why are you so disheveled?" asked Blanche Parry mildly. "Did he lay a hand on you?"

"He did not," Elizabeth insisted. "But . . . as he spoke to me," she went on slowly, conceiving her story as she went along, "I began to see him in a different light. I remembered that he had betrayed his beloved wife, and I suddenly wondered if he would not do the same to me after we were married."

Kat turned suddenly away, mortified, knowing that she had supported Thomas Seymour's outrageous pursuit of Elizabeth whilst he was a married man, and had thereby assisted in heaping pain upon the kindly Catherine Parr.

Elizabeth went on. "Thomas began to protest that the same would never happen with us, but the more he protested, the less I believed him." She was warming to her story now, for in her heart Elizabeth knew that had she been possessed of a clearer head, this imaginary conversation between herself and Thomas might well have taken place. "I understood that I had somehow become bewitched by him, in the same way that Catherine had been." She looked directly at her nurse. "And Kat . . . and even you, Parry."

Her servants stood stock-still. This fifteen-year-old girl was speaking a truth that none of them could gainsay.

"Then," Elizabeth went on, "we were interrupted by Lord Seymour's servant, who came shouting into his rooms —"

"You were in his bedchamber!" cried Kat, recovered from her chastising.

"— that someone named Sherrington's house had been searched," she went on, ignoring her waiting lady, "and that the 'armory' at Holt Castle had been discovered. Lord Seymour, enchanted though he was by my presence, grew alarmed and, without even a proper farewell to me, bolted from the room. I was flabbergasted, confused. Then hurt, then angry," Elizabeth embroidered. "Finally I realized that Thomas had only confirmed my worries about his character. I left immediately" — she paused for effect — "and on the way home I was accosted and chased by some drunken men."

"Oh, my sweet Elizabeth!" cried Kat, coming to put her arms around the Princess. "You're not hurt?"

"I escaped them unharmed, Kat," she said calmly, "but that is why I look so disheveled and probably smell like a goat."

Kat and Blanche exploded with relieved laughter, but John Ashley and Thomas Parry, Elizabeth could see, were exchanging worried looks.

"Was nothing more said of Sherrington's house or Holt Castle?" inquired John Ashley.

"No. Of what significance are they?" asked Elizabeth.

There was a pause as her servants gathered their thoughts.

"If I'm not mistaken, a man named Sherrington is chief counter at the Royal Mint," said Parry, though he could not seem to make more of the fact. "And Holt Castle," he went on, "I cannot say."

"'Twas an 'armory' found at Holt Castle, Parry," interjected John Ashley accusingly. "Have you been paying no attention to the gossip being whispered of your hero Seymour? That he's been planning a revolt?"

"A revolt!" cried Elizabeth.

"He's spoken of nothing like that to me," insisted Thomas Parry indignantly. "We spoke only of Elizabeth's holdings and properties —"

"We hear what we wish to hear," muttered John Ashley, disgustedly, "see what we wish to see."

Parry took a threatening step toward John Ashley.

"Gentlemen!" shouted Kat. "It will do us no good to fight amongst ourselves."

"You see," said Elizabeth pointedly, "the Admiral's influence works its evil on all of us, even without his presence."

Everyone was silent as they contemplated the Princess's words and saw the truth in them.

"I fear we are all in great danger," said John Ashley finally and with quiet certitude.

No one contradicted him. Blanche Parry's lips began to quiver.

"You two," Kat ordered the husbands, "leave us now. We must get the Princess out of these wet things and to bed."

"Bed! How shall I sleep, knowing what I've done?" cried Elizabeth. "We must talk to one another, all night if need be, and make sense of what is happening!"

The sudden sound of heavy pounding on the riverside door silenced the members of Elizabeth's household and froze the very blood in their veins.

"Guard of the Privy Council! Open up!"

Though the shout was muffled, each of them understood both the words and their terrible implication.

"Get her into bed. Hurry," whispered Parry to Kat Ashley and his wife. "We'll see to the guard."

"No," cried Kat. "First to your rooms. Put on your nightclothes and slippers. 'Tis the middle of the night and we, of course, know nothing of Thomas Seymour's shameful doings."

"Right," said John, moving quickly with Parry into the upstairs corridor. "And you into your nightgowns, ladies," he reminded them.

"John, Parry," cried Elizabeth after them. They turned back at her words. "I'm sorry. So very sorry."

They nodded. Then they disappeared. Elizabeth gave Kat and Blanche a desperate look.

"No more time for sorries now, Elizabeth," said Kat in a businesslike tone. "Let us get you out of these clothes."

The five of them, all in gowns and slippers, feigning the grogginess of having been roused from a dead sleep, came slowly down the great stairs. They were whispering urgently amongst themselves, for only moments remained before they would be face to face with the Council Guard, and from then on anything they might say would surely be used against them.

Kat said, "All here promise to reveal nothing of what transpired 'tween the Princess and Lord Seymour. Agreed?"

The quartet murmured, "Agreed," then Thomas Parry added with heartfelt passion, "I would rather be pulled limb from limb by four horses than divulge a word that would hurt our Elizabeth."

This caused tears to spring to the girl's eyes. But Kat saw and, stopping to grasp Elizabeth's shoulders, shook them once.

"No tears, Elizabeth. Shock. Outrage, perhaps. But *no tears.* We have done nothing wrong."

"All right," said Elizabeth, wiping the moisture from her cheeks and eyes. "If only we had more time to —"

"Well, we haven't," hissed Kat, "so we will do our best. You in the lead," Kat ordered Elizabeth. "'Tis your household and we are but your servants."

They came to the bottom of the stair and arranged themselves with the Princess in the fore, followed closely by the two couples. In the foyer half a dozen armed soldiers and their captain stood waiting at attention. The leader stepped forward as the party of five approached.

"What is the meaning of this visit at so ungodly an hour, Captain?" Elizabeth said sternly to what appeared to be the Guards' leader.

"Lord Thomas Seymour," he began, then gulped as though reluctant to continue, "has this night been arrested for conspiring against the King of England, and divers other treasonous crimes against the State. All accomplices and parties with whom Lord Seymour is known to have collaborated —"

"Accomplices?" cried Elizabeth.

"We collaborated with no one," said John Ashley decisively as he stepped forward, shielding Elizabeth's body with his own. "We protest this intrusion and demand you leave here at once."

"I have my orders, sir," said the captain of the Guard, his confidence bolstered by those orders.

"From whom!" demanded Kat Ashley.

"From members of the Privy Council and the Protector himself," answered the captain. At a tiny movement of his head his men broke into two groups of three.

"Katherine Champernoun Ashley and Thomas Parry, identify yourselves."

"No, no!" cried Elizabeth. She flew into Kat's arms.

The woman's body was rigid with fear but her voice was unnaturally calm. "No tears," she said quietly. Into Elizabeth's ear she whispered, though the words were strong as a battle cry, "We have done nothing wrong." Then she pushed Elizabeth to arm's length and stepped forward to stand with Parry who, grim-faced, was avoiding Blanche's eye. Three of the soldiers surrounded the pair.

"Where are they being taken?" Elizabeth demanded of the captain.

"Tower of London," he answered.

"The *Tower!* Arrested and taken to the Tower?"

"Not arrested, Princess. Detained for questioning is all."

Suddenly the remaining three soldiers arranged themselves around Elizabeth and she felt her heart leap to her throat.

"Where are you taking her!" shrieked Kat, unable to disguise her terror.

"Hatfield Hall," said the captain, visibly relieved to have answered thusly.

"Thank God," muttered John Ashley as he took his wife in his arms and embraced her fiercely. Thomas and Blanche Parry too were locked in a final embrace as the guards began to pull their prisoners away.

"I love you, Kat!" Elizabeth cried as the most important person in her world disappeared from her sight. "Take care, Parry!"

But they were gone.

There was only time for a wrap to be brought for Elizabeth and hasty preparations made for her things to be transported downriver to Hatfield before she too was hurried aboard a royal barge.

Elizabeth never took her eyes from the dock of Crosby House where Blanche Parry and John Ashley stood waving, steadfast and pretending a confidence they could not, in this unreasonable circumstance, be feeling. For in matters of treason against the Crown, they knew, innocence was as useless as wings on a wagon. Elizabeth's fate and the fates of her loved ones were, she realized, firmly within the hands of her enemies. What, she wondered, feeling herself succumb to black and utter hopelessness, was a fifteen-year-old girl, devoid of all friendly guidance or counsel, to do?

We have done nothing wrong, Elizabeth said to herself silently. Nothing wrong. Perhaps, she prayed, as the barge made its way downriver that winter's morning, if she repeated the phrase again and again, she would finally believe it was true.

Chapter Twenty

At least I am at Hatfield, thought Elizabeth as two soldiers escorted her down a long corridor. It was the slimmest of all consolations in her present miserable condition, but the house was one she knew well, having lived in it the better part of her infancy and childhood. She considered it her home.

Now, feeling somewhat ridiculous and more than a little indignant to be so closely guarded, she was shown into the writing room and found herself confronted by a man who could be none other than her inquisitor. She experienced a thrill of alarm when she recognized him, for Lord Robert Tyrwhitt was husband to Queen Catherine's stepdaughter, a woman who had doubtlessly watched the entire sordid affair between Elizabeth and Thomas Seymour unfold and destroy her beloved mistress.

This will not go well for me, said Elizabeth to herself as she stood before the man. His face was round, his nose and lips bulbous. He was short, and she, being tall for her age and sex, found herself eye to eye with him. She thought briefly that this equality would be to her advantage, then remembered Kat saying short men tended to harshness as a way to compensate for their deficiency in size.

"Princess," he said tonelessly, and executed the most minimal bow permissible without obvious insult. She noticed that he appeared sharp and well rested, eyes twinkling with fervor for the coming task. She, in contrast, was fighting weariness, having spent the previous night riding alone through London, avoiding rape and harassment, being taken into custody by soldiers, and beginning the confinement of house arrest. She had been given less than an hour upon her arrival at Hatfield Hall to dress and gather her wits about her before this, the first interrogation.

"My lord Tyrwhitt," she intoned in a modulated voice she hoped sounded haughty.

He fixed her with a cold stare. "As you are aware," he began, "Thomas Seymour has been arrested for conspiring to overthrow the Crown."

Elizabeth winced at these words, hardly believing that they could be true.

"We are in possession of intelligence that you and your closest personal servants, Katherine Ashley and Thomas Parry, conspired with the Admiral, without the consent of the Privy Council, to marry. Further, there is evidence that said armed rebellion, against Seymour's brother the Protector and the King of England, was planned with the express purpose of enabling the Admiral — having married you — to place himself as your king and consort on the throne of England."

"Not true!" cried Elizabeth, having immediately lost her composure.

"*Furthermore,*" Tyrwhitt powered on, ignoring the girl's distress — indeed, perhaps encouraged by it — "this night past, the Lord High Admiral was seized as he attempted the kidnapping of your brother."

"What?" Elizabeth went suddenly numb with shock. Her ears began ringing in her head. "Kidnap Edward?"

"These and other crimes against the State, Princess," he continued, "constitute *high treason*. It is my duty here today," Tyrwhitt said, his voice rising to a crescendo, "and in all of the days that shall follow, to learn the part that you and your servants played in this appalling conspiracy!"

Much to Tyrwhitt's pleasure, Elizabeth burst into tears. She covered her face with her hands and, with knees shaking, allowed him to help her onto a stool that had been placed in the center of the room. There he watched her with a sour expression as she slowly regained possession of her senses.

"It would be wise," he began again, "if, as we progress in our 'conversations,' you consider your honor and the peril that might ensue, for you are but your brother's subject, and together with your beloved retainers" — he paused for the effect this would and did have — "vulnerable to the fullest extent of prosecution that English law allows."

"Neither I nor my servants," Elizabeth began, sniffing back her tears, "conspired for my marriage to Thomas Seymour." She swallowed hard and continued in a quavering voice, "Nor did we have knowledge of his rebellion or his kidnapping of my brother the King."

"This, then, is your stance?" queried Tyrwhitt in a sarcastic tone.

"'Tis no 'stance,' my lord Tyrwhitt. 'Tis the whole truth of it."

"When I first spoke of Thomas Seymour's planned revolt, your face registered no shock at the statement whatsoever, as it clearly *did* when I mentioned the attempted abduction of King Edward. Why is that, Princess? Had you or your servants foreknowledge of this rebellion?"

"No!" she cried, feeling the ground fall away under her feet. This man was clever, and he was determined to have Elizabeth incriminate herself, and Kat and Parry, in treasonous plots that could see them all executed.

"I repeat," she said, using the only tactic she could conceive, "no one in my household had any knowledge of the plots you have described."

Tyrwhitt gazed at Elizabeth with a look of withering contempt. "I believed you a more intelligent person than such a simpleton's answer indicates."

Elizabeth reeled with the insult but was speechless, unable to summon the words of righteous indignation that would have rescued her from this humiliation.

"That will be all for today," Tyrwhitt announced dismissively. "We will begin again tomorrow morning."

"What news have you of Kat Ashley and Master Parry?" Elizabeth asked pleadingly.

"No news. They are in the Tower, as you already know, and if I am not mistaken, their interrogator is Lord Rich."

"Dear God," was all Elizabeth could manage at the sound of Richard Rich's name, for the Lord Chancellor was well known as the cruelest inquisitor and torturer in all of England.

"I suggest," continued Tyrwhitt, "that you consider your answers very carefully, for the consequences —"

"I know the consequences, my lord Tyrwhitt," said Elizabeth, rising to her feet.

"Yes, of course you do." His tone was condescending. "They are the same ones your mother suffered for her many indiscretions." He smiled almost pleasantly, taking great pleasure in the Princess's humbling. "Sleep well."

She had wished to have the last word in this meeting, if only to say, "Good day, my lord," but Elizabeth found that her throat was choked, as if a hand were gripping it tightly, and therefore was forced to turn in silence and be led away by two soldiers like a common criminal.

Grateful to be lodged in her old rooms, Elizabeth lay abed exhausted but unable to sleep. First and foremost she agonized over Kat, no doubt lying in a dark, filthy, and rat-infested dungeon. Of no royal blood, there was no reason that Kat should be treated with any but the harshest of measures. Elizabeth squirmed and cringed between her clean sheets, imagining the horrors her nurse might even now be enduring. But worse still was the fear that Kat's loyalty to her charge and her silence on all incriminating matters would lead to the woman's torture. *Kat tortured!* Elizabeth sat up in bed, unable to lie still with so ghastly an image before her. It was not unheard of for women to be placed on the rack, have their limbs torn from their sockets. . . . And poor Parry. A man, so better able to withstand indignity and torment, but he deserved such treatment no more than Kat did.

Elizabeth's only comfort — if it could be called that — was that the three of them were equally responsible for their current predicament. If it were simply her own infatuation and rash behavior with the Admiral that had landed them in so much trouble, she could never have lived with herself. But Kat had promoted Elizabeth's affair with Thomas, and Parry had as well. She wondered at their motives, if they had not somehow perceived some glory or riches in it for themselves. Perhaps Parry, she mused, but certainly not Kat. Kat had simply adored the Admiral, wished for Elizabeth a passion that she herself, in her marriage to staid and upright John Ashley, did not possess.

Kat and Elizabeth were kin. She must find a way to deliver her out of harm's way!

Tomorrow, thought Elizabeth, her own interrogation would

certainly prove more aggressive than today's. Robert Tyrwhitt was ruthlessly determined to trick her, confuse her, break her spirit. If he had his way, Elizabeth would seal Kat's and Parry's fate even more quickly.

Oh, how has it come to this! Elizabeth silently cried. She jumped down from her bed, moved to the window, and threw it open. Unfazed by the bitter night air, she gazed out at Hatfield's great wood, now shrouded in darkness. Such terrible calamity, and all derived from a single source. Like the Egyptian sun, thought Elizabeth suddenly, Thomas Seymour was, to those around him, a source of light and heat and worship — indeed, a source of *life*. All were drawn to his power, believed they could not survive without his love. And all would ultimately perish in his final blaze of glory.

But surely he had loved her, she insisted to herself. What she had felt in his arms for those few moments in the boathouse had certainly been genuine. She'd felt the hardness between his legs. *She* had inspired that. And if she had, she suddenly wondered, what then? Was such arousal not the same condition stimulated by a prostitute? Is that what she was? A whore? Had her good name and reputation been sullied forever, the lives of her precious friends imperiled for nothing more than common carnal desire?

Frustration, remorse, and loathing for herself arose in Elizabeth's throat like some poisonous bile, but there could be no relief from it. She must swallow it again and again, for she had earned it, this foul reward for her acts of dishonesty, betrayal, and lust. She closed the window slowly and climbed back into bed. Indeed, thought Elizabeth, she deserved the misery. All of it, and much, much more.

Chapter Twenty-One

Robin Dudley regarded his father with abject disbelief. Standing before the man he had adored, even idolized, he beheld now an underhanded deceiver, one who would, to further his objectives, use base trickery on his own son. But under the angry gaze of his boy, John Dudley was sanguine and altogether unruffled.

"It was something that had to be done," he said. "'Twas imperative that Thomas Seymour be brought down. You know that as well as I."

"But Elizabeth — you knew she would be implicated. You let me — you *led* me to help destroy her!"

"She is not yet destroyed, Robert."

"Not yet destroyed! She is under house arrest. Her servants are jailed in the Tower. They are accused of plotting treason with Seymour!"

"Elizabeth was a very foolish girl. She wished to marry, against the Council's wishes, an extremely dangerous man. The Admiral surprised even his most vehement detractors with his attempt to kidnap the King. Heaven only knows what he had planned for the boy. I have no way of knowing what was in Elizabeth's mind, and neither do you. She may have been planning to marry Seymour secretly. Perhaps then he would have murdered the King, risen up with his army, disposed of Princess Mary, and taken the throne with Elizabeth by force."

"You may think that of Seymour, Father, but surely you cannot believe such things of Elizabeth. She's just a girl infatuated with" — Robin was growing more and more agitated — "that monster, but she was not to blame. She doesn't deserve the fate of a traitor. And what of her servants? Kat Ashley has been a mother to Elizabeth, and now she resides in England's most fearsome prison, interrogated by Richard

Rich! And all because *I* spied for you. You tricked me, Father. Used me. How could you do it?"

"How?" said John Dudley, his eyes narrowing and his voice growing chilly. "Very easily, Robert. You see, I place the future good of England before the good of Princess Elizabeth."

"But Elizabeth *is* England!" Robin blurted, even before he knew what he was saying. The moment the words were out, he knew how ridiculous they had sounded. His father regarded him with what Robin supposed was disappointment, even pity.

"Your Elizabeth," John Dudley began, "is no more than a minor princess. When King Edward comes of age he will sire heirs to the throne. Sons, daughters. They will take precedence over Elizabeth, and their children after them. If perchance Edward dies without issue, Mary is next in line for the succession, distasteful a thought as that may be. You can be assured she will marry — probably a Spaniard — and die trying to birth a gaggle of Papist brats. Each of *them* will take precedence over Elizabeth, who, if you remember, was not so long ago considered just another of Henry's bastards. Your friend is quite unimportant in the greater scheme of things, and you would do well to forget her. She is doomed, can you not see that? If not to execution or life imprisonment for her complicity in treason, then to a life of relative obscurity. With her reputation sullied so severely, the best she can hope for is marriage to a lesser foreign prince, never setting foot in England again. But you, son, your whole life is ahead of you. You have privilege, rank, close access to the royal family. You are one of the King's favorite companions! And what of your betrothed? I see you and Amy Robsart enjoying as large and happy a family as your mother and I have had. Rejoice, Robert! You've a brilliant future."

But Robin Dudley felt anything but celebratory. He was nauseated with remorse and shame for the dishonor and threat of torture and death he had brought down on Elizabeth and her loved ones, and seething with bitterness toward the one who had led him astray.

He said simply, "I had thought more of you than this, my lord, much more." Then without asking leave to go, Robin Dudley turned his back on his father and left his presence. He knew he must find a way to see Elizabeth again and right the terrible wrong he had done her.

And he would never, ever trust his father again.

Chapter Twenty-Two

"Tell me about this letter," instructed Lord Tyrwhitt as he paced before Elizabeth, now seated, back straight, on the stool in the center of the interrogation room.

"It was one that Kat Ashley had written to the Admiral."

"When?"

"I do not remember precisely."

"An estimate. Last spring, summer, autumn?"

"Do you wish to hear what I have to say about the letter?" asked Elizabeth, trying to stifle the choler that was threatening to destroy the equanimity with which she had so far conducted herself this morning. She had decided to feed her inquisitor tidbits of information that he might find interesting but that were not, in fact, damaging.

"What was said in this letter, Princess?" he asked, relenting momentarily about the date on which it had been written.

"In it, Kat Ashley suggested to the Admiral that he should not come to my residence . . . 'for fear of suspicion.' I believe that was the phrase that was used."

Indeed, Elizabeth was terrified that Kat's letter might somehow come to light and cause no end of trouble.

"For fear of suspicion," Tyrwhitt repeated. "That suggests —"

"I know what it suggests to you, my lord Tyrwhitt," Elizabeth interrupted. "In fact, I have brought it to your attention to let you know that I chastised Kat Ashley roundly for using such a phrase, for by using it she was acknowledging that suspicion about myself and the Admiral even *existed* in the minds of others. *Wrongly* acknowledging. So, you see, the reference in the letter implied no guilt."

"Your chastisement of Kat Ashley proves nothing, Princess, except that even then you feared exposure for your secret meetings with Seymour."

"There were no secret meetings!"

"So you say. And were there no conversations between you and your servants about the feasibility of your marriage with Seymour?"

Elizabeth hesitated. This was dangerous ground, but she had decided to give Tyrwhitt another small piece of gristle upon which to chew.

"There were times," she began, "that the subject arose, but Mistress Ashley was always careful to advise me, in the most responsible fashion possible, that marriage with anyone, including Thomas Seymour, was not to be considered without the consent of the Council."

"You call Katherine Ashley *responsible?*" Tyrwhitt was no doubt recalling the tales his wife had brought home to him of Elizabeth's reckless behavior at Chelsea House. A responsible lady would never have allowed such goings-on. "I am here to tell you, Princess, that Katherine Ashley and her 'familiar,' Thomas Parry —"

Elizabeth shot Tyrwhitt a scathing look, for by the use of that word he insinuated Kat was a witch. But what could she expect? Tyrwhitt was a wretched man.

"— were two of the most foolish, indiscreet, morally unfit, and downright sinful caretakers ever to have been employed in the King's service. These two allowed and encouraged your liaison with Thomas Seymour, even whilst he was married to your stepmother!"

Elizabeth said nothing, just sat upright, jaw tightly clenched as the accusations flew around her.

"Princess Elizabeth," Tyrwhitt said finally in a softer, kinder voice, "considering your age and your lack of experience . . ." He paused for a long moment, and her battered soul prayed that such softness was the beginning of a respite from his harshness, prayed that she had somehow convinced him of her goodness and innocence. He went on, "Considering the difficult beginnings of your life, and of course the great esteem in which your brother the King holds you . . ."

Elizabeth held her breath.

". . . if now you would simply confess your crimes and any secret understandings about your marriage with Thomas Seymour, then all the evil and shame brought down upon you in this last year would surely be blamed on your servants."

"There were no *crimes!*" Elizabeth shouted. "No 'secret understandings'!" Her face had gone quite red and she found that, without knowing it, she had risen from her chair. Heat radiated from her body. If she had had an iota less control of herself she would have reached out and throttled the fat-necked Tyrwhitt.

"Sit down, Princess," he ordered her.

"I think I prefer to stand," she announced defiantly.

"Did you know," he said with a distinct touch of glee, "that there are rumors about London and the countryside too, that you are lodged in the Tower, pregnant with Thomas Seymour's child?"

The words shattered Elizabeth, silenced her. Her backbone seemed to melt.

"All of the King's subjects believe his sister is . . . well . . ."

Elizabeth was past appreciating Tyrwhitt's restraint from finishing that damning sentence. She found she was quickly losing her strength and purpose and resolve. Her mind scattered and she groped for something to say, anything that would mollify her inquisitor, keep him from again speaking such ghastly words as he had just spoken.

"I did once have a conversation with Thomas Parry, perhaps in May or even June . . ."

"Yes?" Tyrwhitt motioned with a finger for the scribe to take careful note.

"He did ask me whether, if the Council gave consent," Elizabeth said slowly, "I would consider marrying the Admiral."

Tyrwhitt smiled triumphantly. His techniques were working. Her will was beginning to crumble. "And what was your answer?" he demanded.

"My answer? My answer . . . Lord Tyrwhitt, I am feeling suddenly unwell. May I be excused?"

"Certainly, Princess." Her interrogator seemed pleased with the progress they were finally making. He would let her go now and entice more out of the girl later.

When the guards entered to take charge of the prisoner, Tyrwhitt surprisingly waved them away. He went to the open door and beckoned to someone. Lady Browne, a plump middle-aged lady, swept into the writing room and awaited her orders from Lord Tyrwhitt.

"Will you escort Princess Elizabeth to her rooms," he said, sounding kind and utterly reasonable. "She's feeling ill."

"Of course, my lord." Lady Browne turned to Elizabeth. "Would you like to hold my arm, Highness?"

"Yes, please," said Elizabeth, and without a backward glance allowed herself to be led from the room.

The two women were silent until they began climbing the stairs and were well out of Tyrwhitt's earshot. Still, Lady Browne whispered.

"I have news of Mistress Ashley."

Elizabeth whirled to face the lady, who wore a kindly expression.

"I know you fear she's in a stinking dungeon, but she is not. Her lodgings in the Tower are clean and safe, and she has not been tortured."

"Oh, Lady Browne!" Elizabeth wished to throw her arms around the woman but restrained herself, for such an outburst of affection by the disgraced Princess would only mean trouble for the individual upon whom it was lavished.

"Tell me," Elizabeth said instead, whispering softly, "what have you heard of my . . . pregnancy? You know, of course, that the rumor is false."

"Yes, I know, Highness. But the lie is indeed spreading. A woman, an old midwife, was taken into custody. She told the story of how she was hired, and blindfolded, taken on the river to a house — whether great or humble she could not tell — and made to do her work on a fair young lady of about fourteen. The baby was born alive but then, as she tells it, miserably destroyed." Lady Browne was clearly shaken by the repeating of such sinister gossip. "As the midwife had heard of your 'condition,' and because of the secrecy of the proceedings and the age of her patient, she surmised the young woman who gave birth might have been yourself."

"And this story is circulating in London?" asked Elizabeth, horrified.

"And in the countryside, too. Oh, dear Princess," whispered Lady Browne sincerely, "I wish you only the best. And to that end I recommend you bare your soul to Lord Tyrwhitt. If you do not, I fear it will go badly for you and your servants."

"Thank you," said Elizabeth. "Thank you for your kind words, Lady Browne." They had reached Elizabeth's door, where two soldiers stood guard. The women exchanged a final desperate look, for only those of their sex knew the grave weakness of feminine circumstance.

"Rest well, my dear."

The door was opened for her and Elizabeth stepped into her room. When the door closed behind her she fell on the bed and gave herself up to weeping, and praying that somehow she might be struck dead, and that Jesus would come and take her soul up and away to Heaven.

Chapter Twenty-Three

"I will see my brother!" shouted Thomas Seymour through his cell door for perhaps the thirtieth time that morning.

With each and every demand, his guard's response had changed, from a deferential "Your message will be taken posthaste, my lord" to a placating "I shall see to it" to an irritated and sarcastic "Anything you say, Admiral."

The demand to see his brother was, in fact, the only thing Thomas Seymour could on this, his third day of incarceration in the Tower, think to say. All of his raging and threatening, his shouts of abuse at his jailers and cries to Heaven at the unfairness and illegality of his arrest, had fallen on deaf ears. They were treating him — him, the High Admiral of the Navy and uncle of the King of England — like a common criminal. If he could just see and speak with the Protector, there was nothing that could not be explained away. All would be restored to normality. All would be forgiven, as it was between brothers.

"When will my message be delivered to the Protector?" Seymour hissed through the door.

This time the jailer did not even bother to reply. He would be sorry, this arrogant fellow, when Seymour was a free man again. No one realized that his arrest had been meant only to frighten him. A slap on the wrist for attempting to override the Protector's control. They had played this game endlessly as children, first in fisticuffs and wrestling when they were young boys, later in complicated mock battles with wooden swords in the forest behind Wolfe Hall. Edward was the eldest and for many years the tallest, but once Thomas had grown, his shoulders had broadened and his muscles hardened, and the contrasts had evened out. Then the battles had become those of wit as well as might. Edward's capacity was in brilliant planning and execution of his intricate schemes, though he was oftentimes foiled by Thomas's instinctual maneuvering and reckless bravery. But always at the end of the day the two had walked back to their father's house arm in arm and laughing at their day's contests. It was true that in recent years, as the stakes had risen and moved into court and Council, competition had become more bitter and acrimonious, and with Edward's marriage to that detestable shrew, much of the fun of their lifelong rivalry had died a painful death. Still, they were tied irrevocably by blood, as they were also tied to the King.

No harm could come to himself, of this Thomas was sure.

"I will see my brother!" he shouted.

This time, to his surprise, the heavy wooden door creaked on its rusted hinges and opened.

Finally, he thought, Edward has decided my punishment has been sufficient. Thomas rose from his cot and assumed a posture that was at once respectfully attentive and altogether arrogant. He could not let his brother know that he had suffered from this imprisonment. He would make a jest of it. Arm in arm and laughing they would walk from this cell, Thomas glaring at the jailers who had made his incarceration so unpleasant. Once free, he would take stock and perhaps this time move more carefully with his plans, trust no one but himself.

But the man who walked though the cell door was not Edward at all. Thomas recognized him as John Billings, a lower secretary of the Privy Council. Perhaps, thought Seymour, his belly suddenly gripped as though by a tightening hand, the whole Council is coming in after the secretary. I shall have to face all of my enemies at once, here in this humiliating circumstance. But now the jailer was closing the door behind Billings. No one else was coming in to see him after all.

"My lord," said Billings in the monotonous voice that had always irritated Thomas in Council meetings.

"Where are the others?" demanded Seymour.

"The 'others,' my lord?"

"The Council. If my brother has not visited me, then I assume the Privy Council will come in his stead."

209

"I have come from the Council," said Billings. "I alone."

Seymour's look of derision was so transparent that the secretary flinched visibly with the insult. He composed himself quickly, however, as though drawing strength from his purpose. Indeed, a moment later that purpose was revealed as he removed a rolled parchment from his pouch and unfurled a long document onto Seymour's table.

"What is this?" asked Thomas warily, the invisible hand once again clenching his guts.

Billings read, "'A Summary of the Articles of High Treason objected to Lord Seymour, High Admiral of England.'"

"High treason?"

"Yes, my lord. On three-and-thirty counts."

Thomas sat and pulled the candle close to the document and he quickly began to read. He was charged with endeavoring to get into his own hands the government of the King, of intending to control the King's marriage, of bribing certain members of the Privy Chamber, and threatening to make the blackest Parliament ever known in England.

By God's precious soul, he thought, Wriothesley and Clinton have spoken out against me. And Dorset. He was one I held as a friend.

He went on reading, disbelief growing into fear. They accused him of prejudicing the King against the Protector, and of plotting to take the King "into his custody." He had paused on that article to read it again, and Billings, peering over his shoulder, added, "Your man, Fowler, informed us that you said how easy it would be to steal the King away, for the palace was so inadequately guarded."

"I said that, meaning only that better precautions should have been taken."

Billings shrugged, for the excuse was ridiculous in light of Seymour's later actions.

Thomas continued reading. He was accused of having ten thousand available men and sufficient money to support an insurrection. Of endeavoring to make a clandestine marriage with the Princess Elizabeth. Of having married Queen Catherine scandalously soon after the death of the King.

"Idiots!" he cried aloud when he'd read that last.

"I will tell my lords of the Council what you think of them," said

Billings with an imperiousness that was growing with Thomas Seymour's discomfiture.

"You tell them," said Seymour, "that they can stick their summary of my 'treasonous' crimes one by one up their hairy bungholes!"

"I think you'd best finish your reading, my lord," said Billings coolly.

This he did. Articles 23 and 24 addressed his dealings with Sherrington and the embezzlement from the Royal Mint.

"Sherrington," Thomas muttered contemptuously.

"Indeed, Master Sherrington confessed all his crimes in the Tower and implicated yourself."

"Bastard," Thomas said to himself and continued reading.

Articles 25 to 31 spoke of his aiding and abetting pirates and profiting from their activities. Damn right, thought Thomas, feeling suddenly rebellious. He had made the most of his position as Admiral. It was the only post his high and mighty brother had deigned to give him when he'd stolen the reins of government from Henry's council of sixteen regents. What *if* Edward had sent him out with specific orders to capture Black Jack Thompson? Any man in his right mind would have taken advantage of the position, as others naturally took profits from grants and leases.

Seymour pushed back his chair and stood up, his face red and seething. "How dare they use such things to accuse me of treason!" he roared.

"How they dare, my lord, I do not know," replied Billings calmly, "but that they *have* is a fact."

"You tell my brother I must see him," Seymour threatened, towering over the smaller man.

"I shall tell him, my lord." Billings sidestepped the Admiral, rolled the document up again, and placed it in his pouch. He turned and knocked on the cell door. Momentarily the jailer came and unlocked it. "The princess Elizabeth is under house arrest for her part in this," said Billings as an afterthought, "and several of her servants are housed here in the Tower with you." The expression on Seymour's face did not change perceptibly with this intelligence. "And the young King is mourning the loss of his favorite hound."

211

"God blast His Majesty's bloody hound!" thundered Thomas, hurling himself at the door.

Safely on the other side, Billings called through it, "Good day, my lord!"

Seymour pounded the cell door in a violent fury. He could hear the jailer and Billings sharing a laugh. They were laughing at him!

Thomas sat heavily on his cot, weighed down as though the thirty-three articles of treason had been hung like a too-heavy mantle about his shoulders. He could imagine the Privy Council sitting round their long table to draw up the document — his enemies gathered like vultures over a feast of carrion.

What would be his fate? Catherine was dead. Princess Elizabeth, herself in jeopardy, was of no use to him. The King and his brother, God damn their souls to Hell's eternity, had abandoned him in his time of greatest need.

When at last it became clear that he was lost, beyond all hope of salvation, Thomas Seymour, High Admiral of the King's Navy, put his head in his hands and wept like a child.

Chapter Twenty-Four

Elizabeth had endured more than a week of long and tedious interrogations at Lord Tyrwhitt's hands, he attempting to wrest from her lips a confession of complicity in Thomas Seymour's marriage plans, or knowledge of his rebellion. As the time passed the Princess found herself weakened, for she was running low on tidbits that might appease him but give him no fuel to fire his case against Kat, Parry, and herself. Tyrwhitt, she thought as she lay abed waiting for sleep, was as sharp and ferocious a lawyer as he could be, with perfect memory, flawless logic, and unflagging ruthlessness. Her tears had no effect on him, and when his demeanor softened and he became kind, Elizabeth had learned, this was the time of greatest danger, for a trap was surely being laid for her.

She was tired, so tired, and had never in all her life felt so alone. She tried to recall her lessons with Grindal and Ascham, call up the Socratic and Platonic wisdom she had studied so assiduously. All of her requests to be allowed her Greek texts, so that she could ease her mind with translations, had been ignored. She felt herself sinking deeper and deeper into an abyss from which there was no escape, with only a death as horrible and ignominious as her mother's to end it.

More and more the idea had preyed on her mind that the people of England were thinking ill of her, and this troubled her no end. Why, she wondered, did she have such a care for the men and women of town and country? They were poor and common and powerless. They had no say in the running of England, for the men in Parliament who were said to represent them truly voted as they pleased. Why then did Elizabeth burn with humiliation at the thought of their disapproval of her? Was it simply the *cruelty* of the gossip that was even now in the lowliest country taverns being repeated and spread like a virulent infection? Or was it the comparison with King Henry's whore, the traitor Anne Boleyn?

All of this, together with the awful shame of having dragged her loved ones down to such depths with her, made the days almost unendurable and her nights marathons of guilty ruminations and sleeplessness.

Then, like a taper being lit in a darkened chamber, an idea burst upon Elizabeth's mind. It came from nowhere in particular but seemed, if not brilliant, then at least feasible. Perhaps it might in some way help her. She rose from the bed and, throwing her robe round her shoulders and sliding into her slippers, she moved silently to the writing table and lit several candles. The moment she sat down and placed the quill in the inkpot and nib to parchment, the ideas began to flow freely from her mind into her fingertips. She had never been so thankful that her penmanship was flawless, for such a correspondence as this must impress its reader with the perfection of its style and grammar as well its content.

My Lord Protector, I appreciate your great gentleness and good will towards me in this time of urgency, and understand your counsel as an earnest friend that I should declare what I know in this matter.

The Protector, if not his wife, had shown Elizabeth due respect in the past, and he was indeed the highest authority in England whom she might personally petition. She wrote on meticulously, declaring all she could without incriminating Kat or Parry or herself, reiterating those items she had shared with Tyrwhitt — things that she perceived sounded far more believable in writing than they had as spoken answers under her inquisitor's evil eye. She "confessed" that Thomas had offered herself use of Seymour House when in London, and that the Admiral had on several occasions inquired as to the state of her patents and her household expenses, perhaps with an eye to their future together. Never, however, had she consented to plans of marriage with Seymour or anyone else without the Council's consent.

Elizabeth looked up from her writing. She had filled an entire page but had not yet begun to convey the most important thoughts for which she had begun this exercise. She carefully blotted the first page with a half-round blotter and set it aside, drawing another sheet of parchment in front of her. She dipped the quill tip into her inkpot and, taking a deep breath to fortify her, continued writing.

Master Tyrwhitt and others have told me that there are many rumors abroad that besmirch my honor and honesty, the worst of which is that I am in the Tower and with child by My Lord Admiral. This is a shameful slander against my name and also therefore against my brother the King's Majesty. I heartily desire, Your Lordship, that I may be allowed to come to the Court so that all there may see me as I am.

Written in haste from Hatfield this 19ᵗʰ of January.

Your assured friend,

As she completed the last flourish of her signature Elizabeth found her eyes growing heavy, as if the very act of writing, decisively and boldly, had returned to her a small measure of control over her destiny, and in so doing tranquilized her soul. She blotted the page, folded the two together, and sealed them with a large clot of red wax. Then she climbed into bed and within moments fell into a peaceful slumber.

Chelsea's day room. Sun streamed through the tall windows, falling in long bright panels on the floor. Two figures sat under windows and, wishing desperately to be in their presence, Elizabeth crossed the illuminated Turkey rug that was Queen Catherine's pride and joy, careful as she placed her feet on the brightness, that the sun's heat not burn her. She crossed the light patches and finally saw the figures clearly. They sat at a large sewing frame, both stitching on a tapestry of which the details were not yet visible. One of the figures was Kat Ashley, an expression of fierce determination on her face, as though the embroidery were of the most vital importance. Elizabeth was happy to see her dear companion, but Kat did not look up from her work. Then Elizabeth turned her head and recognized that the one who sat across from Kat was a man. *A man embroidering!* But no, 'twas not a man at all *but a woman in men's clothing.* 'Twas Catherine Parr, and Elizabeth's heart swelled immediately with joy and love for her, shocked though she was to see the Queen Dowager so attired. Indeed, Elizabeth addressed her then, saying, "You make a fine man, Your Majesty." Catherine smiled up at Elizabeth warmly, and with her eyes invited her to sit at a third stool round the tapestry.

Now she could see the exquisite handiwork. Scenes of armies and battles, gardens of trees and birds and flowers, King George and the dragon. But the wonder of the tapestry, the greatest wonder, was that *it moved!* The armed soldiers were marching in their battalions against one another, the birds flitted from tree to tree, and King George with a mighty thrust of his lance impaled the green-eyed dragon. A *living tapestry!* Elizabeth looked up smiling with the magic of it and saw Catherine smiling too, though she did not return Elizabeth's gaze but stitched on, seeming peaceful in the extreme.

Suddenly Elizabeth's joy vanished as she was struck all at once by remorse for past deeds and mortal terror for the future.

"I beg your forgiveness, Majesty," she heard herself saying in a dolorous tone.

Still Catherine did not look up but replied calmly, "No harm done, my dear."

"No harm done," repeated Kat Ashley. "No real harm done."

Now beneath her fingers Elizabeth saw a fearsome dragon, larger and more hideous than the first. It moved on webbed and sharp-clawed feet across the tapestry, expelling smoke and fire from its long scaly muzzle. Her heart lurched at the sight. Suddenly she felt a sting of pain as its fire blistered her skin. She snatched back her hand and looked up at the two women dearest to her in all the world. Kat and Catherine were gazing at her with deep and abiding love. And something more.

Encouragement, passionate and earnest.

Fierce strength blazed from Catherine's eyes. "Do it, Elizabeth," she urged.

"Do it, Princess," Kat echoed.

Elizabeth looked down. The dragon rampaged through the garden, trampling a hedge of red roses — Tudor roses, she thought — slaughtering birds, setting the trees afire. . . .

216

"Do it, Elizabeth. You can do it."

Suddenly she realized that she held a long embroidery needle between her fingers. The dragon, long hideous tail swishing behind him, was heading for a pretty turreted castle. Elizabeth's heart pounded. Her hand trembled. But she gained control, inhaled deeply. Then with a small cry, she plunged the lancelike needle through the dragon's heart. It let out a terrible shriek and fell thrashing to the ground.

Triumph surged through Elizabeth's being, and great, soul-filling joy.

She looked up again. Kat's and Catherine's faces were aglow with pride. Then they began to laugh. Elizabeth's heart swelled and she began laughing along with them. Their laughter echoed through the day room as the sun enveloped the female triumvirate in a halo of blazing light.

Morning light was pouring into Elizabeth's eyes, the heavy curtains of her bedchamber having just been thrown aside. She blinked awake but dared not move for fear of losing the dream. She had learned that keeping every muscle in place when awakening from sleep, and recalling the details of a dream immediately, fixed the memory of the images in her mind. And this was a dream she must not forget! She closed her eyes again as the maid bustled about the room, remembering the strangeness — nay, the *magic* of the dream — the tapestry moving and alive, the dragon's fiery breath burning her hand, the upswelling of triumph when she'd slain it. This feeling she savored now, a sense of controlling her fate, something she had never, in the whole of her life, felt before.

And Catherine Parr dressed as a man! What could that possibly signify? Had it anything to do, she wondered, with her own recent disguising as a boy? Or was Catherine instructing Elizabeth to act like a man? The Princess, like most people, was a believer in dreams and premonitions, and of the stars' influences on the lives of men and women. For Catherine to have come to Elizabeth with so much sweetness in a dream of such potency, the meaning was clearly that the Queen Dowager had forgiven her.

Elizabeth heaved a great sigh of contentment.

"Rise and shine, Princess." These words, spoken with harsh authority by Lady Tyrwhitt, who had just bustled into the bedchamber, were as a chill wind that swept away Elizabeth's warming coverlet of private thoughts, leaving her naked to the woman's sarcasm. "Did you plan to sleep the day away?"

"No, madame," replied Elizabeth tartly. "I was planning to rise and dress for the *privilege* of spending my day in your delightful husband's company."

Lady Tyrwhitt bristled, and Elizabeth pulled the sheet over her mouth so the woman could not see her smile. The Princess was in fact more than ready to greet the day – – and even her inquisitor — fortified by the strength and forgiveness of the Great Queen, Catherine Parr.

Chapter Twenty-Five

Thumbscrews. Thomas Parry had never in his life had occasion to see such devices, but as he was marched into the same dank cell in which he had been interrogated day after day for more than a week, there was no doubt in his mind that what sat benignly in the middle of the trestle table next to his chair were indeed those infamous instruments of torture. Instantly his bowels began churning and he prayed they would not turn to water.

He had to this point, he believed, stayed altogether faithful to Princess Elizabeth, repelling the aggressively invasive questioning of Lord Rich with stouthearted equanimity. Nothing he had said could have incriminated her. He had simply denied any wrongdoing, indeed denied any contact with Thomas Seymour other than the most innocuous — that which would have been expected of a servant of the Princess whilst she and her household were living under the Admiral's roof.

The Lord Chancellor had proved a truly fearsome inquisitor. Had Parry overstepped himself, he knew, Rich would have slammed shut on him like a spiked trap on the leg of a wild animal. But Parry had withstood all assaults. Stayed strong and loyal to Elizabeth.

Now, with one glance at the thumbscrews, Thomas Parry's resolve began to crumble. Till today, there had been no talk of torture, and though any imprisonment in the Tower implied its possibility, somehow Richard Rich had lulled Parry into believing it unlikely.

Parry suddenly felt a fool, tricked, like a child. It was a measure of Rich's abilities in this occupation, he realized. Lowering the victim's guard, allowing him a false sense of security. And then the thumbscrews, a silent reminder of the true course of this interrogation.

By the time Lord Rich stepped into the room, elegant in black velvet doublet trimmed with gold braid, fingers covered in heavy gem-encrusted rings, Thomas Parry had lost his nerve altogether. The thumbscrews, small and unprepossessing as they appeared, were merely a reminder of the more hideous forms of torture that the English had over the centuries perfected. Thomas Parry, during his life of privilege and position, had never suffered any sort of physical pain save that of a rare headache, the cramp of an ague, or a strained muscle. Now, with the thought of his fingers being crushed in these screws, his body being torn apart on the rack, red hot irons being applied to his skin, his eyes, perhaps his anus, he began to tremble violently.

Richard Rich smiled a brief and terrible smile. "Today," he began, "I wish you to expound upon Thomas Seymour's 'familiarities' with Princess Elizabeth whilst she lived at Chelsea House. Until today, Master Parry, you have denied remembering any and all such activities, though rumors of such improprieties were rampant in that household. Do you think" — he paused to gaze down at the thumbscrews — "that this morning your memory might be significantly improved?"

Thomas Parry opened his mouth to speak. His lips flapped several times but no words were forthcoming.

"Very good," said Lord Rich, twirling a heavy gold ring round and round on his finger. "I think perhaps we are making some progress."

If truth be told, Kat Ashley had, during her incarceration in the Tower of London, suffered more from the cold than any other discomfort. Her quarters could more rightly be called a small bedchamber than a cell. Besides a bed, table, and chair, there was a reasonable window that looked out upon Tower Green, and a woven reed mat on the floor. Her meals, though simple, had been edible. Her jailers had been kind. More than one of them had whispered inquiries about Princess Elizabeth, and Kat assumed that her own preferred treatment stemmed from her charge's popularity with the majority of the English people. Even Richard Rich's interrogations, though persistent, had proven considerably gentler than Kat had feared they would be.

It was just the cold that was aching her bones and freezing her fingertips and nose, she thought as she waited for the guard to take her to what had become her daily deposition by Lord Rich. The small fireplace in her room would have been adequate had she been supplied with enough coal. But all pleas for increasing her portion of the stuff had been ignored. The fires she made were pitiful, burning out before she could even get the blood flowing into her hands. She spent most of her time when free from Rich's questioning crouching in bed with the covers pulled round her. She would fall asleep shivering and wake shivering. It occurred to Kat that this was perhaps a refined form of torture, though as the days passed and chilblains turned her fingers raw, it seemed less and less subtle after all.

She was, of course, in all waking moments tormented by thoughts of dear Elizabeth, alone and helpless, assailed by her enemies, vilely accused of treasonable offenses that might lead to her permanent imprisonment or even her execution. Sweet Jesus!

If she were entirely honest, Kat knew she must hold herself in good part accountable for this disaster. She had come finally to understand how completely she had been blinded by Thomas Seymour's charms. Upon reflection in her cold prison she realized he had had the ability to hold an almost mystical sway over people's hearts and minds. She knew she was not alone in this weakness, and though the thought did not eliminate her self-loathing, it did assuage her somewhat that a woman as superbly levelheaded as Catherine Parr had been similarly affected by the man.

Now her fate and Elizabeth's were wholly uncertain, but with news of Thomas Seymour's articles of high treason — thirty-three of them! — coming by way of her jailers, hope of exoneration seemed every day more doubtful. Kat's only weapon, and Elizabeth's and Parry's too, was deniability. Everything that Richard Rich claimed to know of Elizabeth's dealings with Thomas Seymour was founded in gossip. She had been told that the Admiral had so far confessed to nothing. And the one article claiming that she, Parry, and Seymour together had conspired for him to marry Princess Elizabeth was entirely unprovable.

Kat heard voices outside her chamber. The heavy lock turned and the door opened. She stood, fully expecting the guard who came to fetch her each day for her interrogation. She was startled, therefore, to see Lord Rich stride purposefully into her room. He looked too pleased, thought Kat with sudden alarm, for he'd not worn this particular expression during any part of her questioning. She had not long to wait for an explanation. With a small flourish Rich produced a written document and placed it on her table.

"Your coconspirator's testimony," he said simply.

Kat was stunned, did not move or utter a sound.

"Thomas Parry has confessed to everything, Mistress Ashley. To negotiations with Thomas Seymour for his marriage with Princess Elizabeth, and to allowing to go unchecked . . . 'sexual horseplay' between the two whilst they were living under the Queen Dowager's roof."

"He admitted nothing of the kind," said Kat Ashley very decisively, meeting Lord Rich's gaze. "You have compiled a scandal sheet derived solely from rumor."

"Have I?" said Rich almost amiably. "Why don't you have a look for yourself? You will see it is written in your friend's own hand."

Kat stood unmoving for a long moment, then dropped her eyes to the document. Indeed, the handwriting appeared to be Thomas Parry's. But this could easily be a forgery, a trick! If she believed Thomas had confessed, *she* would have to confess. She raised her eyes again to the Lord Chancellor's gaze.

"I do not believe it, my lord. This document is false."

Silent, Rich dandled the ring on his finger very slowly, never taking his eyes off Kat. Then he made a signal to the guard outside the open door. A moment later a pale, shaken Parry entered Kat's chamber. The treachery of his miserable act was written across his face.

"What have you done, Thomas Parry?" she murmured, but she knew too well what the answer was.

"I . . . I," he stuttered.

"False wretch!" she cried, taking a threatening step toward him. "You swore you'd sooner be drawn limb from limb by horses than betray her!"

"I'm so sorry," said Parry. There were tears in his eyes.

"Sorry!" she spat disgustedly.

Thus confronting her old friend, Kat never noticed that Lord Rich had brought to her table several sheets of parchment, a quill, and an inkwell. Now she saw him studying her as a cat studies a mouse before the strike. He held out the quill and smiled a wicked smile.

"Your turn," he said.

Chapter Twenty-Six

The two confessions lay before the Princess on the day room table. Robert Tyrwhitt stood behind her, looking over her shoulder. Neither of them had spoken for some time as Elizabeth studied each document carefully, examining a passage from one, then comparing it with the other. Her face registered no discernable emotion, but she was in fact seething with outrage that she had, after all of her own restraint and courage in the face of a relentless inquisition, been betrayed by Parry.

Betrayed by Kat.

The written testimonies of her servants — they could not possibly have been written by anyone else — laid bare in excruciating detail everything that had transpired in Chelsea House: Elizabeth's infatuation with Seymour, how she blushed simply to hear his name spoken; the bedroom romps with Thomas, and later Catherine; Kat's own infatuation with the Admiral, his note inquiring after her "great buttocks"; the bizarre incident in Chelsea's garden in which Catherine had pinioned Elizabeth's arms whilst Thomas had torn the gown, leaving her half naked, then made ribbons of the dress with his dagger. Kat and Parry used almost identical words to describe the scene in which the Queen Dowager had found Elizabeth in her husband's arms. Dozens of meetings between Parry and the Admiral were confessed to, in which Elizabeth's and Seymour's adjoining properties, her grants and household accounts, were discussed with an eye to their future marriage, this despite a lack of consent from the Privy Council for that marriage. All that was missing, thought Elizabeth with equal measures of bitterness and relief, was a description of her rendezvous, in disguise, with Seymour. At least Kat and Parry had had the presence of mind to keep *that* secret. Still, her humiliation could scarcely have been more complete.

But this was nothing compared to the fear that was rising round Elizabeth like a roaring spring tide. By now she was no longer reading, though to buy herself time she pretended to continue rereading and comparing certain paragraphs.

She had been grievously betrayed by those she had believed in most. But then, she mused, was she not inured to betrayal? She'd been abandoned by her mother, bastardized and ignored by her father. She had loved and trusted the Queen Dowager, who had changed, almost overnight, into a madwoman. She had given her heart and soul to Thomas Seymour, and he had used her, tried to rape her.

But Kat and Parry? How could they have given evidence that would destroy her, destroy themselves?

"Well, what have you to say now, Princess?" said Tyrwhitt smugly.

All at once, as if from a distance, Elizabeth heard a voice. Three words were repeated, at first softly so as to hardly be discerned, then louder and louder till her ears were ringing with them.

"No harm done. *No harm done.* NO HARM DONE!"

Elizabeth's back straightened suddenly and she lifted her eyes from the pages.

Images of her dream replayed in her mind — the fire-breathing dragon menacing the countryside, castle, and rose garden. Did the monster signify Lord Tyrwhitt and Richard Rich, who, with their relentless interrogations and accusations, threatened to lay waste the succession and altogether destroy the great Tudor dynasty? Was Elizabeth the dragon's slayer, meant to stand strong against these ruthless enemies of the State? Become the hero who would save her family, save England?

"No harm done." Kat and Catherine had insisted as much in the dream. No real harm had been done! Everything suddenly became clear. All the black murkiness of the past week was, as in the dream, brilliantly illuminated — as brightly as Queen Catherine's Turkey carpet had been by the sunlight streaming through Chelsea's day room windows.

Elizabeth's mind raced, revisiting the confessions piece by piece. They demonstrated obscenely bad judgment on the part of her servants, and her own unconscionable recklessness and complete moral disregard. But none of it, realized Elizabeth, the idea expanding in her head, was seriously incriminating. *None of it was treasonable.* Elizabeth bit the inside of her lip to keep the smile from breaking across her face.

"Well?" Tyrwhitt demanded.

"These are serious charges," she replied evenly.

"They are indeed," he said indignantly, for he could suddenly and clearly sense Elizabeth's lack of fear, and he was confused by it. "I am told that when Thomas Parry was brought into Mistress Ashley's presence," Tyrwhitt goaded her, "he received a vicious tongue-lashing for admitting his crimes and hers, and *yours*, Princess."

Elizabeth nodded sagely and spoke carefully in reply. "It was a great matter for Parry to promise such a promise not to betray me . . . and to break it. Poor man." She could feel the heat of Lord Tyrwhitt's frustration and anger rising against her steadily increasing calm. In that moment Elizabeth felt her soul open like a flower on a warm day and she knew with certainty that all would be well in the end.

"Give me a quill and parchment, my lord," she said. "I think it is time I write you a confession."

When the Duke of Somerset entered the game room, King Edward was sitting partnerless at his chessboard, staring vaguely in front of him. The Protector approached him. There was no time for pleasantries. "In a moment the Council will come in here to ask for a bill of attainder against Thomas, the bill to be thereafter debated in Parliament," he said. The boy's expression did not change, nor did he look at his uncle. "They are all of one mind in this matter, Edward. It is my feeling that the charges are so many and so serious that the Parliament will uphold the bill and Thomas will be condemned to death."

Somerset took the seat across the chessboard, forcing his nephew to look at him. "Despite all of that, you . . . and I" — he paused for a moment — "have the right to show leniency to my brother. We have the right, once he is condemned, to pardon him."

Edward took a sip of watered wine from his goblet but remained silent, in this way insisting that his uncle make his choices altogether clear.

"We are both aware, Edward," Somerset proceeded uncomfortably, "that I have not always consulted you on matters of state."

"On almost none," said Edward tersely.

"On almost none," the Protector agreed. "But on this matter particularly, Your Majesty, it is imperative that you and I appear as of one mind. You cannot commit to leniency and I to —"

"I *know* what 'of one mind' means, my lord," Edward interrupted with irritation.

"Forgive me, Your Majesty," Somerset intoned, hoping to sound submissive. "It is just that I am — you can imagine — most distressed by these circumstances. So I will just ask you now, given the choice between pardoning the Lord Admiral and allowing his . . . execution, which would you choose?"

The eleven-year-old glared at his uncle with so furious and vengeful a look that Somerset found himself squirming in his seat. Then Edward spoke, and though it was the reedy voice of a young boy, something in it — its ice cold steel or perhaps its natural and absolute command — recalled the voice of King Henry the Eighth.

"Let him die," said Edward. "Let him die."

Chapter Twenty-Seven

What month, thought Robin Dudley wryly, could be more perfect for an execution than March? All was grim and gray, biting wind, sinister clouds scuttling across the steely sky. Tower Green was, in fact, brown, and the scaffold upon which Thomas Seymour would soon end his life was a barren platform with only enough straw beneath the block to soak up his blood.

Robin's father was showing a gravely reserved face to the small crowd that had gathered on the lawn outside the Chapel of St. Peter ad Vincula, but his son had seen him as they'd left the family's apartments at Hampton Court, and John Dudley had been nothing less than jovial. He was glad of Thomas Seymour's death, for this signaled to him the ultimate demise of his brother the Duke of Somerset. Indeed, the talk swirling round them now was less to do with the man who would here soon die than of the forces and designs that had brought him to the scaffold today. The Protector and the King were both absent, and it was well that they were, for much of what was murmured this day was about the pair of them: how young Edward, when asked his opinion of his uncle Thomas's crimes, had said, rather unconvincingly, how sorrowful the case was to him, but had never spoken one word in the man's defense, perhaps remembering more clearly the shooting of his dog than Seymour's past generosity and companionship. Some considered the King's cold-bloodedness, and wondered what kind of ruler he would come to be. "A heartless king," one man was heard to say, "would a cold country make." Even Henry, mad and violent as he was at his end, had seethed with passion for all things, and England had been the better for it.

Of the Protector few good words were said. When asked for his participation in his brother's prosecution, he had begged "for natural pity's sake" to be allowed to withdraw. Though the Admiral's treason had been obvious, and any support his brother might bring be therefore suspect, now men were crying "fratricide." It was said that Somerset had shown uncommon mercilessness in refusing to see Thomas during his imprisonment in the Tower as his fate was being argued in the Council and Parliament. Few men knew, thought Robin, that the brothers' separation had been masterminded by his father, and fewer still realized the cold joy the Protector's befouled reputation brought to John Dudley's heart.

The executioner took his place on the scaffold, soulless eyes staring out from holes cut in the black hood. His arms were bare and, mused Robin, less powerful than he would have imagined. Would stronger arms mean fewer cuts, a less gruesome killing? This was Robin's first beheading, one for which his father had insisted he be present. It could never be said of young Dudley that he was squeamish, but the part that he had played in Seymour's demise, and the grief he'd thereafter brought down upon Elizabeth's head, caused in the boy a reticence to attend that had surprised John Dudley.

"You will come and see what happens to traitors," he said.

"*Your* father was executed for treason," Robin argued.

"Unfairly. Sometimes . . . mistakes are made. Not in this case." He had smiled thinly.

Preceded by a chaplain and flanked by twelve guards — did they expect the prisoner to attempt an escape? — Thomas Seymour was led across Tower Green. It was, thought Robin, strange to see the Admiral devoid of his devil-may-care smile and belly-shaking laugh. John Dudley was right. Thomas Seymour was a dangerous villain who deserved this death, but as the Admiral climbed the scaffold's several stairs, Robin Dudley hoped he would never in his life again be responsible for such a dreadful thing as this.

The humiliation of this moment, decided Thomas Seymour, is a hundred times more horrifying than my death shall be. At least on the interminable march from the Tower to the scaffold the phalanx of guards in their tall feathered helmets had surrounded him, prevented the smug, gawking noblemen from observing his miserable expression. But now he stood facing the crowd and they all could see him in his utterly humbled condition. Seymour knew that most men took pride in a "good death," but he was tired and had no stomach for a final show.

My life, he thought, arrogance flaring briefly, *has been the show.*

The Council had denied him an open trial. Instead, a bill of attainder had been drawn up, a foregone conclusion of his guilt. By the time the Archbishop of Canterbury had come to the Tower to hear his statement, defense was useless, and he'd refused to answer all but the first three articles against him. These he claimed were false, as was the charge of treason. He asked once again to see his brother and was denied. He demanded once again an open trial and was denied.

He loathed his family and these godforsaken noblemen, Thomas thought as he peered into the sea of faces, and he loathed England too. They expected him to stand here and confess his guilt, gracefully accept the justice of his sentence, and pray for forgiveness.

Well, they could stuff their forgiveness!

Seymour swept the crowd with his sullen gaze, hoping to find his brother so that he might with his eyes murder him with contempt. But Edward Seymour was absent, coward that he was, and thus denied Thomas the one last act that would have given him any joy or comfort.

He barely heard the chaplain read the final benediction, for the blood had begun to pound in his ears. As in a dream, Thomas silently handed the executioner his customary payment.

"Tell them to get it over with," he hissed to John Martin, who stood to one side. Then he beckoned the servant closer and whispered in his ear. "When I am dead and you carry my body away, find in the sole of my shoe two letters. Deliver them."

"Yes, my lord," whispered Martin, then stood back.

With a last look at the world that had betrayed him, Thomas Seymour knelt and, pulling his great red beard forward, placed his head upon the well-worn wooden block. 'Tis smooth against my neck, was his bemused thought.

It was the last he ever had.

Chapter Twenty-Eight

As Hatfield Hall came into view Robin Dudley felt his heart ease. It was not the house, though he knew it to be one that Elizabeth dearly loved, but the great wood and lush fields surrounding it that soothed his soul. Here the Princess and he had spent countless hours at play. Since earliest childhood, hardly able to straddle their horses, they had ridden every road and rut of this forest and field together. He loved coming to visit Elizabeth here, and here she was at her best.

Suddenly, as though he had conjured her with his thoughts, Elizabeth appeared at the door waving. He'd not told her he was coming this day — this grievous day — but it seemed as if she'd been expecting him. Her smile was sad but welcoming nonetheless.

He swung down from his horse and approached her. They clasped hands and there was a sweet familiarity in their greeting. He saw that she'd been crying.

"Is it done?" she asked in a dolorous tone.

"Done. Two quick strokes. He seemed not to suffer."

Elizabeth's face quivered strangely, as if only by conscious effort would the parts of it continue to hold together.

"Did he speak before he died?" she asked carefully.

"No. But something did happen."

"What, what happened?"

"He'd whispered something to his servant just before. . . . When the servant was later questioned as to the Admiral's words to him, he confessed that Seymour had directed him to search the soles of his shoes."

"Was anything found?"

"Two letters. One to your sister Mary . . . and one to you. I haven't brought it," he said quickly and apologetically. "My father took them both, will bring them to the Council."

Elizabeth's eyes were pleading.

"They were nearly identical in content. Seymour was warning both princesses to beware of the Protector. He wrote that Somerset was making plans to estrange you from your brother and induce him to deprive you and Mary of your right to the succession."

Elizabeth was silent for a long moment. "Is it true? Should I beware of Lord Somerset?"

Robin hesitated. Angry as he was at his father, loyalty to his family was paramount, and John Dudley's plans — every day gaining strength and momentum — were to usurp Edward Seymour's place by the throne. He believed the Protector ill suited for the job and frankly malicious. It was possible, even probable, that Thomas Seymour's warnings to the Princess were well founded.

"Despite the source," Robin answered finally, "I would take the warning seriously. I would let the Lord Protector know that your eyes are open and that you are watching him carefully."

"He knows that already," said Elizabeth with some pride.

"How so?" asked Robin, pleased for this show of spirit in the previously dispirited girl.

"Since my 'confession' . . ." She paused for ironic effect and smiled mischievously.

"The famous confession that cleared you and your servants of any complicity in Seymour's plans?" Robin added. "Robert Tyrwhitt was fit to be tied, I understand. Swore that you and Kat and Parry had planned your stories in advance. 'They all sing the same song,' he was heard to mutter very angrily. How did you do it, Elizabeth? Word is circulating all round London and the countryside that you *outsmarted* Lord Tyrwhitt."

Elizabeth smiled mysteriously. "I received my inspiration from a dream," she said.

"A dream?"

"My teachers, my *saviors,* were Kat and Queen Catherine."

Robin stared at Elizabeth quizzically.

"They gave me wisdom and encouragement." Tears glittered in her eyes at the memory. "They gave me strength."

"Then bless them both," said Robin emphatically, his own tears threatening to spill.

"Indeed," said Elizabeth. Steering them away from a display of emotion that might open a veritable floodgate of the same, she went on, "I can tell you Lord Tyrwhitt *was* very angry, and conceived of punishing me by placing his wife, Lady Tyrwhitt, in my service. 'Twas on this matter, in fact, that I lodged my first, though not my last, complaint with Lord Somerset."

"What did you tell him?" asked Robin, amazed at Elizabeth's boldness.

"That by denying me my long-devoted servant Kat and replacing her with the Queen Dowager's stepdaughter and confidante — a lady openly contemptuous of me — he was humiliating me and worse, announcing to the people that I somehow deserved, through my lewd behavior, such a detestable keeper."

"You said *that* to the Protector?" Robin asked incredulously.

"In *one* of my letters to him. In another," she went on, "I demanded Kat and Parry be returned to my service, and requested that a public proclamation be issued to clear my name immediately, to silence the talebearers spreading lies about me."

"Elizabeth!"

"I want my good name back, Robin!" Then she paused. "Though I may not deserve it."

He had seen the pain in her eyes, even as she was relaying her triumphs. He was therefore taken aback when she said, "You look so sad. I would think you jolly on the day my lord Seymour died."

"Oh, Elizabeth . . ." Robin found the words choking his throat.

"What is it? There's something you're not telling me."

"I am afraid to tell you."

She questioned him with demanding eyes.

"You'll hate me for what I've done!"

Elizabeth looked suddenly fragile, like a pale, porcelain-headed doll. "Perhaps," she said quite seriously, "you should not tell me, then."

"But I *must*, else I cannot live with myself."

Elizabeth turned away from Robin Dudley that she should not see his face when he began to speak, and walked slowly but deliberately down the winding path of the formal gardens. On this late winter day little here was green or cheering to the soul, but perhaps, she thought, moving would ease the pain of what terrible news was to come.

"'Twas *I* who spied on Thomas Seymour, Elizabeth!" Robin blurted the words, the only way they would come. "The intelligence of his plots and rebellions that *I* gathered was what led to his arrest."

Elizabeth stopped dead. Robin's words were like knives sinking into her flesh. Still she refused to meet his eye, and when she spoke again, each syllable echoed in her own ears.

"How did you come to spy on him?" she asked.

Robin was silent for a long while, and Elizabeth knew that this was perhaps the most difficult part of his confession.

"I knew from our meeting on the road outside Cheshunt that you and he were corresponding regularly. That you had plans to meet with him . . . alone. I was frightened, Elizabeth. I knew how dangerous he was, and I knew you would never listen to reason from me."

"And?" she said coldly.

"And so . . . I told my father of your plans."

"Oh, Robin —"

"I'm sorry, Elizabeth. No," he corrected himself, "I'm *not* sorry! Seymour was in fact planning to kidnap, perhaps kill your brother, he was planning treason, and —"

"You promised you would never tell a soul!" she cried. "You promised me —"

"I know, I know. Let me finish, please."

She could feel the fury at yet another betrayal rising with the blood into her face, but she contained herself and let Robin go on.

"When I told my father of your plans, he told me of his suspicions about the Admiral's illegal activities. He said he needed hard evidence to stop him, and only by stopping his rebellion could we keep you out of harm's way. I never dreamt — and only now I see how stupid I was not to have — that his arrest would put *you* in jeopardy."

"But your father knew!"

There was a long terrible silence before Robin Dudley replied. "Yes, my father knew."

Without warning Elizabeth's eyes filled with tears that could not be contained any longer. She turned and saw Robin's face. His cheeks were wet, his expression shamed and altogether wretched.

He had been miserably betrayed *by his own father.* Worse, the betrayal had nearly cost Elizabeth her life. Now her heart ached for Robin as mightily as it did for the many betrayals she herself had suffered.

"Is there more?" she asked fearfully.

"Good heavens, no!" he exclaimed.

As their eyes met, the pain and tribulation they had known — stretched and expanded to their limits of endurance — burst suddenly, and the two of them exploded with simultaneous laughter. It rolled and pealed round them, brought them to tears, coursed through their bodies, and finally cleared in their minds a place for forgiveness.

Elizabeth could see now — it was quite evident — that what Robin had done had been meant for her protection. Indeed, though he could not know and she would never tell him, his timely actions had likely saved her from Seymour's rape. Most important, she knew, her heart swelling with comfort and happiness, he had shown the utmost courage with his terrible admission today. Robin Dudley was an honest man, and nothing, *nothing* could be more important.

All tears and laughter had finally ceased.

"Do you forgive me, then?" Robin asked.

"I *thank* you," she said simply, and he did not question her reply.

She could see his body relax, and his expression too. They walked side by side now, easy with one another, even in silence as it had always been. They strolled to the edge of the great wood, allowing its ancient towering strength to refill and refresh them. Finally Robin spoke.

"My father says you will never rule England."

"I think he is right. Too much stands in the way."

"Be that as it may," said Robin, pausing to face her, "consider me your man, Princess. Count on me . . . always. Will you promise me that?"

"I promise," she said, most seriously.

With poise unexpected from a sixteen-year-old boy, Robin took Elizabeth's hand and raised it to his lips. He kissed her fingers as a man would his sovereign's. But then he could not seem to let her go.

Elizabeth turned her hand gently and caressed Robin's cheek —

this man, this boy, this dearest of all hearts. She carefully pulled her hand away. "I think," she began, "that in coming years I shall envy Amy Robsart very much indeed." Elizabeth saw what she thought was pain flicker across Robin's features. "But never mind. We are best friends," she said forcefully, so that the tears would not begin again.

"And always will be," he agreed staunchly.

Elizabeth felt a lightness, almost weightlessness overcome her, and the pain that had for so long consumed her, body and soul, began to dissolve away.

"Shall we ride?" he asked suddenly. "I think it will do you good."

"I think, Robin Dudley," said Elizabeth, smiling with great and newfound joy, "that you know me very well."

Epilogue

The embezzler **William Sherrington** obtained a full pardon for himself and had his house, lands, and position at the Royal Mint restored to him. He ended his life as the sheriff of Wiltshire.

Owing to Elizabeth's persistence with the Protector, **Kat Ashley** and **Thomas Parry** were released from the Tower and restored to the Princess's service. Kat remained Elizabeth's closest waiting lady and ally until she died fifteen years later.

With the death of his brother Thomas, the ascendancy of **Edward Seymour,** the Lord Protector and Duke of Somerset, ended. During the civil revolt of 1549 his popularity plummeted while **John Dudley,** flaunting his new title as Duke of Northumberland, flourished. Further reduced by his rival's successful scheming, Somerset was relieved of his duties and confined to the Tower. He was succeeded as Protector by none other than Northumberland. Somerset temporarily regained his place on the Privy Council and, in a gesture of submission, married his daughter to Northumberland's eldest son and namesake, John Dudley, but he was secretly plotting to bring the new Protector down. The plot failed. Somerset was convicted of a felony and beheaded in 1552.

King Edward the Sixth lived under Northumberland's protectorship and together, rabid Protestants, they instituted some of the worst persecution of Catholics in English history. When King Edward was sixteen years old, he died an excruciatingly painful death, some believe of tuberculosis. In the weeks preceding his death, the Duke of Northumberland schemed with **Lord Dorset** and, in secret, married their children **Guildford Dudley** and **Lady Jane Grey.** Though it was not Jane's or Guildford's wish, it was their fathers' greatest desire that the pair should rule as king and queen. They succeeded briefly. For nine days the fourteen-year-old Jane was queen of England, thus upsetting the lawful succession of **Princess Mary.** No one counted on popular support for the Catholic princess nor on her ability to muster an army of her own. But she and her troops routed Northumberland and Dorset, and as **Queen Mary** (later known as "Bloody Mary" for her persecution of Protestant heretics) she took the throne. The Duke of Northumberland, his son John Dudley, and Lord Dorset were beheaded for treason to the Crown. A victim of Dorset's and Northumberland's failed schemes, little Jane Grey, nine days a reluctant queen, and Guildford Dudley were executed on Tower Green.

Catherine Parr's death of childbed fever may have ended the life of an extraordinary Renaissance queen, but her influence lived on through Elizabeth. Despite the Queen Dowager's lapse into what can only have been temporary insanity during her marriage to Thomas Seymour, Catherine managed to imbue Elizabeth with strength, character, and political skill sufficient to see her through the rest of her life.

Dowager Queen Catherine and Thomas Seymour's orphaned infant daughter **Mary Seymour** was wholly unwanted by her relations. She was cared for briefly by the Duchess of Somerset and later the Duchess of Suffolk, but history soon lost track of the girl and she died in obscurity at an unknown date.

After a reign of five years during which she married her Spanish cousin, Philip II, Queen Mary died childless. In 1558, in a transition both peaceful and joyful, **Princess Elizabeth** ascended the throne. As **Queen Elizabeth** she ruled gloriously for forty-four years. Many believe the Seymour affair figured significantly in her distrust of powerful men and her remarkable decision never to marry.

Robin Dudley, whose grandfather, father, and two brothers had all been executed for treason against the Crown, lived on to be named Earl of Leicester, with grants, properties, and great houses bestowed upon him by his childhood friend, now queen. Dudley became Elizabeth's lover, suitor for her hand in marriage, confidant, Privy Councillor, and one of the three most trusted advisors throughout her long reign. Dudley was perhaps the most reviled man at court, not so much for his behavior as for his unshakable influence with the Queen. When the Spanish Armada attempted its invasion of England in 1588, she entrusted to Lord Leicester the greatest of honors possible — leadership of all her land forces. He died shortly after the Armada's spectacular defeat, and thus the deepest, most passionate, most enduring friendship of Elizabeth's life ended.

Author's Note

While I am deeply indebted to a number of excellent historians without whose research this book would have been impossible, I have always been astonished that this episode of the Tudor story has been largely ignored or given short shrift by them. Alison Weir in her recent biography of Elizabeth *(The Life of Elizabeth I)* allows the subject three brief paragraphs and draws exactly one conclusion about the events. Even among the texts that view the Seymour affair as significant enough for a detailed account, there are next to none that go beyond the facts and provide an analysis of the individuals and relationships involved in the most fascinating psychosexual interplay, the most virulent sibling rivalry, and the deadliest family feud of the sixteenth century. Thomas Seymour ranks as the number-one bad boy of Tudor history. A textbook-perfect sociopathic/charismatic personality, he ran roughshod over the Renaissance landscape, severely altering every life he touched.

In any account of a history that goes back 450 years there are sure to be gaping holes — that is expected. But in the period spanning the death of Henry VIII (1547) and the execution of Thomas Seymour (1549), I found in most cases glaring omissions and inconsistencies, inadequate analyses and faulty conclusions.

This is particularly true of the idea that Seymour might have played a role in his wife's death. Despite the fact that on her deathbed she was clearly furious at her husband and berated him in front of many people, only Carolly Erickson *(The First Elizabeth)* admits that "the circumstances were highly suspicious." Seymour did not allow Catherine to see her physician for three days after their daughter's birth, and the will that she dictated during the agonizing postpartum period *was never signed.* Still, Anthony Martienssen *(Queen Katherine Parr)* sloughs off the idea that

Thomas Seymour may have hastened Catherine's death and takes the High Admiral at his word, quoting a letter he wrote to Lord Dorset. In it Seymour claimed to be "so amazed" by Catherine's passing that his affairs were thrown into confusion, for he had "neither anticipated nor expected it." This from a biographer who earlier described Seymour as a man with "serious defects of character" and "an overriding passion for power and wealth, but with no objective than his own self-aggrandizement." He was "devious . . . consumed with jealousy for his brother . . . and his prime motive in seeking Catherine as a bride was to supplant his brother as Protector." Why would Martienssen so blithely accept a description of this scoundrel's emotions surrounding his wife's death?

William Seymour's *Ordeal by Ambition,* an otherwise well researched account (by a descendant of the Seymours) of the family's rise and fall, says "There was loose talk at the time . . . that Thomas poisoned her." The author easily dispels this story about the Queen Dowager's final days by attributing it to what he clearly feels is a biased report. Though Catherine's stepdaughter, Lady Tyrwhitt, was the closest eyewitness to the events, Seymour dismissively describes her as "not a particularly pleasant woman." Her evidence against Thomas, "whom she cordially disliked, was *damaging and ungenerous*" (italics mine). The biographer admits that Catherine's will was unsigned and made orally, but he declares unequivocally that "the witnesses were persons of the highest character." Then in the very next paragraph, of the man whom he has just defended against the possibility of foul play, he says, "Seymour lost all sense of proportion. He scowled upon the world with lineaments of jealousy, rage and doom. . . . His actions . . . were scarcely those of a heartbroken widower. Still less can he be excused for his eager pursuit of the Princess Elizabeth, almost before the grave had closed over that gentle and lovely lady. . . . Thomas compromised himself beyond redemption by his gasconades, and worse still his overt treachery." Is this a man we should trust to secure "witnesses of the highest character" for the oral and unsigned last will and testament of the richest woman in England?

Of Elizabeth's response to Thomas Seymour's sexual advances, Neville Williams *(The Life and Times of Elizabeth I)* declares, "For all his charm the Admiral had become repulsive and she [Elizabeth] determined that he would never come across her alone." In the *very next sentence* he says, "During her pregnancy Catherine Parr's jealousy of the Princess increased, and at Whitsun 1548 she caught Elizabeth in Seymour's arms." So much for Elizabeth's determination to stay away from her repulsive stepfather.

The most egregious omission, and the mystery that propelled me into examining this story in the first place, was the Queen Dowager's state of mind during this period. How was it, I asked myself, that a woman of Catherine Parr's intellectual and moral stature as well as her peerless decorum and unparalleled kindness could have become the mad creature who would pinion her stepdaughter's arms while her husband, armed with a dagger, ripped Elizabeth's dress from her body and slashed it to ribbons? Virtually none of the historians ponder this question.

As to Thomas Seymour's effect on Elizabeth, Paul Johnson *(Elizabeth I)* concludes, "These episodes, when they emerged, caused Elizabeth great embarrassment. But they do not amount to much." Most historians believe that after Catherine's death, although Kat Ashley encouraged the marriage to Seymour, and Parry met a dozen times with him to discuss the details of such a match, Elizabeth wanted nothing to do with the Admiral and even refused to correspond with him. Johnson claims that "at no point did she seriously think of marrying him." I asked myself, how could a girl who had risked the love of the only woman she had ever called mother by succumbing to passion with Seymour suddenly — now that he was free to marry, and she encouraged by her closest retainers — ignore his very existence? Only Erickson states that the Princess "may have given him secret encouragement." This seems a most logical possibility to me.

There is much dispute as to the extent of Elizabeth and Seymour's sexual involvement — how far they went, and whether in fact the rumors of her pregnancy were true. In no history book is more said of the events leading up to her expulsion from Chelsea House to Cheshunt than that Catherine discovered the Princess "in Seymour's arms." I cannot believe that a woman who loved her stepdaughter so dearly would send her the very next day from her sight, never to lay eyes on the girl again, unless the "embrace" was serious indeed. But this is one "hole in history" that only writers of historical fiction are allowed to fill. I can only hope that my take on the subject is believable, satisfying, and as true to the facts as humanly possible.

The readers of my first two novels in this series, *The Secret Diary of Anne Boleyn* and *The Queen's Bastard*, have questioned me endlessly — or come to their own conclusions — about what in these stories is "historical" and what is "fiction," so I'll take a moment here to expound on *Virgin*.

Until the moment of Elizabeth's expulsion from Chelsea House after her tryst with Seymour was discovered by Catherine, the characters and events adhere very closely to the historical record. We do know that the Princess went to Cheshunt and thereafter became quite ill. It's recorded that she and Catherine corresponded cordially during that time and that the Queen Dowager's pregnancy was unremarkable.

That Elizabeth and Thomas Seymour continued their personal relationship after Catherine's death, however, is conjecture, though Erickson suggests it is *possible* that they did. The clandestine meeting at Seymour House and the Admiral's attempted rape are literary invention, though in light of his character and the later desperate measures he took, it seems a plausible scenario.

While there's no proof that Robin Dudley spied on Thomas Seymour at his father's behest, we do know that it was John Dudley who brought to the Privy Council much of the damning evidence of Seymour's illegal activities that ultimately led to his trial and execution for treason. By this time Elizabeth and Robin had been close friends for six years, and she might well have confided to him her passion for Seymour. The rivalry between the Seymours and the Dudleys was firmly in place, and the excessively ambitious John Dudley was willing to resort to extreme measures to bring his enemies down. While I've clearly taken literary license here, I believe everything written is well within the realm of possibility.

The guiding inspiration behind each of these books has been Elizabeth and Robin Dudley's deep and abiding love for each other, one that lasted through their lives till his death. By the time she ascended the throne at age twenty-five, these two had already passed through countless fires together, forging the powerful foundation of that relationship. While the pages of history fail to link them during this critical episode in Elizabeth's life, I have every reason to believe they shared its agonies and dangers as well as reaping from it several invaluable lessons.

Please forgive this author her indulgences and flights of fancy, but conjecture extrapolated from fact is, after all, the very heart of historical fiction.